Danny O'Leary clawed his way up from 'working the doors' of some of Essex's and East London's most violent pubs and clubs. By his early twenties, he was working the security behind the notorious Epping Forest Country Club – an immensely popular nightclub that, at its height, welcomed thousands of visitors a night, including many well-connected people and a host of celebrities. From there, Danny went on to organise security for Waterstones and HMV during their celebrity in-store appearances and, eventually, the personal security of a number of celebrities, including Katie Price, Courtney Love, P Diddy and Katy Perry.

A Violent Gentleman is his first novel.

A VIOLENT GENTLEMAN

Danny O'Leary

ORION

First published in Great Britain in 2021 by Orion Fiction,
an imprint of The Orion Publishing Group Ltd.,
Carmelite House, 50 Victoria Embankment
London EC4Y 0DZ

An Hachette UK Company

1 3 5 7 9 10 8 6 4 2

A CIP catalogue record for this book
is available from the British Library.

ISBN (Hardback) 978 1 4091 9881 9
ISBN (Trade Paperback) 978 1 4091 9882 6
ISBN (eBook) 978 1 4091 9884 0

Typeset by Input Data Services Ltd, Somerset

Printed and bound in Great Britain by Clays Ltd, Elcograf S.p.A.

www.orionbooks.co.uk

A VIOLENT GENTLEMAN

Prologue

Devils take all shapes and forms. Angels too. At six-foot-nine, Jeremiah O'Connell came in two sizes, big and tall, and he could be devil one minute, angel the next. His clothes were expensive but practical, beard tidy not fussy; his hair was part-way to getting long, and it framed an action-hero square face and grey eyes. When he laughed, which was often, the sound was filthy, smoky and joyful. But if you called him a nasty bastard, you wouldn't be the first, and nor would you be the last.

One problem. Jerry wasn't psychic. If he'd been psychic, then maybe he'd have stayed away from Cedar Tree Avenue on that warm LA night.

Then again, knowing him, maybe not.

Part One

Chapter One

Cedar Tree Avenue was typical for this part of LA: long, straight and shabby, with sparse palm trees either side of a wide street and a canopy of power lines overhead. Neglected buildings were either dull grey or a beige the colour of soggy cardboard. Sidewalks were strewn with litter and abandoned furniture.

This was a street where breeze blocks and corrugated iron were the preferred building materials. Where the twinkling lights and vibrant colours of Santa Monica, Westwood and Beverly Hills were close enough to touch but might as well have been a thousand miles away for all that they meant to those who called it home.

At night, it was even less appealing. *Christ*, Jerry had thought, looking left and right as he drove, taking in the neglect, *what a shithole*. He was hunched over the steering wheel of the Prius, a nondescript silver thing that he hated but drove anyway, because sometimes you had to bite the bullet and play safe by keeping things inconspicuous. He'd affixed an Uber sticker in the rear window, just to complete the picture.

Ah. There it was. The strip club he was looking for. It went by the name All Fur Coat, except the 'T' of 'coat' was missing.

All Fur Coa . . .

He selected a space and reversed into it, adjusting a wing mirror in order to ensure that he could see behind as well as ahead. Old habits.

And now to the task at hand.

He pocketed his phone and was just about to go to work when something outside caught his eye. From where he was parked, he could see the club's front entrance, but also a side door. Now, Jerry knew a lot about clubs. Having started his working life on the doors back home in Essex, what he didn't know about clubs wasn't worth knowing – so that side entrance would be used by the girls. Probably there was a more private and secure rear door for when they wanted a smoke, but they'd use that side entrance when they needed to score – just for ease, just for the speed of it.

Right now, there was a geezer hanging around it. A Latino-looking guy, he wore a black denim jacket, black jeans, hair slicked back. A tattoo poked out from the neck of his T-shirt, curling up behind his ear. But it wasn't the clothes that gave him away. It wasn't the dark, leathery skin, pitted, like he'd been left out in the sun. It was just the look of him: the watchful eyes. The mouth, crooked and spiteful. Not far away was a black Ford Falcon, sprung low. Gleaming and ostentatious, it was a drug dealer's car.

Even so, Jerry probably wouldn't have given it another thought but for the fact that the guy looked so agitated. Like he had something more than just a drug deal on his mind.

Jerry took a deep breath, checked his watch and decided that the job could wait a few minutes. He was going to see how this panned out first.

He didn't have to wait long. The door opened, out came a girl and right away the neck-tattoo guy was in her face, closing off her retreat into the club as he backed her up against a wall. His face was contorted, voice raised but not quite shouting. His shoulders were thrust back, fists clenched by his side.

Jerry exited the car and wandered across, pulling his camel-hair coat around him. It was the girl who saw him first.

Neck Tattoo noticed the way her eyes widened, and he wheeled to see Jerry approach. 'What the fuck do you want?'

There's a time and a place to steam in and knock a geezer down, but this was not that time. Jerry would probably never see the girl again and the last thing he wanted was to make life harder for her by clomping her boyfriend. Instead, he simply stared. That was it. Just stood and stared, flint-eyed.

And when Neck Tattoo looked back at Jerry, he saw no fear, no heightened state, no fight, no flight – nothing. Jerry might as well have been ordering a skinny latte for all the emotion he showed. He'd learnt his trade back in the day; he'd learnt it on the job. The hard way. And nobody knew better than him that the moment you showed fear you were dead.

'I was just going to give her phone back,' said Neck Tattoo, all but backing down in the face of Jerry's hulking presence. 'That's all.'

The girl's eyes flitted from Jerry to Neck Tattoo and then back again. 'Give me it then.'

7

'I don't have it with me,' growled Neck Tattoo over his shoulder.

'You called Janice,' she said. 'Told her you were here to return my phone.'

'I just wanted to speak,' said Neck Tattoo. He was trying to sound bruised. Lying.

Jerry cleared his throat and then spoke for the first time. 'Look, mate, leave it for the night is my advice. Get the phone another time, hand it in to the club. Time to move on, yeah?'

The girl jutted her chin in thanks, turned and slammed back into the club. Neck Tattoo sniffed, and although he looked mollified, Jerry could see that his eyes blazed. For a moment or so, the two of them stood looking at one another in the otherwise empty parking lot, the night still and warm around them.

'Time to move on, yeah?' repeated Jerry meaningfully.

Neck Tattoo looked at him for a moment more and then brushed past, stomping to his car. Jerry watched as it fired up with a blatting sound that seemed to vibrate the air around them, followed by a blast of music. With a screech of tyres, it pulled out into the traffic of Cedar Tree Avenue, leaving a mini cyclone of fast-food wrappers in its wake.

Jerry thought that was the last he'd ever see of that guy.

He was wrong about that.

Chapter Two

Jerry ambled towards the strip club entrance, pulled open a door and moved into a vestibule area, where a doorman sat on a bar stool looking at his phone. Jerry tried to hide his contempt, resisting the urge to tell the guy to get his arse outside, which was where he should be. Standing. Watching. Being a fucking doorman. Not sitting inside texting like a kid.

The guy looked up at Jerry, down at his phone and then, in a double take, back at Jerry. In the next second, he was scrambling to his feet, broadening his shoulders and narrowing his eyes. 'What up?' he croaked.

From behind him came the muffled thump of the strip club music. The phone went away, hands into the pockets of his bomber jacket. Making it clear to Jerry where he kept his weapon – whatever that might be.

'All right, mate?' said Jerry. 'You open for business, are you?' He was taking the piss, but it went clean over the head of the doorman.

'Always, always,' nodded the doorman, 'just as long as you're not after trouble . . .'

Jerry held up his hands. 'Just here for the booze and the birds, mate.'

The doorman held the door open for him and he moved through into the foyer. A woman in a booth took his money. He passed into the main club and took in the scene: dancers gyrating at poles on a central stage; sleepy-eyed waiting staff; a clientele who looked like part of the furniture. The over-all feel was one of lethargy, boredom. The afternoon after a heavy night when the world has nothing more to show you.

He took a seat, ordered from a waitress who introduced herself as Ashley, and then, when she returned with the bottle, asked her, 'You got a girl here called Commodore?'

Commodore. Fucksake. What a stupid name.

'Yeah, Commodore's here,' replied Ashley warily. 'Who wants to know?'

'A fan. I've been told her dancing is utterly sublime,' said Jerry, tongue-in-cheek, affecting the voice of a connoisseur. Taking the piss again. He kissed his fingers. Grinned.

Ashley wasn't having it. 'She's new.'

'Word travels fast.'

'All right. Well, you're in luck, she's on soon.'

Jerry sat back, drank his beer in three long slugs and then ordered another one, Ashley even more wary now, which was just as he intended. Sure enough, from the corner of his eye, he watched the arrival of a guy he decided was probably the duty manager. Jerry knew the type: scrawny little guy with a wispy beard, cheap, shit suit and shoes that didn't match. The kind of guy who'd take advantage of the women.

In turn, the duty manager beckoned to Ashley to join him.

They spoke briefly, the waitress glancing over at Jerry, nodding, before the manager was joined by a bouncer in black cargo pants and trainers. More conversation. More glances towards Jerry. Ashley departed to go about her business. The bouncer and the duty manager remained, just at the periphery of Jerry's vision but staring his way.

Now Jerry looked over, maintaining eye contact. Next, he stood, turned and very deliberately repositioned his chair so that instead of facing the stage, it now faced the two men. He regained his seat, lifted his beer bottle and saluted them, mouthing *Cheers*.

They gave no response, just stared. The manager said something to the bouncer. The bouncer nodded and made his way over to Jerry.

He was a big guy: goatee beard, thick dark eyebrows. Probably knew his way around a fight. As he arrived at Jerry's table, Jerry stood, reached for a chair, pulled it out. For a moment or so, the two men faced one another, and then the bouncer sat, Jerry doing the same.

'What can I do for you?' asked the bouncer. His gaze was steady, but light glanced off a line of sweat on his forehead.

'You've got a girl here called Commodore, yeah?' began Jerry. 'Don't answer that, it's a rhetorical question. I know you have. Thing is, she's leaving with me, so I'd appreciate it if you'd let Commodore know that we're going, like, now. Tell her to pack a bag, take anything that's hers. She's not coming back.' Jerry checked his watch, the flash of his gold Rolex not lost on the bouncer.

The bouncer regarded him. His expression barely changed. 'Fallen in love, have we?' he said.

'It makes not a blind bit of difference to you *why* I'm taking her. Just: I'm taking her.'

The bouncer pulled a face, shook his head. 'Commodore's not free to leave. We set her up here, which means she works for us until such time as she's paid off her front money, and she's nowhere near doing that. What I'm saying is, she ain't going nowhere.'

Another bouncer had appeared and was standing a few tables away, hands clasped in front of him, still as a statue. Jerry gave him the once-over, reflecting that you could always tell if a geezer knew what he was doing by the way he held his hands. Behind his back or down by his sides? Forget it, guy was an amateur, you might as well have them in your pockets. In front was a bit better, but the real pros had them up high to make it easy to deflect.

Meantime, the girls on the poles were still dancing, but at the same time were looking across. Even the few customers had raised their eyes, their attention arrested by something that was only slightly less commonplace than the sight of naked flesh and the taste of warm beer – the threat of imminent violence.

'And now,' said the bouncer, as though he had regained the upper hand, 'I'll have to ask you to go.'

A moment passed. Their eyes locked. Jerry didn't move.

'I'll tell you what, I'm going to give you my card,' said Jerry. It was already on the table. He slid it over.

'Just says "Jeremiah O'Connell", and a number,' said the bouncer without picking it up.

'That's all you need,' said Jerry. 'Make a few calls. I'll wait for you to speak to whoever you need to speak to.'

12

It took about ten minutes or so. Then the bouncer with the goatee returned. 'Commodore will be out in a moment,' he said flatly. His eyes betrayed nothing, but Jerry saw the tension in his shoulders. A vein that stood out on his neck. Both tells that Jerry knew well – signs of one predator sizing up another.

'Well done, mate,' replied Jerry.

The bouncer gave him an appraising look, seemed about to say something, but thought better of it and then moved away. Moments later, Commodore appeared, pale and drawn. Her eyes were tired, and she wore streetwalker clothes.

'They say I have to come with you,' she said blankly.

'They're right, darlin'.'

Hope for the best, plan for the worst – that was what they always said. He was prepared for a fuss. Tears. Screaming, maybe even fists, and he was ready to carry her bodily out of the door if needs be.

Instead, she just looked at him with tired, dark-rimmed eyes that no amount of caked-on make-up could disguise. She might be beautiful again, maybe, at some point in the future. But right now her world had robbed her of looks and life. Drugs had brought her low, and when she asked, 'Did my father send you?' and he told her yes, the look on her face was one of relief.

In short order, he made the call, drove to The Saddle Ranch further along and delivered the girl into the grateful arms of her father. An envelope was handed over. 'There's a lot of money in there,' said the father.

Jerry shrugged. 'Price was agreed. Twenty grand for her safe return. You got her back, you pay up. Simple as that.'

His face darkened. 'Not planning on quibbling about it now, are you?'

The man seemed to remember himself, shook his head, and when he handed over the envelope, it was with a look of gratitude, of relief. He watched as Jerry stowed the envelope in his inside jacket pocket, got in the car and took off.

For his part, as he took off along Cedar Tree Avenue in the shitty Prius, Jerry was looking forward to a drink at the Naughty Pig on the Strip.

Which was when it happened.

Chapter Three

The thing that happened was in fact two things that took place in quick succession. The first was as Jerry drove and found his eyes going across the street to a gas station, his attention arrested by a guy he saw standing on the forecourt.

It was Neck Tattoo, the geezer from the parking lot at All Fur Coat. Except he was no longer alone. With him was a second bloke who wore a hoodie and was taller – north of six foot – but otherwise similar in appearance. Another Latino. Before they both climbed into a black beat-up Ford van parked nearby, Neck Tattoo tossed a pack of smokes at the new guy, and then something else. What looked like a roll of black duct tape.

Jerry slowed, watching as the van pulled out of the gas station, headed in the opposite direction – back down the street in the direction of All Fur Coat. At the same time, his mind ticked over the possibilities. Thinking that he didn't want to jump to conclusions; that it could be something or it could be nothing. And even if it was something, then was it really *his* something? After all, he'd done his bit back at the club, and if the stripper couldn't keep out of trouble, then perhaps she was beyond help, like maybe she'd made the wrong career choice.

And maybe that duct tape was for home repairs.

Except no. Not that. And he'd made it his business as soon as he'd got involved back at the club.

Fuck it.

He checked his rearview and swung the Prius in a U-turn, changing lanes, pulling close to the sidewalk and keeping an eye on the van up ahead.

And then the second thing happened, when suddenly – and way too late – he saw a flash of a child on a bicycle, heard a bang – no, *felt it* – and hit the brakes.

Jerry was not one to panic. He rarely broke a sweat and he never worried. But there was a first time for everything – he'd never hit a child with his car before.

In moments, he was out of the Prius and round the front. A little girl, eight or nine years old, was lying on the ground, bike beside her. For a terrifying second, she was still, and Jerry felt the air close in around him. But then – thank fuck – she stirred and, slowly, groggily, pulled herself into a sitting position. He crouched to her and she scuttled away. He held up his hands, palms out, like, *I mean you no harm*, desperate to help her but not wanting to scare her further. She looked like a waif, dressed in an outsized LA Lakers basketball shirt and jeans. Her jeans were torn at the calf. Must have been from the accident because he could see fresh blood. She had a bump on her forehead, too.

But what really floored him was the look in her eyes as she pulled herself to her feet. Not pain, humiliation or anger just a terrified, hunted look – a look so terrible that he was momentarily taken aback.

All of which meant that he was painfully slow to recover as she took off along the sidewalk in an unsteady, half-limping run, leaving her mangled bike behind.

'Hey,' he managed, rising to his feet, still in a state of shock. 'Hey darlin'. Stop.'

But she was gone, swallowed up by the darkness as she dashed towards an alley between two boarded-up stores.

His hands were in his hair. He'd have to go after her. He had to find her. It was like a physical need in him to make things right.

At the same time, he saw up the street, where, in the distance, the van was indicating, making a turn – pulling into the All Fur Coat parking lot.

He thought about the little girl, and then he thought about the duct tape, trying to decide what to do and realising there really was only one choice.

Chapter Four

Jerry pulled into All Fur Coat in time to see the two Latinos, Neck Tattoo and Hoodie, leaving their van and making their way over to the club's side entrance. As they approached, the door opened and the girl appeared, only this time she was more cautious, staying in the doorway, ready to duck back inside if they cut up rough.

Jerry saw her hand outstretched, her mouth forming words. She wanted what they'd no doubt promised: the phone.

The two Latinos had stopped an unthreatening distance away. Jerry used the opportunity to reverse into a space, killing the engine and watching to see whether his arrival had been noted.

It hadn't. Neck Tattoo and Hoodie stood with their backs to him but slightly at an angle. Neck Tattoo was smiling, trying to put the girl at her ease, full-on charm offensive. At the same time, his mate was throwing looks left and right, and Jerry saw a bulge in his jacket pocket – a duct-tape-shaped bulge.

Now it felt as though Neck Tattoo had won the girl's confidence. He'd enticed her out of the doorway at least. A beam of light at the frame blinked off as she stepped out into the night and the door shut behind her.

In the car, Jerry murmured, 'No, darlin', no,' certain that she was putting her head into the lion's mouth but needing that last bit of confirmation before he made his move.

He got it when Neck Tattoo popped a cigarette in his own mouth and offered her one. She stepped forward to take it, just as the fella seemed to discover that his packet was empty. He gestured to his mate, like, *Have you got cigarettes?* and the mate produced one from inside his jacket. Just one.

And that was it. That was all Jerry needed.

He unlatched the door of the Prius, was out and moving over, swiping the cigarette out of the girl's mouth.

Neck Tattoo reacted right away. 'Oh, man, you again. Fuck off, hombre.' Beside him, his mate bristled and his presence no doubt gave Neck Tattoo courage. There were two of them now. They probably thought that together they could take Jerry, but they didn't know Jerry.

'You,' he said to Neck Tattoo, the leader. He proffered the cigarette. 'Put this in your mouth right now.'

Neck Tattoo sneered. 'I ain't doing shit, hombre. Now fucking turn around and walk away.'

Like a proper amateur, Neck Tattoo touched a hand to the back of his jeans, telling Jerry where he kept his knife and which hand he favoured. Simultaneously, Jerry took a step to the side, closing the distance and bringing Hoodie in front of Neck Tattoo, lining them up.

Neck Tattoo now had his hand at his belt, about to draw.

Behind them, the girl looked confused. 'What's going on?'

Jerry held up the cigarette. 'Laced with something, darlin',' he told her.

'What?' The colour drained out of her face.

And now Jerry pointed at the bulge in Hoodie's pocket. 'And what's in there, eh?'

Everything happened at once. The girl gasped, turned and ran back for the safety of the club. Neck Tattoo swore and reached for his blade. Hoodie stood between them, his mouth agape.

And Jerry attacked.

He grabbed Hoodie, yanked him forwards and headbutted him. He put all of his height, power and experience into that butt and knew that the nose was broken and the guy would be blind with watered eyes. He grabbed the geezer's hood, dragged it over his head, gathered it in his fist and thrust his dazed body to block Neck Tattoo. For a moment, the two Latinos were in a tangle, and then, as Hoodie dropped to the deck, Jerry grabbed Neck Tattoo's arm, twisted it and put him down to the tarmac.

Neck Tattoo was mewling and crying as Jerry dragged him to the van and pulled open the doors. Somehow, he'd known what to expect and there it was, right in front of his eyes: a mattress, a screen and a small studio light. The guy writhed and screamed as Jerry took it all in. Again, Jerry put him down to the tarmac and was about to stamp him when he had a better idea. At his feet was an empty Coke bottle, spiderwebbed with cracks. Jerry reached for it, jammed it into the guy's open mouth.

Then kicked his mouth shut.

The bottle shattered. Jerry stepped back as the bloke gagged and spluttered, spitting his teeth out like bloodstained Tic Tacs, glass slicing through lacerated lips. At the same time, he tried to move away, fearing further violence, attempting to make his way underneath the van, like a cat crawling away to die.

Jerry looked down at him dispassionately and then turned, returning to the second bloke, who still lay out cold close to the side entrance of the club. He dragged him back to the van, slapped him awake and dumped him down next to his mate, who lay still, blinking, but in agony.

'Come look at your mate's face,' said Jerry to Hoodie, whose nose was spread across his face.

The guy took one look at the scarlet pulp that had once been his friend's mouth and paled.

'Right then,' said Jerry. In his hand was the laced cigarette. 'Now smoke this.'

Jerry waited until he'd lit up and was smoking before he decided to leave. Before he did, though, he made sure to take their IDs, just in case they had any ideas about calling the police on him.

He always stayed one step ahead.

Chapter Five

The girl slid from the bed, dragged on a T-shirt and took a seat at the dressing table to apply lipstick. The money, paid upfront, nestled in her purse and the deed was done. The lipstick was her way of saying, 'We're done here.'

'So how did a stone-cold fox like you end up as a hooker?' he asked from the bed.

He'd been nervous before, all *aw-gee-shucks,* playing up the out-of-towner, fish-out-of-water bit. But now he wore a sated look, the kind of grin you might call 'shit-eating,' if you were so inclined.

'I'm not wife material,' she replied in the mirror. Her stock response.

'Oh yeah? You girlfriend material then, maybe?' he offered.

'I'm using wife interchangeably with girlfriend,' she said, smiling to offset the weariness she heard creep into her voice. 'Wife, girlfriend: neither are me.'

'See, where I come from, a girlfriend can also be—'

'A mistress? Yeah, I get that. Fact remains—'

'As does my question.'

She sighed. 'Look . . . Steve. An hour ago, you weren't

bothered *why* I was a hooker, right? Just as long as I was one.'

He conceded the point. 'But I sure was thinking it.'

She shrugged and dropped the lipstick into her bag. Time to wrap things up. 'This is LA. Maybe we have better-looking hookers than you do in Arizona.'

'Utah,' he corrected, with a little irritation.

And *damn*, because she prided herself on the details.

'Did you have fun, honey?' she asked instead, hoping the conversational swerve wasn't as jarring for him as it felt to her.

'Oh yeah, I sure did,' he said, yawning, stretching. 'How about you?'

'No doubt about it,' she said, grabbing her bag and standing. 'But all good things come to an end.'

A turn off Sunset, a two-block journey to a street lined with palms and Noah was home, wrestling with the door to her bungalow, edging inside and nudging it closed with her hip.

The bungalow was small and the air con blasting too cold gave it a chilly, unwelcoming feel, like the house didn't want her around. She felt her heart sink a little as she moved through to the kitchen to dump her bag of groceries on the counter.

Silence. Just the sound of groceries relaxing in the bag, distant traffic. She found herself thinking about Jacqui, or Jakki, or however her housemate had been spelling – beg your pardon – *styling* it that week. She'd used to rag on Jacqui for the name-styling thing. Even so, she was just about the closest thing Noah had to a friend.

Jacqui had started out as a dancer – as in, pole and lap, not *Cats* at the Pantages – and that's what she'd been doing when she and Noah first became housemates. She'd been good fun in those days, regaling Noah with tricks of the dancing trade, like the one where she'd pretend to show an interest in a guy by opening his jacket, surreptitiously checking the label and if it wasn't designer then moving on to the next mark. 'If they're wearing a tie, you twirl the tie, like so . . .' She had demonstrated with a magician's hand, 'until you can see the label.'

'Okay,' Noah had said. 'But not all rich guys are so . . . obvious, right?'

Jacqui had looked confused, and like everything else that Jacqui did, she did it in a big way, raising her shoulders, spreading her hands, knitting her eyebrows together theatrically, as a look of total perplexity made a tour of her features. 'Obvious? It's "obvious" having a label in a suit? What? You think that's flexing?'

'No, but you know what I mean. Um, I don't know, Mark Zuckerberg? Bill Gates? You see those guys and they're wearing polo shirts and T-shirts, beige chinos, dad stuff. They don't *look* rich, do they?'

Jacqui had rolled her eyes. 'That's because they're Mark Zuckerberg and Bill Gates. They can afford to not give a shit. Their face is their passport. Anybody else, they have to look the part, have to dress it. That's what you're looking for, kid, I'm telling you.'

Jacqui had tried porn. That didn't go well. Some of the girls in porn made good money – the ones with thousands of followers on Twitter, who made it onto Howard Stern, who starred in rap videos. Most didn't do so well, and Jacqui was one of those. Porn, in the end, was a flameout, a wrong-turn career move from which she had emerged battle-scarred and bloody, and if not with a full-scale coke habit, then definitely with an increased appetite for it.

Meantime, Noah had been doing well, pulling in the big bucks. She did her best to carry Jacqui along in her wake, even introducing her to her madam, Vera, but that had crashed and burned. A chaotic and strung-out Jacqui had chosen the day of her meet with Vera to be even more chaotic and strung-out than usual. Back at home in the aftermath, she seemed to resent Noah all of a sudden. Noah had watched helplessly, heart breaking, as her previously warm and funny friend became increasingly bitter and vocal about it.

'You think you're better than me,' Jacqui had raged during one of their fallouts.

But Noah didn't think that and never had. She just thought she'd made better choices. Comparatively better anyway. And she wanted help paying the rent.

Then there was the way Jacqui had left. The final argument. Noah had gone in hard; in return, Jacqui had replied in kind, called her 'poison'. They'd both said regrettable things, but neither had apologised, and two days later, during which time silence had hung over the bungalow like a shroud, Jacqui was gone. Not a word then. Not a word since.

And Noah missed her. She had some money saved, so rent wasn't a worry for a while, but even so, she wished she'd tried harder to repair their relationship; wished she had been more understanding. And even though she knew all the stuff about it being better to be alone than stuck in an unhappy marriage, she found her gaze going around the silent house and had a hard time believing it.

Noah shook herself. She wasn't by nature a person given to gloom and introspection, and she didn't want to start now. Okay, so *do* something. She'd already punched the clock. No more work tonight. So fuck it. Time to get trashed.

Chapter Six

As blowjobs go, it wasn't exactly award-winning stuff. Then again, what did you expect from a desperate, destitute junkie?

In his hand, he held a vial. It was about an inch long and the circumference of a pencil, the kind used for perfume samples, except that inside this one nestled a rock of crack that in the mind of this junkie, and others like her, was easily worth a quick blowjob sandwiched between the paint-sprayed walls of a piss-stinking alley.

After he was finished (and the exact details of that particular process had been agreed in advance), he watched with pleasure the face she made as she swallowed. When she reached out with a trembling and desperate hand, he made her beg and cry until she threatened to go to the boss, at which point he relinquished and let her snatch the vial from him. The look in her eyes was a look he knew well. Like a hunted animal finally finding sanctuary.

Just then a shadow fell across the mouth of the alley, and he looked up to see a familiar figure. In an instant, the junkie was gone, flashing him a crooked, knowing smile, and he turned, buttoning up his jeans, to speak to the new arrival. As he did so, he sensed someone else at the far end of the alley, swivelled and saw his suspicions confirmed. He was boxed in.

Now it was his turn to swallow.

The two sentinels were dressed similarly: black jeans, over-sized black sweatshirts, thick chains. The first guy had drawn his gun from the waistband of his jeans.

'Someone wants a word with you,' he said and then stepped aside. Behind him was a third guy: older, white, and cut from an entirely different cloth. Not for him the street uniform. He wore a navy suit and dirty off-white sneakers. His hair was long and unwashed, and with his slight stoop and downcast gaze, he had the look of a man who was dreading returning home to face the music. This was the bossman.

His name was Ronson Beaufoy.

And yet, when he raised his eyes, they glittered with malice, the smile he wore signalled danger more clearly than any clothing, and his voice when he spoke carried terrible promise. 'Well looky here,' he said.

'Boss, listen, please, I was going to make up the money. I just fancied a blowjob.'

Beaufoy looked around as though unable to identify the source of the voice, before calling to the man at the far end of the alley, 'Sasha, make sure you find that junkie and beat the living shit out of her, won't you? Do it out front so that we all know what happens to those who think they can get away without paying. Remind them that . . .' and here he looked up as though to address a higher power, paused a moment, then bellowed, *it's a cash business.*'

His words seemed to climb the walls of the alley and escape

over the roofs of the adjoining apartments. In their wake, just traffic noise and far-off sirens.

'No, let me do it, boss,' stuttered the dealer. Sweat glinted on his forehead, his voice cracked with mounting panic. 'I'll fuckin' get her. I'll beat her like you want. I'll make sure it'll never happen again.'

'Oh, it's never going to happen again.' That smile once more. From inside the dishevelled linen suit came a long blade – known in the community as The Knife. 'You can be sure of that.'

At a nod from Beaufoy, the two heavies moved in and grabbed the dealer. He was a guy they knew well, a colleague, a friend, even. They'd stood on corners, shot the shit, played Xbox, shared innumerable blunts and plenty of women; they'd called each other bro and looked out for each other on the streets.

But all of that meant nothing and they felt nothing, knowing that it would be the same if the roles were reversed, as they turned a deaf ear to his pleas, ignoring his whimpering as their leader advanced.

The knife was held low and it stayed low as he began his work, and the faces of the two men were blank as the pleading and then the whimpering turned into screams that escaped the sheer walls of the alley and were heard in the adjacent buildings and in the small parking lot out front.

But nobody called the cops. In response, blinds were drawn and apartment doors eased shut. The residents of Sunshine Heights knew better than to get involved with Ronson Beaufoy.

Chapter Seven

The Naughty Pig was the destination whenever Noah wanted to rinse the pipes. True, it was a touch redneck for an LA joint, lots of red strip-lighting, maybe too much noise from the pool sharks and their girlfriends, TVs competing with hair metal from the jukebox, like, *hey, 1982 wants its bar back.* Even so, she felt comfortable here. *I like it. So sue me.* Besides, at home was just an empty, silent house. Not for the first time since Jacqui had left, Noah wondered whether having a coked-up and broke housemate was better than no housemate at all.

She took a seat, rested her elbows, hooked her boot heels on the stool and ordered a drink. She'd been coming here for about two years, knew the barman, Jake, who in return remembered that her favourite drink was Jack Daniel's and Coke on the rocks. She sat playing with it for a moment or so, mulling over whether to throw it back or make it last.

Ah, what the hell. Down it went. Along the bar, a big guy in a camel-hair coat had arrived and taken a seat, leaving a few stools between himself and her – *Good stuff, my friend,* she thought, *keep your distance.* Jake approached him, about to take his order, but without looking, the big guy pointed down the bar towards her, the noise in the bar not enough to drown out his voice when he spoke. 'Serve the lady first.'

Delivered the way it was, Jake's feathers remained un-ruffled. Noah wasn't sure how she felt about that. *Serve the lady first*. Jesus.

Then again, the second thing most noticeable about this guy besides his size was his voice. He was an English guy. A Londoner, maybe, his distinctive accent enhanced by a rasping, growling delivery.

She opened her mouth to object, but he stopped her before she could speak, 'Don't go saying nothing just yet, darlin'. Hear me out if you would. Here's the deal. If you're sitting there having just knocked back that JD and Coke in impres-sive time and looking very much like someone in need of a second, then I'm buying.'

Normally, it would annoy Noah to the point of actual physical violence if a guy spoke to her like that. Any other day and the word 'darlin'' alone would be enough for a little mouth-sick.

Normally. But there was something about the guy, a look in his eye, or maybe the fact that he was English . . . some-thing, anyway, that produced a smile instead. And when they made eye contact and held it, she found herself more bemused than irritated by him. And that was a first.

Even so, that was it – for a while at least. She drank and messed about on her phone, at the same time keeping an ear on the conversation along the bar, where the big guy ordered drink after drink, tossing nuts into his mouth and chatting to Jake.

He talked, she noticed. He liked to talk. But he also listened. His eyes were crinkled, intent on Jake when it was the barman's turn to speak, nodding with understanding and prompting him with further questions, rather than jumping in with his next unfunny quip or self-aggrandising statement, something most other men seemed to do – something Noah hated. And Jake liked the guy, you could tell. He'd gravitate back to him, upending the bottle of Scotch without being asked, bringing more bags of nuts.

A waitress in denim hot pants approached, plopped a tray of shivering empties on the bar and gave the big guy a quick cuddle, momentarily disappearing into his coat.

'Everybody being nice, darlin'?' he asked her, with a meaningful side-eye at the rowdy pool players.

'Sure, Jerry,' she grinned, blowing hair from her face and turning with a fresh tray of drinks. She caught Noah's eye. They shared a look, and for a moment Noah wondered if the waitress was about to say something. Found herself wishing she would. But then the tray was hoisted upwards and the waitress was gone.

Twisted Sister on the jukebox. Noah tossed back the last of her JD and Coke and ordered another just as one of the pool players approached, hitting on her.

'Hi, honey, can I buy you a drink?'

'I'm good, thanks,' she said.

'You waiting for someone?'

'Whatever I'm doing, I'd prefer to do it alone, if it's all the same to you.' She flashed him her very best winning smile. 'Maybe another night, huh?'

The idea was to stay firm but keep him sweet, maybe even

flatter him a little, defuse any rejection he might be feeling. Sure enough, it worked. Off he went, a little flushed, but with his dignity intact. She cast a glance at the big guy – Jerry – who raised his drink, toasting her diplomacy, and she raised it back.

Moments later, Jake appeared, elbow lifting as he poured a ribbon of Jack into her empty glass. Without thinking, she knocked it back.

Okay, she thought, seeing that she'd released a tiny rainfall of spilled JD on the bartop, *keep it tidy, Noah, better not get too trashed . . .*

But it was too late. She was wobbling . . .

'Careful, darlin', careful.'

Seeing that she was about to go, and manfully resisting the urge to shout, 'Timber!' and let her fall, Jerry scooted along the bar as the girl lurched to one side. Either way, she stopped herself in time, warding him off with a held-out hand.

'I'm fine, I'm fine,' she said, although it was more of a slur, 'I don't need any help.'

Trouble was, she was drunk, and since he was the one who'd been buying her drinks, he felt partly responsible. Question now was whether she was a good-natured, funny drunk, or the other kind.

'You wouldn't be doing that, you know, if you knew anything about me,' she continued. 'I'm poison.' She held up both hands and wiggled her fingers, though what on earth it was supposed to mean, Jerry had no idea.

'You're not poison, darlin', you're just a bit pissed,' said Jerry.

'Pissed?' she spat, rearing back. 'What am I pissed about? What could I possibly be pissed about?'

'It's what we say back home, darlin'. We say pissed; it means drunk.'

'What?' she said, drawing the word out like *whaaaaaaat*. 'Pissed. It means angry. Irritated. Ready to smash somebody in the face. And anyway, pissed or trashed or whatever I am, you still wouldn't be looking out for me if you knew what I do. Have a guess. Go on.'

He tipped his chin to the bar and lowered his voice before he spoke. 'So what, you're a lady of the night? No one's judgin' you here, darlin'. We all just use the assets we're born with to better our circumstances.'

She reared back and looked at him, and he realised that he was about to discover if she was a good-natured drunk or not.

Chapter Eight

Morning, and Jerry surfaced slowly from sleep, daylight warming his eyelids. He hadn't closed the blinds last night. The sun danced in the room. Thick planks of it lay across the sheets.

He scratched his beard, swung his legs from the bed and heaved himself upright, brow furrowed, pushing his hands through his hair as he made his way from the bedroom into the lounge area. There, he stood and took stock, looking from the sliding doors that led to the balcony, across the room and to the kitchen area. A set of stairs led to a small mezzanine, where a desk and computer were set up. To his left was the door to what was a disproportionately huge bathroom. Otherwise, the apartment was just as Jerry liked it: big enough for him – and maybe one or two more if he had guests – but not too big.

A lot of his belongings had stayed back in England. What he had with him here was mainly stuff he'd bought since settling in LA. Pride of place in the centre of the room was a low marble coffee table. On it was a laptop and a couple of glasses that he picked up with two fingers, pincer-style, to take through into the kitchen area. His coat was slung over the back of the couch, and he retrieved that, too, on the way past, preferring to sling it over the back of a breakfast bar stool ready for hanging up, rinsing the two glasses and placing them to one side.

Back in the main living area, he cracked open the balcony doors, breathing in mid-morning air that was so thick with warmth you could practically chew it.

An embankment dropped from beneath his balcony to the road below, while to his left and right — and at a suitably discreet distance — were balconies belonging to other apartments in the complex, all boasting the same great view over West Hollywood. He toasted it with a cigarette, paying tribute to LA. There were those who said the city was 'fake' and 'insincere', apparently anathema to a Brit like him. But the fact was, he liked it that way. Hardly mattered to him if the clerk didn't mean it when they wished him a nice day. Far as he was concerned, it was just nice to be nice. Plus, he liked the fact that there was so little jealousy. Aspiration, yes. Ambition, most certainly. But not jealousy. Not in the resentful, begrudging way of back home. Pull up to a valet here, and they'd compliment you on your car. Back in London, people would be just as likely to key it.

Did he feel at home here? Any more than actually 'at home'? That was another question for another day.

He knew better than to flick his fag butt over the balcony, that was for sure. Fire risk. It went back into the apartment with him.

He returned to the living area, glanced at the bedroom door, listened. He checked his watch, saw that it was 10:36

a.m. On the wall was a clock set to UK time. The time in the UK was 6:36 p.m. according to the clock. Not too late, then.

He dropped to the sofa and flipped open the lid of the laptop. Moments later, he was FaceTiming home, and a few rings after that, Katie appeared.

Katie was twenty-seven. An adult, as she constantly reminded Jerry, but still his baby sister.

'What's happening, darlin'?' he asked.

'All right, Jerry,' she said, and he grinned at the sound of her voice. Nobody sounded like him in Los Angeles. Plenty of English voices, of course. But he could go for weeks on end without hearing Estuary English – the accent everybody mistakenly called cockney but wasn't. Katie had no idea what it meant to him. Just hearing it gave him a lift.

They talked for a while, just catching up, Jerry asking how things were with the beauty course, how she was getting on with her part-time job at the petrol station and asking, *How's Mum?* Asking her questions, gently probing. Did she have a boyfriend? No. Did Mum have a boyfriend? Yes, a bloke called Keith. And there was something about the way Katie behaved when she talked about Keith that raised a flag with Jerry, but he kept it to himself and was glad that he did, because in the end it was good between them, and when Katie said goodbye, she rewarded him with a smile, blowing him a kiss into the bargain. It was nothing to her, but everything to him, and he felt like a dog having its belly rubbed.

The call ended. Jerry reached, snapped the laptop shut and then settled back into the sofa, thinking.

He picked up his phone. Scrolled to his contacts and found

Mad Micky Walker. Should he get in touch? Ask Micky to do a bit of digging?

For long moments he sat in silence. Sun dappled the wood flooring, far-off traffic a steady hum, background music to a reverie that took him overseas and back in time.

And then his guest appeared.

Chapter Nine

Noah had spent a bit of time in bed pulling herself together before schlepping through to see if things were as she remembered them from last night. But when she went through into the living area, he'd been sitting on the sofa looking pensive, and so she'd stood there for a moment or so, unsure what to do, not quite wanting to interrupt his reverie, until . . .

'Hello,' he said at last, turning his head to look at her and making her wonder how long he'd known she was standing there.

She greeted him back, coming into the room. 'Who's that?' she asked, pointing to a photograph that peeked from behind the clock: him and a bunch of other guys, all smartly dressed, standing outside a white-painted building. All the guys were either tall or beefy, or a combination of both; Jerry towered over them.

'That's me and the boys from the Epping Forest Country Club. We were bouncers there,' he explained. 'That's how I got started out, darlin'.' He walked over, pointing at faces. 'That's Wayne the Thug. That's Yum Yum, that's Mad Micky Walker . . .'

'Mad Micky Walker?' she repeated. 'That's quite a name.'

She was grateful the silence had ended. Brooding guy wasn't what she needed right now. She wanted good-natured dude back in the room. And if there was one thing that she did remember from last night it was that he liked to reminisce about the past.

On cue, he brightened. 'Oh yeah, Micky was with me at the Country Club. You know you were asking last night how I'd got into the bodyguarding game?'

'Was I?' Her nose wrinkled as she struggled to remember. That's right. He'd been a bodyguard, working Hollywood. It was coming back to her now. But he was no longer a bodyguard. Now he was something different. A problem-solver. Somebody you went to when you had problems that couldn't be solved by any other means. And by the looks of things he was doing very well at it. But bodyguarding. There was definitely bodyguarding in there. 'Yeah,' she agreed, adding, not entirely truthfully, 'I remember.'

He grinned. 'Coffee?' She nodded gratefully and he stood, moving through to the kitchen area, talking at the same time. 'Well, it was Micky that got me into that game. Years ago, this was. See, there was this huge grassroots football tournament over at Colliers Wood football ground. Thirty-two teams, all different nationalities, getting together to play football – that's soccer in your lingo – and for the ten years they did it, it had been a war zone. You can imagine: you've got USA against Iraq, all these Middle Eastern countries that hate each other, Japan against China. Every year, fucking World War Three. They couldn't get security that was any good, the police had to attend. It was bedlam.'

'And this was the crowd or the players?'

'Both, like. So anyway, the geezer that ran it, a geezer called Mark, he knew Mad Micky Walker, who worked at the events firm who put it on, and he asked Micky if he knew anyone who could run the security and so Micky asks me, "Do you fancy it?" Tells me all about it, how it's a war zone and stuff. I'm running the door at the Country Club, so it sounds like a walk in the park to me. I say, "Sure. No problem, I'll give it a go, I'll get the lads together." "Actually, there is a problem," says Micky. "See, it starts at eight o'clock . . ." "Well, that ain't a problem. . ." "Eight o'clock in the morning," says Micky. How do you take it?'

'Black, no sugar, please.'

'Coming up. Well, eight o'clock in the morning *is* a bit of a problem, as it happens, because we're doing the doors at the Country Club until four o'clock in the morning, after which we've got to get over to Colliers Wood. So anyway, I told the boys to wear black shirts on the door at the club. We had to go straight from there to the tournament, with just time for a bit of breakfast first, and if there was a tear-up that night – and, believe me, there always was a tear-up at the club – and we got blood over us, then I didn't want it showing up on our shirts.

'So, we turn up, and the very first game, World War Three breaks out. One of the sides was Japan and there were flying kicks going everywhere. The Japanese manager actually pulled out a corner flag and was swinging it around. It was that mad.

'Now, for many years these footballers had ruled the roost. They were used to softly-softly security, bit of diplomacy, "calm down, lads", all of that. But we were all bouncers, still in "door mode" from like four hours ago, with bits of dried blood on our shirts, and we weren't in any mood to take shit from a bunch of footballers. So we run on the pitch and start giving them a hiding. We just beat the granny out of anybody fighting, and that was it.

'But what happens? Because everybody's seen what they're going to get if they make a fuss, there isn't a single problem for the rest of the weekend. Peace broke out. And Mark, who ran it, was going, "I can't believe it, we've always had the police out, riot police, the works." And I'm like, "It's easy, you just don't tolerate any nonsense. You nip it in the fucking bud – we're not here to babysit."

'Well, Mark got me to more events and that grew into me doing work for a big bookshop chain back home, where I'd be doing security for book signings. And the way it happened was that I'd be better at the job than the other security. Celebrities would turn up, see me at work and want me bodyguarding for them, and I'd pick up jobs that way. And, in a funny kind of way, that's all down to Micky.'

'But you're a bodyguard now?' she asked, trying to dredge up memories of last night's conversation.

'No. I told you . . . Bloody hell, you really were out of it, weren't you?'

'Yeah, I was.' She cleared her throat, waited a beat. 'And I need to know if . . . Well, did we . . .?' She cleared her throat.

'Did we what?'

'Don't be an asshole, okay? You know what I mean. Did we or not?'

He shook his head. 'Nah, you're all right. Well, you weren't all right last night. But no, we didn't do anything. I wasn't drunk enough for you to take advantage of me. Even though you were all over me, like.' He preened a little.

She rolled her eyes, hanging on one hip, her arms crossed. Then, 'You guessed I was a working girl.'

He shrugged. 'We were in a bar on the Strip. It wasn't a tough call.'

She pursed her lips. 'And did that have anything to do with it – the fact that we didn't . . .'

He chuckled. 'No, darlin', I've slept with plenty of ladies of the night – many different professions – don't you worry about it.' He winked. 'Sometimes I've even paid.'

She nodded. It figured. 'And you're all right, are you?' she asked. 'You don't have a hangover?'

He came across and handed her a coffee. 'I don't get hangovers.'

'Well I do, thank you. Mind if I get some air?'

'Make yourself at home,' he said, sitting back on the sofa and pushing his hands through his hair as she inched open the balcony doors and stepped outside to lean on the railings and gaze across the valley.

After a while, she returned. 'How are the neighbours?' she asked.

'Ah, well, that's the trick. I don't have any.'

She did a double take. 'You're putting me on.'

'Well, all right, there's still an old geezer in the end one, but nobody's buying the apartments right now.'

The glint in his eye told Noah that there was more to the story. 'Yeah. Come on. And . . .?'

'Just that the gaff is—'

'Gaff?'

'The apartments, right? The abodes. They're very expensive.'

She shrugged. 'So? This is LA . . .'

'Yeah, but when lawyers do their research, it reveals what you might call *terminal* levels of subsidence.'

She pulled a face. 'It's falling down?'

'No, I never said that, did I? Just that there are ways and means you can have little adjustments made to the specs, know what I mean?'

She looked at him, cottoning on. 'You'll end up with the whole complex to yourself?'

'Who knows?' he smiled. 'I'm playing the long game on this one.'

'Okay. Colour me impressed.'

She'd finished her coffee.

'Tell you what, darlin', you fancy going out?' he said. 'I've got a little job to do. Maybe get some breakfast an' all? What do you say?'

She looked at him, wondering if she was right to feel that this was a rubicon moment. After all, she didn't socialise with clients, not unless they were paying.

Except he's not a client, Noah.

No, worse, he's a guy who picked you up in a bar.

Or maybe you *picked him* up, *how's about that?*

She thought of her empty bungalow. She thought of guys from Utah and Arizona, 'in town on business'.

'Sure,' she said at last, 'on one condition.'

'What's that?'

'You don't call me "darling", "honey", "babe". Nothing like that. I get enough of it in a professional context.'

'I don't know about that,' he said doubtfully. 'It's just the way I talk.'

'Those are my terms.'

He seemed to consider for a moment, then, 'I'll try,' he said. 'No promises.'

Chapter Ten

'I've got a condition, too,' Jerry said.

They stood at the door of the parking garage below the apartments. His fingers hovering over the keypad, ready to allow them entry.

'What is it?' she said.

'You have to drive.'

'Oh, you're one of those Brits who hates driving in LA?' said Noah, folding her arms and looking, she hoped, definitive. 'Well, no, sorry. I'm not for hire as a chauffeur to traffic-averse Limey guys. You want me to come with you – you can do the driving.'

'No, I'm not one of those guys,' said Jerry. 'Just that . . . Tell you what, I reckon I can make you change your mind.'

'You won't,' she said, firmly. Her arms remained folded, but a smile hovered about her lips.

'In about three minutes' time, your mind will change, I promise you,' he assured her. 'Soon as we get through this door.'

He keyed in the code, the door swung open and they stepped through into a warm, musty and dark space. Away from her stretched the parking garage, mostly empty, which was just as she expected, given that most of the apartments were vacant; even so, there were a number of vehicles on view, and nearest to them was a collection of motorbikes: Ducati, Moto Guzzi. Triumph, Harley-Davidson . . .

'All yours?' she asked, archly. But the answer took her by surprise.

'Yeah.' He stood to one side, but not, she noticed, running a proprietary hand over them. Content to let her admire them. Proud but not possessive. 'But look, that ain't the half of it,' he told her.

'My mind hasn't changed.'

'I said three minutes.'

'You said as soon as we walked through that door.'

'Your mind's changed,' he grinned. 'You just don't know it yet. Now, walk this way if you would.'

They moved further into the garage, with Noah wondering what she was supposed to see in the dark – only for lights triggered by the movement to flick on in bright winking strips. Noah looked at Jerry, who in turn threw her a look. *Changed your mind yet*? She rolled her eyes.

And then her gaze went to what lay before her, illuminated by the automatic lighting: a dozen cars or more. Some of them were covered in tarpaulins, some were a little dusty, others were showroom ready. But what struck her most was that, firstly, they were all well-kept, treated with pride by their owner; and, secondly, they were almost all vintage. Just looking at them was like taking a trip back in time. And from what she could see, they were almost all in immaculate condition.

The daughter of a car fanatic, she saw a Buick, a Corvette, a Ford Mustang, a Pontiac, a Dodge Charger, a Dodge Viper, a Chrysler Imperial and a Porsche 911. The kind of cars you expected to see driven by Steve McQueen, Sean Connery or Michael Caine. Hell, even The Green Hornet. Cars that were like living reminders of a bygone age that, in reality, wasn't better than the one in which they lived now, but felt like it was.

'Jesus fucking Christ on a bike,' she said.

'Yeah,' agreed Jerry. 'That's about the size of it.'

She moved between them, unable to stop herself from reaching out and touching, as though they might be holograms, her fingers brushing the sea green of a Cadillac DeVille.

'And these are yours?' she said, aware that for some insane reason she was talking in a hush all of a sudden, as though in church.

He nodded.

'You've changed your mind, haven't you?'

The eyes she gave him said it all.

'I knew you would. You should see your face. You told me last night that you loved your cars, remember? Come on, it's a beautiful day. What better way to spend it than cruising in one of these?'

'You're right,' she said, shaking her head, perhaps knowing she had been played and maybe not caring too much. Something occurred to her. 'Why do you need a driver anyway?'

'DUI,' he said.

'All right then.' She pointed. 'We'll take that one.'

'Ninety-eight Oldsmobile,' he said. 'Now that's a good choice.'

48

Chapter Eleven

Her name was Jane. She was nine years old, and right now she stood staring at the yellow police tape that criss-crossed the mouth of the alley on Cedar Tree Avenue.

The alley itself ran between two blocks, each of which was divided into several retail units: a liquor store, a Day & Night Food Mart, coin laundry, smoke shop, discount clothes store. Serving both units was a sparse, untidy parking lot, where kids, mainly older than Jane, hung around on bikes or in groups outside the stores. Most of them lived in one of the two apartment blocks that lay behind the units: on the left, Oakwood. On the right, Sunshine Heights.

That was Jane's life: the stores, the apartments, and school, if she could be bothered to go, which was rarely.

And now, and not for the first time, murder.

They said that the man they called the bossman – Ronson Beaufoy was his proper name – had done the killing. They said that he had cut up a dealer called Blaze for reasons that Jane didn't understand but involved something called a blow-job. The older kids who hung around the liquor stores all found Blaze's killing very funny. They would laugh loud and long, each, it seemed, trying to outdo the other for how funny they found it that Blaze was knifed for a blowjob, not to mention the fact that the bossman hadn't just cut him up, but had in fact *cut off his balls*.

But to Jane their laughter sounded hollow and false. The louder and more raucous it was, the less joyful it sounded, the more fearful. Sometimes it felt as though she were the only one who understood this. She would look at the faces of the other kids when they gathered in groups, some older, some even younger, and she'd be looking for signs that they, too, saw through the fakery of the laughter, but saw none. Even so, she knew better than to scream out, 'They're lying! They're scared!' even though that's what she wanted to do, because she, too, was scared.

Instead, she had pedalled, day and night. Occasionally, she lost herself in a daydream, and that's probably why she'd been hit by the car. But at least that accident had taught her a lesson; it had taught her to keep her wits about her.

Being careful, that was the thing. That was what she had to do from now on. Maybe being scared kept you careful and being careful kept you alive. Maybe.

Losing her bike, though – that was the real punishment. Suddenly she felt at once more vulnerable and yet still invisible. More ghostlike. Somehow it didn't matter if the other kids noticed her when she was on her bike; being on foot was a different matter altogether.

She wandered off, leaving the murder scene behind. 'The cops don't care.' That's what she'd heard after it had happened, and they were right. She hadn't seen a cop since they took the body away. The police tape meant nothing. Soon, the younger kids would tear off strips and tie it around their bikes, riding around the lot with the tape trailing like black-and-yellow kites. In due course, the street would reclaim the alleyway. That's what she thought as she moved off, child of the street, wondering as always where to go and what to do next.

And that's when she saw the car.

It was an open-top car being driven by a woman wearing dark sunglasses, wisps of blonde hair escaping a ponytail to frame a pretty face. Jane's eyes slid past the woman and to the passenger, recognising him immediately despite that fact that he, too, wore sunglasses.

It was him. It was the man who had hit her with his car. The big guy who spoke with the funny accent.

Right away, she turned and darted off.

Chapter Twelve

He told her the story on the way to Cedar Tree Avenue. Well, an edited version of the story, in the sense that he told her about Commodore and the little girl but didn't mention the fight with the Latinos – he wasn't sure she was ready to hear quite how severely he'd dealt with them. Not yet anyway.

Soon enough, they arrived, and she swung into the parking lot in front of Sunshine Heights and was about to kill the engine when he stopped her. 'Not this one.' He was paying particular interest to a group of six or seven kids hanging outside the stores, two of them on bikes, one of them sitting on a car hood. To the left of the shops, the mouth of an alleyway was criss-crossed with yellow police tape.

'You don't like this space?'

'Not much. Reverse into that one over there, would you?'

She pulled a face. 'You must be joking. Nobody reverses into a space in LA.'

'Just humour me.'

She sighed but did it anyway, and then, when they'd parked, now facing the storefronts and apartment blocks, said, 'Why do I get the feeling that the reason you like to reverse into a space is because you might need to make a quick getaway?' She indicated the police tape.

'There's that, yeah,' agreed Jerry. 'Normally. But not today. Today I just want a decent view.'

He looked over at the kids, who were in turn checking out the new arrivals.

Noah interrupted his thoughts. 'So the girl ran off in the direction of the apartments?'

'Yeah, that's about the size of it.'

'You go after her?'

'I tried. No luck.'

'So? What does that mean for . . .' She tailed off.

'You can help me find her,' he said.

'Um, well, even if I wanted to, and even if I could, why do you want to find her? She got up and ran away. It sounds like it wasn't even your fault.'

He shrugged, looking away across the lot at nothing in particular. 'She was just a little girl. Shouldn't even have been out here on the street on her bike. As for me, I should have been paying more attention.'

'These things happen.'

'Yeah, these things happen. And when they do, I don't just shrug my shoulders and walk away. It's not the way things are done. Not the way I do things anyway.'

'And what are you going to do if you – by which I mean I – manage to find her?'

He nodded. 'I've got something in mind.'

Chapter Thirteen

Jerry found himself looking at the police tape, wondering what it meant. Again, not his business. Without the tape, Noah might have used that alley to reach the apartments behind, but she'd gone a different route, taking the approach road. There stood a sign: *Sunshine Heights*. Jerry looked at the building now. Like most LA blocks, it was squat, off-white and fronted with walkways. What struck him most was the lack of life, of activity. Usually you'd expect to see guys hanging out in the balcony, shooting the shit, watching the world go by, maybe with a beer or two on the go. However, all three walkways were empty.

Something else struck him. All the doors were shut. Most of the windows were blacked-out as well, as though the curtains were drawn. The whole place – in fact, when he looked, *both* buildings – had the same distinctive look. He hadn't noticed yesterday, probably because it was night-time and he'd just knocked down a little girl, but they looked deserted. Not abandoned. Just empty. Devoid of life.

He felt a stirring in his gut that he recognised as concern for Noah and was reaching for the door handle when he saw

54

her. She had reappeared from around the side of the building and strolled over to the car to lean on the door. 'I've found her. Well – not quite found her. I know where she is.'

They took Noah's route into the apartments, where Jerry was struck again by the strange sense of lifelessness about the place. 'It's like the birds don't sing round here.' He spoke under his breath, head turned even as his eyes moved ceaselessly, all senses on high alert. He hadn't been expecting this. 'What do you think the problem is, then?' Remembering that he was still a stranger in this town, that maybe there was something about the area he didn't understand.

They took the steps up to the first-floor walkway. 'Not sure,' she replied, 'but I felt the same thing.' They were on the walkway now. 'This is it.' She gestured along the doors. 'This is where I was told she lived.'

'Then it's time to start knocking.' He was about to do just that when they heard something from further along the walkway. Raised voices.

Jerry and Noah looked at one another, eyebrows raised. In the next moment, a door was flung open and a little girl appeared.

It was her.

She came belting out, face red with tears, sobbing. In the next instant, she caught sight of Noah and Jerry, her eyes widened further in distress, and she hurtled off in the opposite direction.

'Was that the girl you were looking for?' It hardly seemed necessary to ask.

Jerry, nodding, went to the balcony rail, casting around in

vain. She'd vanished. Instead, he went to the door of 22B, where whoever was responsible for scaring the girl was currently conspicuous by their absence.

He knocked.

The door opened promptly. Just a crack, mind. Enough to reveal a woman. She was about his age but looked much older, thanks mainly to her lifestyle choices – or should that be 'choice', singular. You didn't need to know much about drugs to recognise an enthusiast when you saw one. Perhaps that also accounted for the fact that when she first clapped eyes on them, there was a look of hope about her, like perhaps they had come with fresh supplies – a spark that died the instant she got a better look at Jerry.

'What do you want?' Her eyes settled into birdlike hoods. Her mouth became a thin line. Only the slight tremble of her hand on the door indicated a physical and mental frailty.

'Was that your little girl?' He gestured down the walkway with his head.

'What business is it of yours if she was?'

'Just that I was hoping to speak to her, darlin'?'

'Well, you can't. Fuck off.'

The door slammed.

And Jerry stood, knowing that to expect any other outcome had been a triumph of optimism over experience.

He and Noah had turned to go, wordlessly deciding to regroup and talk tactics in the car, when the little girl reappeared. She stood, some distance away, regarding them with curiosity. If there had been any doubt before that it was the same girl, there wasn't now: scrap of a thing, dirty blonde hair, oversized Lakers shirt. And, if anything, she looked even more neglected than she had the last time Jerry saw her, which took some doing, when you considered she'd just been knocked down by his car.

Noah watched, eyes darting from Jerry to the girl. Now, the one thing that Noah knew about Jerry was that he loved to talk. They'd stopped for gas on the way over and he'd struck up at least three conversations at the gas station. He was an equal-opportunities chatterbox, too. You didn't have to be a good-looking woman. You could be a slightly infirm guy who needed a bit of help with his groceries. You could be the gas station attendant. The cashier. Noah had been in his company less than twenty-four hours and already he'd talked to half of LA. And yet . . .

Here he was, standing on the walkway, unsure what to say. It was almost like he was . . . shy.

Sure enough, he turned, seeking Noah out with his eyes. 'Any time you want to step in? A couple of words maybe, just to put the little angel at her ease, know what I mean?'

But the girl spoke before Noah could step up. 'You ran me over,' she said to Jerry.

'Well, that's what I came about, darlin'.' He took a step forward, about to bend down and get to her level, but it was the wrong thing to do, because something in the girl's attitude changed and it was clear to see that she was about to make a run for it.

'*No*,' called Noah quickly, 'don't go. What's your name, darlin'?' She found herself playing up the Texan accent of her birthplace. Normally she tried to disguise it, but there were times, like now, when you could do a lot worse than sound like Dolly Parton.

'Jane.' The girl looked past Jerry and seemed to take in Noah for the first time.

'We need to speak to you,' Noah told her. 'I guess we also need to speak to your mother . . .' It came out more as a question directed at Jerry. After all, she had no idea what he was planning . . .

'It's not a good time,' said the little girl, finality in her voice. 'Maybe you could come back tomorrow.'

And with that, she was gone once more.

Alone again, they looked at each other, then turned to go. 'Well?' Noah took the steps. 'What now?'

'We come back tomorrow,' he replied.

'And do what?'

'I've got something in mind.'

'What?'

'Just hold your horses, I'll show you soon enough.'

They had reached the bottom of the stairs.

And then stopped.

In front of them stood two men: one, a black guy in standard gangbanger gear: black jeans, oversized sweatshirt hiding who knew what at the waistband and a gold chain across his chest. The other man was white and more distinctively dressed in a rumpled navy suit.

Jerry had seen them first, and once again Noah saw a change come over him. He didn't move, yet his bearing altered. His eyes were fixed, not on the gangbanger but on the guy in the suit. His eyes narrowed a little, his eyebrows bunched, a brittle tension settling over the two men as each sized the other up. Never before had she seen anything similar happen: a meeting of two men who had wordlessly, and yet entirely mutually, decided that they were natural enemies. There was something almost elemental about it.

'Can I help you?' asked Suit Man, breaking the wordless stand-off. His hands were clasped in front of him, head tilted slightly to one side.

'Help us?' replied Jerry. 'Why? You the caretaker, are you? I think I saw a bit of dog shit in the parking lot. You might want to get your shit bags out.'

Gangbanger shifted. Suit Man's smile was wintry. 'Just wondering what business you have here?'

'What business? Well, that would be none of your business.' Jerry's voice was light, but his eyes told a different story.

In the next second, as Jerry moved his hand quickly to his hip, drawing back his coat at the same time, Noah, thought, *Woah, what are you doing?* until she saw the gangbanger reach reflexively to his waistband and understood: Jerry had forced him to give away the fact that he was armed.

'Some might say that if you're in this building then you make it my business,' responded Suit Man.

'Well, I'm leaving, so no need to worry,' replied Jerry. 'Now, you might want to move aside before my claustrophobia kicks in. It can get unpleasant.'

He flicked his hand as though it had gone to sleep, allowing himself a smile as the gangbanger flinched in response.

Suit Man threw him a look, *Stand down*, saying to Jerry, 'The exit's that way.'

'Obliged,' said Jerry.

Moments later, they were back in the car and Noah gave voice to that second feeling she'd had. 'If I didn't know better, I'd say you enjoyed all that.'

Chapter Fourteen

As she reached for the ignition keys, it occurred to Noah that at no point during the stand-off had she felt unsafe. It was something to do with Jerry – the sense that he could handle whatever life threw at him.

Which is why the next words out of her mouth weren't to make her excuses and leave. Instead, she asked, 'Where are we going now?'

'How about I tell you when we get there?' he offered.

'Okay. So tell me a bit more about yourself in the meantime.'

He sniffed. 'What do you want to know?'

'Well, you're a debt collector now, right?'

He thought about his answer. 'You know what I always say if somebody asks me my business?' he said at last.

'You tell them it's none of your business,' she said, her mind going back to the earlier confrontation.

'No, I tell them I mind my own business,' he replied, 'and normally when I tell them that I mind my own business, they look at me, all concerned that they've offended me. "Oh, I'm really sorry, I didn't mean anything . . ." And I always say back to them, "No, I mean it, that's what I do. I mind my own business."'

She was curling a lip. 'Sounds like a good line. Doesn't sound like much of an answer.'

'No, look, I do a bit of everything, is what I'm saying. But, yeah, debt recovery is the most of it, I have to say.'

'Okay, right. So how do you go from being doorman at the golf club . . .'

'The Country Club. And I wasn't just a doorman. I ran the firm that did the security.' He rolled his eyes. 'But it'll do for now.'

'Sure. Sorry. So there was the Country Club. There was the soccer tournament stuff and that led to bodyguarding. Hey, don't they call it close protection these days? Personal security? Something like that?'

He pulled a disgusted face. 'Nah, nothing like that. I hate all that shit. When I was working the doors, I was a bouncer, not a door supervisor, customer safety officer or a security guard. Doorman, if you like. But I called myself a bouncer. Likewise, I was a bodyguard.'

'Right, bodyguard. Bodyguard in the UK. What I mean is, how did you go from being a bodyguard in the UK to being in debt recovery – I beg your pardon, "a man who minds his own business" – over here in LA, with a garage full of vintage cars and bikes?'

He told her about the jobs with Waterstones and how it led to him picking up work with celebrities. And then, 'You ever hear of a movie producer called Sidney Frankus?'

She nodded. He was one of the few household-name producers, mainly because he had the habit of bankrolling movies that were either wildly successful with the public or adored by critics. A regular tabloid fixture and a big guy – fat, you might even say – he was constantly seen around town with a cigar in one hand and a starlet in the other.

'Right, well, there was him. Fucking pap magnet, he was. I'd been doing a bit of bodyguarding for him when he was in London, and he asked me if I fancied working with him here in LA. Back then, we were getting on all right. I hadn't worked out what he was really like and so I said yes.'

'And what was he really like?'

'You don't want to know. He was a fucking scumbag.' Jerry paused, 'Anyway, so now I'm spending time in LA as Sid's bodyguard. Spending time with him and his staff. I'm a bit of a novelty among all these guys, because I'm from a different world. For me, it was a walk in the park. I'd come from nightclubs, altercations and tear-ups every night, having problems. Now I'm looking after this guy and the biggest problem I've got is overzealous fans and people hassling him for a role in his next movie. Somebody being a bit loud or a bit abusive. All I was doing was applying my talents with a person beside me.

'At first, I was a bit homesick, but it was only as I spent more time out here that . . . well, you know what it's like. The eyes see more. If you're cocooned within your world of Romford – that's in East London – and don't know about LA, the trappings in LA, of nice people, hot women, beautiful beaches, everyone being happy, it feels a bit alien, do you know what I mean? It takes a bit of getting used to. But, anyway, everyone liked what I did and so I got invited out here for good.'

'And what was it they liked, exactly?' she asked. 'That you were good at beating people up?' Right away, she regretted her bluntness, relieved when he greeted it with nothing more than a raised eyebrow.

'There isn't much beating people up in the bodyguarding game, mate. Not if you're doing it right. Most times I didn't need to be violent or aggressive because my size and ability stops the trouble before it happens, which is, after all, what I was there to do in the first place. Sidney liked the little tricks I had. Like I'd carry the torch and shine it on to the paps' lenses so it would fuck with their pictures. I had a little tub of Vaseline with me as well, get it on my thumbs, and if the pap's within reaching distance, I'm putting Vaseline on their lens. They learned to keep their distance. So just by being there, I'm getting the paps to behave better. It's about making sure they keep their distance so that Sidney and his companion can move from point A to point B hassle-free. It's about making life easier for them.'

'So what happened?'

'Well, you know what he's like? All chomping on his cigar, playing the big man. Old-school Hollywood and all that. It dents a bloke's ego, doesn't it, the fact that they can't protect themselves or their girlfriends without a guy like me around? So you got that in the mix, floating about, that kind of resentment. Meantime, I realised I was over it. When I first started out as a doorman, I was proud of being a doorman. Then I became a bodyguard and, I tell you what, I was proud of that, too. There were so many people who just assumed that I was ex-police or ex-military or have some kind of background in security because I was so good at it.

'I'm not blowing smoke up my own arse, you can take that look off your face. It's just a fact, right? I'd been working the toughest doors in London and I knew how to read people. I had the size. I had the right temperament. It was just something I took to, and while I was doing it, I was proud of doing it. I didn't want to be anything else but the best bodyguard.

'But, at the same time, I was pulling off little deals here and there, building up a bit of a property portfolio, creating a passive income, you might say. Just little things, mind, but even so. And, like I say, I got involved with a little bit of debt recovery here, a little bit of problem-solving there.

'Now, these are services that don't come cheap. What's more, they're services that bring me into different circles. All of a sudden, the celebrity that I'm looking after may not be the main event. Sidney used to get pissed off. People would invite him to a party and ask if I was coming. It got to the stage where basically I just got bored of walking in someone else's shadow. It wasn't me any more. I suddenly felt almost embarrassed, hanging around with an arsehole that's full of lies and a fake persona that he presents to the rest of the world. I didn't want to be the hired help.'

'And you decided to live out here full-time?'

'Yeah, pretty much.'

'Family back home?'

'Family, yeah,' he said. 'Mum and one younger sister.'

'You get on with them?'

'Bloody hell, you're nosy, aren't you?'

'And mum . . .'

'I love my mum.' He cleared his throat. 'Who doesn't love their mum?'

'But your life's out here now?'

'That's right. My life's out here now.'

A few moments later, before Noah could interrogate him further, they had pulled up in front of their destination, a car body shop set back from the street. The body shop itself was scruffy. A parking area studded with vehicles in various stages of disrepair was equally unkempt.

Wandering out of the dark interior of the body shop, squinting in the sudden bright sun, was a guy with a gaunt face and sunken cheeks topped by a mop of unruly sandy hair. A tattoo of a snake or a serpent wound its way from the collar of his overalls, up his neck and to just under his left ear. He was wiping his hands on a piece of blue shop towel, talking into a phone that was cradled between his cheek and his shoulder. He raised a hand to acknowledge the new arrivals. *With you in a moment.*

'That's the guy who runs it. Lucas. Best mechanic in LA,' explained Jerry. 'You wouldn't believe it, would you, to look at the place? But if you know your stuff, here's where you come.'

'Well, okay, but how come . . .'

'Oh, he used to have money. Shitloads of it, by all accounts – until he did time on a ringing scam, lost his business, got divorced and acquired a heroin habit.' Jerry described a spectacular fall from grace with a dipping finger.

'He's a junkie?'

'*Ex*-junkie, so it goes. He left the heroin behind, but not the debts. Now he's just a fucking great mechanic with good connections and a shitshow for a bank balance.'

Lucas finished his call, came over and looked admiringly,

even covetously, at the car, barely sparing a look for Noah. Sure enough, talk was of cars and motorbikes for a while, with more than one reference to Jerry's collection, before Jerry asked, 'You done that repair for me, mate?'

'I'll be right back.'

'What's all this about?' asked Noah, watching him go.

'You wanted to see what I had in mind for the little girl, didn't you?' said Jerry.

She nodded.

'Well, here it comes,' he said, just as Lucas reappeared, wheeling Jane's bicycle, now fixed.

'Here you go, Jerry,' said Lucas, 'it's as good as new.'

'Thank you,' said Jerry. He flashed Noah a grin.

Chapter Fifteen

With the repaired bike in the trunk, they took to the road once more. Next on the list was a visit to Noah's bungalow. She wanted a quick change, she said.

When they pulled up in the street outside her home, a minivan stood at the kerb. On seeing it, Noah's demeanour changed.

'What's the problem?' asked Jerry.

'Dunno,' she said, chewing her lip. 'Might be nothing.'

They climbed out of the Oldsmobile, Noah still eyeing the minivan suspiciously. As though to acknowledge her fears, the driver's door of the minivan opened and out stepped a big guy with well-cultivated stubble. 'Hey, Noah,' he called over.

She had put her head down, was heading for the bungalow. 'Just leave me alone, Jeff,' she called over her shoulder.

Jerry was alert. 'Is there a problem here?'

The guy turned to him, his hands upraised. 'Hey, there's no problem here, buddy.' The combination of shades and carefully sculpted stubble made him look like George Michael, but he was well built. Back home, Jerry and his crew had an expression to describe the blokes who were probably good in a fight: 'He looks like he could have a row.'

This geezer – he looked like he could have a tear-up. Jerry knew the type well. This guy would use his size to intimidate the girls, and Jerry could see that Noah – hardly the easily frightened sort – was looking distinctly uncomfortable.

No doubt about it – it was a dynamic he recognised.

And he decided to change it.

Jerry stepped up – *strike first, while the other guy's still gabbing* – when a station wagon swung up to the kerb and parked, doors opened and a couple stepped out.

Jerry checked his approach, and maybe Jeff realised what had been about to go down, how he'd had a lucky escape, because he smiled a little. At the same time, the couple getting out of the station wagon became aware that they'd stepped into the middle of a situation and, looking over, the indecision – *should we stay or should we go?* – flitted across their faces.

Jeff smiled. Noah looked pensive. Jerry decided to take advantage of the fact that he had his back to the new arrivals. 'Mate,' he said in a low voice to Jeff, 'what's that on your jacket? You need to . . .' He mimed brushing something from his own front. And then, just as Jeff reflexively moved his hand to follow suit, Jerry sprang. 'Shit, he's going for a gun,' he bellowed, and clomped the bloke.

Jeff took the punch and dropped like a stunned bull. Over the way, Station Wagon Couple gasped, the woman squealing, the bloke spluttering and reaching for his phone, until Jerry called over, 'It's okay, it's okay, folks. He's out cold, taking a nap. He won't be bothering nobody.' Kneeling on the bloke's head, he pretended to retrieve a gun. 'Tell you what, you go about your business, we'll get the police to look after him, don't you worry about that. Crisis averted.'

With relief, he watched as they did as they were asked, hurrying off up the street. Then he tensed afresh as the door to the minivan opened, and first one booted foot, and then another, appeared.

It was a woman, mid-forties, all in black, but for mirrored aviators. She was short in stature, but even so, there was something commanding about her. 'Jerry – Jeremiah O'fuckin' Connell,' she cried in an Arizonian accent, 'it really is you.'

Jerry's mouth dropped. 'Vera?' he said, squinting, and then was swamping the much smaller woman as he embraced her. 'How you doing, darlin'?' he asked her and then turned to Noah. 'You know Vera, then?'

Noah was nodding and, of course, it all made sense. Vera Marlantes was one of LA's top madams. Most people, if they wanted the services of a sex worker, knew where to go in the city, or how to go online, order one up like a pizza. But if you were rich, powerful, famous, all three, or just one of the above, then you went to someone like Vera. Not only was her name a hallmark of quality – and Jerry knew from first-hand experience that the girls in her stable were absolutely stunning – but it was also a guarantee of discretion. If her clients wanted to tell one another that they used her, that was their prerogative, and a lot of them did, passing on her number, dropping her name, using the connection as a status symbol. But when it came to Vera herself, her lips remained sealed and had done through more subpoenas than anyone cared to mention. Same went for her private life – if she even had one. There was nothing Vera hadn't heard about the goings-on in LA. If it involved sex, drugs or any combination of both, then it would have reached her ears. She herself, however, remained a constant question mark.

And how did Jerry know her? Sidney Frankus, of course. Being a movie producer – and not just a movie producer, but a highly successful movie producer – Sidney was hardly short of female attention, but his sexual appetite was voracious and, after all, Vera's girls were the most beautiful in the city. More importantly, Jerry *liked* Vera. She was down-to-earth and straight-talking – two characteristics Jerry prized. In return, he knew, Vera liked him. They'd always been upfront with each other, and neither took themselves or the celebrity world in which they found themselves too seriously.

'Noah's your girl, then, is she, darlin'? That's why you brought the Rottweiler here?'

The Rottweiler in question was picking himself up off the floor, holding his injured nose, blood leaking from his palm. 'Vera just wanted to talk, that was all,' he said, mouth full of blood and reproach.

'Well, I don't want to talk to her,' Noah sounded on the verge of extreme violence herself.

'Hold up, hold your horses.' Jerry looked from one party to the other. 'And that's it, is it? Just a case of yous wanting to talk to yous, and yous not wanting to talk to yous.'

'What can I say, Jerry?' grinned Vera. She didn't seem overly concerned about Jeff, just folded her arms and leaned back on the minivan like a woman at peace with the world. 'Noah's a popular girl. Lot of clients asking about her. There's a lot of money to be made if she wants it.'

Jerry reflected that he'd heard similar things about Commodore and wondered whether it was a trait unique to LA
– the urge to treat beautiful women like commodities, to be
bought, sold and traded.

'Lot of money for *you* to make, is what you mean,' spat
Noah, hands on her hips.

'I think you have your answer, don't you?' said Jerry.
Rottweiler – the artist formerly known as Jeff – had helped
himself to his haunches. To show there were no hard feelings, Jerry stepped over and offered his hand. In return, Jeff
gave him a wounded but pacified look. 'Tell you what, how
about we all go and have a drink together, and we can talk
. . .' started Jerry.

'Oh no. Oh no,' interrupted Noah.

'. . . About *not* talking,' finished Jerry. 'Let's just go for a
drink, is what I'm saying. And maybe something to eat while
we're at it. I know a great place that does a good monster
platter. You'll love it.'

'Sounds like a good idea,' said Vera. 'Maybe over a drink
you can tell me what happened between you and Sidney.'

'You heard that we parted ways, then?'

'You know full well that there's nothing I don't hear in
this town.'

'Wait . . .' Something had just occurred to him, and he
turned to Noah, who grimaced, knowing what was coming.
'Were you with the agency when I was working with Sidney?'

'You know better than to ask questions like that, honeybunch,' drawled Vera. 'And, Noah, you know better than to
answer, darlin'.'

'All right, keep your hair on. All I want to know is . . .' He

71

looked carefully at Noah. 'Did you and him ever . . . I mean, did he get his leg over?'

'Does it make any difference?' she said. 'To us, I mean?'

'Nah,' he said reflexively. 'We're mates, aren't we?'

She looked sharply at him. 'We're just mates?'

He seemed to think about this, chin jutting as he regarded the sky thoughtfully. 'Yeah,' he said at last, 'why not?'

In response, she felt suddenly weightless, as though an invisible force pressing down upon her, a pressure that, whether she liked it or not, had been present in any dealing with any guy for as long as she could remember, had suddenly been lifted.

She looked at him in wonderment. Did he know what he'd just done? How, with just a few words, he'd blown through her life, a breath of truly fresh air.

He looked at her and winked. 'Now, how about a drink?' he said.

Chapter Sixteen

Night had fallen, and nowhere had it fallen harder than on Cedar Tree Avenue, where the 'All Fur Coa' strip club was lit up, where the night women came out to ply their trade – and where addicts came to score.

Mostly they came to score at the apartments of Sunshine Heights, where the parking lot was almost as empty as it had been when Jerry and Noah had visited some hours before. There was just the odd car pulling in, deals done through cranked-down windows. A lot of the traffic was on foot, sometimes twos and threes, but mainly alone, hands in pockets, trying, and mostly failing, not to shuffle across the lot, either making contact with the kids outside the shops or finding their way to the apartments. The methods of introduction differed, and the dealers in many cases were different again – but they were all controlled by one man: a man who wore a crumpled linen suit and who carried a long knife with a half-serrated blade. He used Sunshine Heights as his base and ran it as his own personal fiefdom.

His name was Ronson Beaufoy. The bossman.

He had not grown up on these streets. In fact, Beaufoy's

birthplace was wealthy Bel-Air, some distance away. But addiction had befallen his prosperous family, and the bubble of family life, successfully maintained by his mother and father so that he and his older brother had remained happily oblivious until their early teens, finally burst for good.

Shortly after that, he had found himself one of the few white faces in Compton, adapting to a new life, new people, new rules. The street was his master now, and he had done what he needed to do in order to survive. And what he needed to do in order to survive was prove himself.

Beaufoy had always been fascinated by serial killers. As a teenager, growing up in Bel-Air, he had marvelled at their deeds, wondering how they steeled themselves to do what they did.

'A lack of empathy.' That was what the books said. The mark of a serial killer. An inability to *feel*.

Perhaps it was the fact that in Bel-Air his empathy had never been tested. Perhaps circumstances – his father's addiction, his parents' break-up, the family's fall from financial grace – had all combined and conspired to leach away what empathy he had. For when it came to acts of violence on the streets, Beaufoy realised, not without a certain amount of satisfaction – as though discovering a new, hitherto untapped skill – that he was that person. Not only was he capable of inflicting great pain, even being creative in doing so, but he enjoyed it.

And here he was in an environment where that particular trait was not one to inspire revulsion or fear. Rather, it gained him respect. By being more vicious, crueller and more ruthless than any other member of the gang he joined, he had saved what was left of his broken, battered family. He had saved them through crime and violence. He gained the respect of the gangs by showing a disrespect for the sanctity of life, by proving himself more willing to transgress norms of the flesh.

He was never the leader, not back then. The streets would not have allowed it. But he very quickly became a feared enforcer, and that was enough to ensure his own prosperity and that of his family.

Ultimately, he took that reputation to another part of the city, more ethnically diverse, and he used his gang contacts to set up a franchise, a new operation, a gang known as CT-40 after the Cedar Tree neighbourhood in which it was based. The coup was hardly bloodless. His takeover of the neighbourhood not exactly without its victims. But he had prevailed, and not only that, but he had made connections in another direction. He had, if anything, transcended his roots, become more and more powerful and more feared, because in his business, of course, power and fear were exactly the same thing.

There had been a moment, years ago, back in Compton, when Beaufoy was anointed enforcer of the gang. It had meant that his period of apprenticeship had come to an end, and he had earned his full quota of respect. As long as he continued to do what was right and did nothing to betray his brothers, then his position was guaranteed. He was a made man.

Shortly after, he went in search of his father, and learned that he had kicked the junk, cleaned himself up and was now living in a modest apartment in Brentwood, working as an insurance adviser.

Ronson had visited that apartment. He had taken a seat in an armchair, listening to the noises of the city from outside the window, and waited for his father to return from work.

His father had thought he was an intruder at first. Realising that it was Ronson, his son, the older man had moved to embrace him, tears bubbling up from inside as emotions collided in whimpers of relief and apology and regret. He pleaded for forgiveness, this man whose inability to control his appetites had sentenced his family to such hardship all those years ago. He hadn't even had the decency to die.

But Ronson made up for that. His father's raw emotion was such that he failed to notice that Ronson had remained unmoved by the reunion, and that he wore rubber surgical gloves and shoe coverings. But he noticed when Ronson drew his knife.

He told his father to undress, and then he used his knife to take all of his father's dignity, his self-respect, his spirit and, lastly, his soul.

It took him several hours.

And when Ronson left, he took the navy linen suit his father had been wearing.

It was just the right size for him.

Chapter Seventeen

Now, Beaufoy had a problem. No, he hesitated to call it a *problem*. More of an *issue*. But one that needed attention all the same. There was the matter of the tall English guy he had spoken to earlier that day. Not a cop – he knew a cop when he saw one. But if not a cop, then what?

According to Shea, one of his right-hand men, this guy had arrived in an Oldsmobile and gone straight to apartment 22B, where Ruth Shepherd, one of Beaufoy's workers, lived with her daughter. Beaufoy had summoned Shea and another of his men, Lucky Strike, to accompany him. It was time to pay that apartment a visit.

On the walkway, he hung back, clasping his hands behind his back, flexing his shoulders, as Shea went forward, knocking on the door.

It opened a crack, Ruth relieved to see a familiar face on her doorstep. 'Have you got the stuff?' she asked. Ruth, as well as working for Beaufoy, was also a client. Most of those who called Sunshine Heights home shared the same status. Theirs was a world of fear and need and addiction, all of it controlled by Beaufoy.

Shea shook his head 'no'.

Panic flared in her eyes. She was desperate for a hit and had been since way before the tall guy came calling. 'But Mr Beaufoy wants me out there selling. I can't sell if I've got nothing to sell . . .?'

'It can wait. Beaufoy wants a word with you.'

She blanched. 'Wants a word with me? What does he want to talk to me about?'

'Let him tell you himself,' said Shea, and Beaufoy stepped forward, Lucky Strike behind him.

Ruth's eyes flitted. Visits from Beaufoy's men were commonplace, but never from the man himself. Her heart hammered in her chest and the sweat she felt prickle her forehead was from fear as much as the withdrawal that was gnawing at her insides.

'Inside, if you will,' Beaufoy indicated she should stand away from the door and all three entered, filling the small, rancid apartment.

Beaufoy cast his eye around. Growing up in Bel-Air, they'd had cleaners. Whether his father's addiction had ever spilled into domestic view, he couldn't really say – all traces of it would have been removed by the help. Relocating as a trio to Compton, his mother had been fiercely proud. The bungalow, like other identical bungalows on their street, was small, and although the front yard was untidy and unkempt, inside was always spotless. The Beaufoy family had never given up. His mother had made sure of that, God rest her soul.

This – this was giving up: beer bottles and coffee cups and dirty plates. Everything that could be used as an ashtray employed for that purpose. The whole place dark and full of stench. Jesus, she raised a kid in this?

Ruth stumbled to the opposite side of the room, the three new arrivals arranged in a line. She stood, trembling, pale and scrawny, wearing an oversized sleeveless Nike shirt over ratty gym leggings, hair in greasy ropes, crooked teeth like moss-covered gravestones.

Beaufoy pushed his hands into the pockets of his suit and raised a foot that he placed very carefully on the coffee table. 'You had a visitor earlier.'

She knew better than to lie. Even if the information hadn't been given to him by either Shea or Lucky Strike, or another of his enforcers, it could have been passed to him by one of the dealers, or one of the users, or one of the other residents. 'Yes. Some guy from Australia and a woman.' She ended, knowing it was better to give less information than more.

'He's British. And what did he want?'

She gave him what she thought was the right answer, based on the two seconds of thought she'd given the matter right after the man's visit. 'A school inspector.'

'A school inspector?' Beaufoy tried the words in his mouth to see if he liked the taste. 'It's been a long time since I heard the words "school inspector". They still have those?'

She shrugged. 'I don't know, do I, Mr Beaufoy? All I know is that he came, asking after Jane. Maybe they sent me a letter, but . . .' She moved her head, birdlike, to indicate the futility of looking for a simple letter in the mess.

'But it's not just the visit that I want to talk to you about.' Beaufoy, hands still in pockets, foot still up on the coffee table, looked pained. 'Because I've been receiving complaints from customers. Transactions have been coming up short. And now you're getting strange visitors.' Those words again, strange in his mouth, as though exotic: 'School inspectors.'

A whimper escaped her lips as, from inside his jacket, Beaufoy produced the Knife.

Not just his preferred instrument of punishment and/or torture, his only instrument of punishment and/or torture. It was about seven inches long. One side of the blade was wickedly serrated, the other clean and sharp. He turned it over for a second or so and then leaned forward to ram it hard into the coffee table.

The sound it made, like a guillotine. *Thunk*. Another whimper from Ruth.

'Come here, please,' said Beaufoy. 'We have a little game that I would like to play. A little game of truth or dare.'

At that moment, a figure appeared in the small passageway leading to the bedroom and bathroom. The little girl. She looked from her mother, to the three men who stood close to the closed door of the apartment, her eyes wide with fear and skittering.

'Ah,' started Beaufoy, 'you must be . . .'

And then he stopped, because although he had planned to take advantage of the girl's appearance and question her, he was overtaken by a sudden and quite unexpected turn of events. Ruth had reached behind her, from her waistband produced a small handgun, and in the next instant had grabbed Jane, and was now holding a gun on her – on her own daughter.

In his time as a gang enforcer and leader, Beaufoy had seen plenty of ghastly sights – acts that plumbed the depths of human sickness and depravity. But even he had never seen a mother pull a gun on her own daughter.

Slowly, a smile spread across his face.

And then, very deliberately, he leaned forward, retrieved the knife from the table and, drawing back his jacket, replaced it in its sheath at his hip.

'Careful,' said Ruth as he did so, but he continued anyway, pulling his jacket back into place and then returning his hands to his pockets.

'What now then, Ruth?' he said amiably.

Her eyes were moving in two different directions. White matter had collected at the corner of her mouth. Her entire body shook. This was a desperate junkie in severe need of a hit.

'Go,' she said.

'But we haven't spoken.' Beaufoy felt a feeling of great calm in moments like this. As though that darkened territory between life and death was exactly where he was born to be. 'I had hoped we could get to the bottom of things, and then perhaps I could leave. Oh, and we've got some gear for you.'

The magic words. For Ruth they cut right through the moment; they overrode whatever else was going on in her stagnating, addled mind.

'But now you tell me you want me to leave,' continued Beaufoy, spreading his hands, looking from Shea to Lucky Strike in exaggerated comical disbelief.

Jane whimpered, 'Mommy,' but Ruth was oblivious to her little girl's distress. If anything, she increased the pressure, pushing the barrel of the weapon hard on the top of her skull.

'Leave the gear and go,' she said.

At this, Beaufoy pretended to consider, until, as if decided, he raked a hand through his hair, fixed Ruth with a look and said, 'Go on then.'

'Mommy.'

'I will. So help me I will.'

Shea and Lucky Strike shifted.

'Go ahead,' goaded Beaufoy.

'Don't push me. I'll do it. I swear, I'll do it.'

'I dare you to. I'll tell you what. You put a bullet in your daughter and we'll leave.'

'Boss . . .' said Lucky Strike from one side, but Beaufoy silenced him with an upraised finger.

'Do we have a deal?'

'The drugs? Will you leave the drugs?'

At that, Beaufoy threw back his head and roared. 'Of course! How remiss of me, I forgot to mention the drugs. Indeed we will leave the drugs.'

'Mommy!'

'Boss . . .'

'Do it then.'

She was breathing hard, finger squeezing, whitening on the trigger, mental pathways blocked by want and need.

Beaufoy reached into his pocket, pulled out a baggie, held it up like a pocket watch, taunting, tormenting her with it.

'DO IT.'

She did.

The little girl fell down, a section of her skull sheared away by the bullet. On either side of him, the men recoiled, disgusted, but as for Beaufoy, the smile never left his face.

'Now I've seen it all,' he said and punched the number 911 on his phone.

On the other side of the room, Ruth fell to her knees, knowing what she had done, the horrible enormity dawning too slowly, and far, far too late, upon her.

The room took its time to settle. In the immediate wake of the shooting, there was no sound, just a terrible silence, before Ruth Shepherd began weeping, the dread realisation dawning upon her, Shea and Lucky Strike reacting with revulsion, and then Beaufoy speaking on the phone, calling in reports of a shooting at number 22B Sunshine Heights.

He and his men turned to leave. They closed the door behind them, and then, as they made their way towards the stairs, they heard another shot from number 22B.

Beaufoy shook his head in wonder and disgust.

Chapter Eighteen

For the second day in a row, Noah awoke with a hangover twice the size of Anchorage and three times as bleak.

She groaned. Last night, when the festivities had died down and it was finally time to hit the hay, she had retired to the guest bedroom, and she was glad of the extra space now. With extra space, nobody could hear you scream. She rolled over and groaned again, wondering what the day had in store.

Meanwhile, in the living room, Jerry was already up, mulling over the previous night's events. Jeff had gone elsewhere. After that, it had been a good evening, with just the three of them: one that had started with beers, followed by shots, followed by almost total monopoly of the bar's juke-box, followed by an outbreak of dancing, followed by a return to his apartment, more drinks, and more dancing. No doubt about it. Had to admit it: a bloody good night.

On the sofa beside him, a crumpled figure lay asleep. 'Do you fancy a cup of tea, Vera?' he asked, giving the duvet-covered shape a gentle nudge. From beneath the cover came a growl that he took to be a yes and he stood from the couch, padding through to the kitchen area to make drinks.

A short time later, Noah appeared, and all three of them sat at the table, sipping tea in companionable silence, until Vera decided it was time to go and summoned an Uber. She gathered her things. 'So what's the story, honeybunch, you coming with me?' she asked Noah.

Noah took a deep breath, trying to decide. *Okay*, she thought, *so maybe it's high time to make like a tree and leave.* After all, those bills weren't going to pay themselves. A girl had to make a living. She massaged her forehead, unable to make up her mind – her drink-fogged, hangover-blighted mind.

'What's your thoughts then? Are you going, or would you like to stay?' Jerry prompted gently, seeing her indecision, maybe trying to jog her into making her choice.

'Well . . .' She looked from him to Vera, who stood waiting expectantly, eyebrows raised. 'Um . . .'

'I'd like to think that Vera and Jeff have forgotten any ideas they had about insisting you work for them.' Jerry's voice was pleasant, and when he looked at Vera, he smiled, but there was no mistaking what he meant. In return, Vera gave him a disingenuous look: *What? Me?*

'It's not that,' began Noah. 'Just . . . I mean, you know I have money to make, right?'

Vera's phone told her the Uber was outside. 'Time's a-ticking, Tinkerbell.'

Noah looked from Vera to Jerry and then back again. She thought of the bungalow, so lifeless without Jacqui. She thought of guys from Utah. She thought of little Jane, the girl at Sunshine Heights. She thought of what Jerry had said on the sidewalk, and the feeling of relief and freedom she'd felt, that weightlessness.

'I'll stay,' she said.

'There's your answer,' he said.

When Vera had left, he turned to Noah, 'Now we've got a bicycle to deliver. You up for that?'

She nodded. Yes, she was up for that.

Chapter Nineteen

'I had a dream last night,' announced Jerry as they drove. Deciding on a change, they'd left the Oldsmobile in the garage, choosing a topless 1964 Chevy Impala instead. It was virtually the only other car in the collection large enough for them and Jane's bicycle, which lay along the back seats.

'A bad dream, was it?' she asked.

'What's the difference between a bad dream and a nightmare?'

'A bad dream is a dream that's not so great; a nightmare's the full-on a bloodthirsty monster is chasing me and I'm wading slowly through mud.'

'All right, well this was neither. It was just a dream. About my dad.'

Noah hung a left, accelerated, shifted up. 'And your pa. Is he still . . . alive?'

'No. That's the thing. He died at fifty-nine. But he'd split up from my mum before that.'

She thought of her own non-existent relationship with her father. He was drink-sodden, constantly angry and, as she'd gotten older, a master of insinuating looks. She'd left home before he could turn looks and thought into action, which he surely would have done, sooner or later. There was nothing her father liked better than to take off his belt. 'Did you get on with your pa?' she asked Jerry now.

He seemed to think about this answer for a while. 'Yeah,' he said at last, 'I got on with him well. I remember things. Like when I was little, we'd be out driving, he'd let me put my hand on the gearstick, put his hand on top and we'd change the gear together. It was a connection. I loved that.'

She smiled, nodded, trying to picture this huge bear of a man as a little boy basking in his father's love.

'I remember I used to be in the back seat of the car sometimes,' he continued, one memory sparking another, 'I'd reach round and hug him in the driving seat, draping my arms around his neck, head on his shoulder. I remember that really clearly. I remember the smell of him. He smelled of Golden Virginia.'

There was silence for a moment. 'Sounds like a good guy, your pa. Were you still in touch with him, when he died?'

'Not so much. I mean, I know I made him proud though. I know it because there was a garage where he got his car serviced and I was friendly with the geezers who worked in there. Anyway, so one night I was out bodyguarding a footballer. We'd been in a club, came out and all the paparazzi are blasting away, getting pictures of him, and I'm there next to him.

'So, like I say, I knew the geezers in this garage where my dad got his car serviced. They had the paper, and I heard that they were like, "Is that your son? Is that Jerry?" And he was like, "Yes, that's him," all proud.

'So he already knew that I'd gone on from being a door-man. He knew that I'd made something of myself. Just wish he could have been around to see all this,' he gestured, meaning the car, LA, the lifestyle.

'At least you knew you'd made him proud.'

'Well, I didn't – not until he died. It was only at the funeral that people were coming up to me telling me these stories.'

'And it was him you were dreaming about last night?'

'Yeah. The funniest thing. I just dreamt about him, and when I woke up, my first thought – you know what it's like, when waking and dreaming is all mixed up – my first thought was, *I gotta go and see him today*, and my next thought after that was, *I can't. He's been dead for ten years*.'

She let him ruminate awhile, before saying, 'You sure lead a different life now.'

'Oh yeah,' he agreed.

And for a moment or so, he was indeed content, thinking about how far he'd come, enjoying the sun, sitting beside Noah in a 1964 Chevy Impala, and anticipating giving little Jane her bicycle back.

But then Sunshine Heights came into view, and any good mood was instantly shattered.

Chapter Twenty

In the parking lot was a police cruiser, next to it a CSU van, beside that what looked like another unmarked cop car. The kids were in their usual spot, but other than a small huddle of residents outside a grocery store, there was barely any interest being shown in all the police activity. Jerry knew why: this was a community in harness, and thinking back to his encounter with Suit Man, he thought he knew who was holding the reins.

At the same time, he was struck by a thought. No, not a thought. A fear, sudden and sharp, like a blade between the ribs, and his eyes were drawn to the apartment block overlooking the lot. Sunshine Heights. Despite its name, it cast a shadow, both figurative and literal. He'd have expected to see bystanders there, people hanging out on the walkway, watching the activity below. Again, there was nothing.

What there was, however, was an open apartment door marked by yellow police tape and guarded by a uniformed cop.

'Hey,' he said to Noah, nudging her, pointing.

'Oh, shit,' she said.

'That's exactly what I was thinking.' He climbed out of the car, striding towards the kids outside the store. 'Hey, mate,' he said, nearing them. 'What's going on, then?' he gestured up at the apartments.

A little white kid on a bike, couldn't have been more than twelve, gave him a laconic, street-hardened shrug. 'Some little bitch got shot,' he said, managing to make it sound as though he were not only responsible for the shooting, but proud of the fact.

Around him, the other kids sniggered obediently, all following the script faithfully.

But, come on, look around, it's not their fault, thought Jerry, swallowing his immediate feelings of revulsion. 'You don't know the girl's name, do you?' he pressed. 'Wasn't Jane, was it?'

'Yeah, bro,' said the kid. 'That was the bitch's name.'

He'd been expecting it, but even so, the news hit him like a punch. Beside him, Noah had arrived. On seeing her, the kids had straightened and openly leered, one of them even flicked his tongue obscenely, but she wasn't paying attention. Like Jerry, she was in shock, thinking, *This can't be. We only saw her yesterday.*

'Is she dead?' asked Jerry. The question came from behind clenched teeth. He found that he was flexing his fists and shoved them into his coat pocket.

'The little bitch?'

'No more of that,' warned Jerry.

The other kids roared with laughter. The twelve-year-old tried to tough it out. 'Easy, bro. They took her to the hospital.' He grinned. 'Her mom sure was dead, though.'

Jerry was still trying to work out what might have happened: Jane shot and in the hospital, her mum – the junkie at the door – dead. 'And it happened up there, did it?' he asked.

A sneaky look flitted across the kid's face. 'Maybe you should be asking your questions to the cops, bro.' He jerked his chin and Jerry turned to see two plain-clothes arriving, a man and a woman – him white, her mixed-race – dressed similarly in suits and white shirts, both wearing sunglasses.

'I was wondering if we could have a talk, sir?' said the woman. Out came the badge.

The kids exploded again, jeering. 'Hey, make sure you tell the cops why you've got her bike in your car!' taunted the kid. 'The little *bitch's* bike.'

Jerry would have liked to throttle the little shit, but the cops were commanding his attention now.

'I'm Detective Sergeant Lowrey,' announced the woman, tucking the badge away, 'and this is Detective Sergeant Baxter.' Her colleague smiled thinly. 'Maybe we could have a quick word in our car?' she gestured at the unmarked vehicle beside the CSU van.

'And why would you need to do that?' asked Noah. From beneath her mantle of shock, she sounded a little mutinous.

No lover of authority, this one, thought Jerry. Probably had a ton of bad cop experiences under her belt.

Lowrey turned her attention to Noah. 'Well, until two seconds ago I was going to ask what you were doing here. Now that you apparently have the victim's bicycle in your car, I guess I'll just go right ahead and ask you about that as well. That okay with you, *ma'am*?'

Noah relented and all four of them moved away from the stores towards the car.

'So it's true, then?' Jerry asked as they made their way over. 'She's been shot.'

Lowrey spoke over her shoulder. '"She" being?'

'The little girl, Jane.'

'Then yes, sir, I'm sorry to tell you, it's true.'

Jerry swallowed. 'And she's in the hospital.'

'She is, sir, in an induced coma. In one sense, she's very fortunate. Bullet travelled the length of the brain – entered from the back, exited from the front – but not into the brain itself.'

'And that's a thing, is it?'

'Much more common than you'd think.'

'Who did it?'

'We don't know that for sure right now, but we think the mother shot her – why, we don't know. Maybe an accidental discharge, maybe something else – before taking her own life.'

'She shot herself, the mum?'

'That would appear to be the case, sir, yes.'

Horrific, thought Jerry, but kept his trap shut.

They'd reached the car and all four climbed inside: Jerry and Noah settling in the rear, the two detectives in the front, twisting round to face them.

'How about we start with your name and address?' asked Lowrey.

Noah bridled once more. 'Well, how about we don't,' she said, 'unless you suspect us of committing a crime.'

'Oh, check Ms Know-My-Rights here. How about the

theft of a bicycle – unless the kids over there have got it wrong.'

'Well, they didn't say the bike was stolen, did they?' replied Noah. 'They don't know shit.'

Lowrey and Baxter exchanged a glance, frowning. Jerry had seen that look on cops' faces before, both in LA and at home. 'Look, all right, I'll tell you my name and address. My friend – that's up to her. But to get us off on the right foot, yeah, I'll tell you who I am.'

Noah cast him a sour look, but Jerry knew what he was doing: they could run the plates of the Chevy and that might throw up more questions than it answered. Far better to be upfront.

Lowrey nodded approvingly and couldn't help but shoot a victory glance at Noah. 'Okay, so how about you do that, sir. Tell us who you are and how come the girl's bicycle is apparently in the back seat of your car.'

So he did. He began to tell them the truth, or at least a palatable version of it. As he spoke, however, he noticed a gangbanger hanging around the Chevy. A guy he recognised from yesterday. This geezer was looking across at the cop car with a half-smile on his face. Taunting Jerry.

Laugh it up. Fucking enjoy yourself while you can, he thought.

'Look,' said Jerry, when he'd finished his tale, 'I know you don't think I had anything to do with this. I know it. You've just told me yourself that the mother did it.'

Lowrey didn't blink. 'Doesn't change the fact.'

'What fact? The fact that we were trying to do someone a good turn?'

He stole another glance over at the Chevy. Still lurking over there, the gangbanger caught his eye, smirked and ran a hand lovingly along the Chevy's bodywork before settling back and folding his arms, behaving for all the world as though the car belonged to him. His eyes went up to Sunshine Heights and Jerry got the impression that there were others there, keeping watch.

Suit Man?

Undoubtedly.

Lowrey, meanwhile, had laughed at Jerry's 'good turn' comment, but there was no joy or mirth in that laugh. It was dry. Baked granite-hard by the streets. 'You don't know this neighbourhood, do you?' She gestured around them. 'Otherwise you might know better than to be returning bicycles, however pure your motives.' She indicated Noah. 'You from uptown as well, are you?'

Noah looked at her, feeling her cheeks burn, as though the cop could see right through her, to the core of her. Like the cop *knew* that she was a hooker. She nodded.

'Yeah, I thought so. Because if you had any understanding of this area, then you'd know better than to be sticking your nose in.' Jerry started to say something, but she quietened him with an upraised finger. 'You may *think* you had nothing to do with what happened up there, but an area like this, it's what you might call a microcosm, and a guy like you turning up, looking the way you do, driving the car you're driving, well, it disrupts that microcosm, it raises eyebrows, causes trouble.

'Think on that, why don't you? Think on that the next time you're deciding it wasn't your fault. Nobody's saying you pulled the trigger, sir. Nobody's saying you didn't intend to do the right thing. But ask yourself, did anybody in this area greet you with open arms?'

Jerry had already come to the same conclusion. No, he had had nothing to do with hurting the little girl.

And yet . . .

He felt hollowed out. Responsible.

'Are we free to go then?' he asked, betraying nothing.

Lowrey swung round to face front in the passenger seat, dismissing them with her back. 'I trust I won't be seeing you around here again,' she said. 'Go back uptown. Stay there.'

Jerry and Noah made their way back to the Chevy, Jerry glad to note that behind them the detective's car was already pulling out of the lot. He cast a swift, surreptitious look around. A couple of cops remained but were occupied talking to residents. Nobody was paying him and Noah any attention, not even the kids at the store. Under his breath, he said to Noah, 'Soon as we reach the motor, get in the driving seat, yeah?'

She nodded.

And now they arrived, where the gangbanger, unperturbed, still leaning against the bodywork with his arms across his chest, smirked. 'Time for you to move on, homeboy, huh? Awful what happened to little Jane and Ruth Shepherd, wasn't it? Terrible tragedy.' He made gun fingers, two shots, *blauh, blauh*, ending by pointing them meaningfully at Jerry and Noah.

Jerry pretended to ignore the performance. He fished in the pocket of his coat for his sunglasses, put them on. 'You enjoying my motor, are you?'

Noah had climbed into the driving seat, as asked.

'It's a nice ride,' said the gangbanger with a look across at her, fully aware of the double meaning in his statement.

'I saw you looking at the bike,' said Jerry.

The gangbanger shrugged.

'Shame I couldn't fit it in the trunk, really,' Jerry continued. 'Just had to leave it there in the back seat.' He left a significant pause. 'See, the trunk's full.'

The gangbanger took the bait. 'Full of *what*, homeboy?'

'What's in the trunk is the real reason I'm here. Something your boss might be interested in.' He jerked his head in the direction of the apartments. 'Merchandise.'

'Shoulda mentioned it when you had the chance, homey,' said the gangbanger, unimpressed.

'Didn't have it then. I brought it to show him today.'

'Show me,' said the gangbanger, sliding along the Chevy until he was closer to the trunk.

Noah's head was still. Her hand was on the ignition.

'Nah, mate.' Jerry shook his head. 'Need to talk to the organ grinder, not the monkey, know what I mean?'

Glowering, the gangbanger looked around and then lifted up his T-shirt to show the butt of a handgun in the waistband of his pants. He pointed at the trunk. 'Open it, homeboy.'

Jerry nodded, as though to acknowledge the point, and then opened the trunk. Curious, the gangbanger leaned in to see.

It took the guy about half a second to realise what Jerry was up to. Which was half a second too late. In one fast movement – an attack-first-and-fast strategy honed over the years – Jerry snatched the gun from the guy's waistband, swiped the butt of it across his temple, bundled him inside and then slammed the trunk shut. A heartbeat was all the time it took.

Jerry stood by the trunk, casting his eyes around the lot until he was happy they hadn't been seen by the two cops. As for the watchers from Sunshine Heights, he couldn't be sure. All he knew was that he had to move fast.

Inside the trunk, the guy was shouting in pain and surprise, yelling to be let out, muffled threats, fists and feet banging on the inside of the trunk.

'Rev the engine,' Jerry told Noah, to drown out the geezer, and then, 'Drive,' as he dropped into the passenger seat, turning the radio on to block out the noise. 'Keep it smooth, but just drive.'

From the back, the banging and shouting sounds intensified, muffled by the radio. Noah's hands were slick on the steering wheel. She was beginning to wonder if she had made a mistake not taking Vera up on her offer.

Chapter Twenty-One

'Jesus, what the fuck are we doing, Jerry?' asked Noah as she drove, trying to keep her voice steady, wondering if it was the hangover, fear or a mixture of both that was making her sweat.

In response, Jerry was calm, shades on, elbow up. 'I got questions that need answers. This numpty in the back is going to give them to me. Here, pull over.' He pointed. 'Just there.' He was gesturing towards an abandoned industrial unit with an overgrown patch of scrubland to one side. 'Stop up there, out of sight. I've got to sort this noise.'

Noah drew to a halt, and a moment later Jerry had left the car, ambled round to the trunk, opened it, and then smashed the geezer inside in the mouth with his fist. Next, he grabbed hold of his hair, pulled his head onto the lip of the trunk and slammed the trunk lid on him. Flesh split and blood bubbled.

A second later and Jerry was back in the passenger seat, beside Noah. She had paled.

'You all right?' he asked.

Noah was not completely alien to the world of violence,

but rarely – make that never – had she seen it dispensed so ruthlessly.

'Was that really necessary?' she asked, as she started the car again.

'Don't worry, the car's fine.'

'I didn't mean the fucking car,' she hissed.

'Yeah, all right, it was only a joke. Look, did you want him making a racket all the way back to the apartment?'

'I mean, couldn't you have just hit him once?'

'It ain't that easy to knock somebody unconscious. This isn't like the movies.'

By now, they were back on the road, and Noah was glad to be putting Cedar Tree Avenue in the rearview at last. 'Why are you getting involved with this anyway? It's not your fight, Jerry.'

Jerry sighed. 'It ain't as simple as that.'

'Why? I mean, it's awful what's happened. I'm angry, too. But this sort of crazy shit is happening to good people all the time. In the world, in this country, in this city, probably on this very street. What does this have to do with you?'

'It's like Lowrey said.'

'Come on. That was just cop talk. That's just the kind of shit they pull.'

'No, it wasn't just cop talk. She knows what I should have known. What I did know, deep down, but didn't act on.'

It was true. After all, he'd realised at once that there was something odd about Sunshine Heights; right away, he'd clocked the feeling of fear that shrouded the place like fog. He'd even met Suit Man. And one thing he knew from past experience was that it upsets the apple cart to go barging into a place like that.

But he had anyway.

'And what you're doing now,' said Noah, 'this is the softly-softly-catchee-monkey approach, is it?'

He had no answer to that. Instead, he said, 'Lowrey thought we'd kicked the hornets' nest by turning up that day. If she's right, then I want to find out what happened next. How did us turning up become Ruth shooting her own little girl?'

Noah's mouth opened to protest, when his phone rang. It was a number he didn't recognise but given recent events thought he'd better answer anyway.

'Is this Mr O'Connell?' asked a voice he didn't know.

'That would be me.'

'You did a favour for a friend of mine. You helped remove his daughter from something of a fix.'

The penny dropped. The All Fur Coat club. Commodore. He had, of course, taken that job hoping to reap the benefits, and it looked like those benefits had now arrived. Sure enough, the caller continued . . .

'I was wondering if you might be able to help me with a problem of my own.'

Jerry closed his eyes, a column of curse words marching through his brain. *Fuck, fuck, fuck, fuck, fuck. Why now? Why now?* This would be worth a lot of dough, an awful lot; it was the prize he'd been chasing, the very reason he'd been at the fucking strip club in the first place (and, no, it wasn't lost on him that if he hadn't been at the club then he would never have knocked over the little girl and . . .)

But no. He didn't bother asking who was calling. Didn't want to know anything that might distract him from his purpose.

'I'm sorry, mate,' he said, sounding assured but feeling rueful. 'It's going to have to wait. There's something I've got to do first.'

Chapter Twenty-Two

'What's your name?'

Jerry didn't expect an answer right way. After all, he reflected, it must be difficult to raise your head when someone's
wrapped a padlocked motorbike chain around your neck.
And since Jerry had done exactly that to the gangbanger, he
allowed the guy some time to get his bearings.

For a moment or so, the guy clawed ineffectually at the
chain, and then looked around, trying to make sense of his
surroundings.

It took him a few seconds, but he got there in the end. He
was in a sauna.

It was Jerry's sauna, and what had happened in the
meantime was that Jerry had decided Noah shouldn't be exposed to any more violence, so he'd dropped her off at the
bungalow.

'There's no DUI, is there?' she'd said, just before getting
out of the car.

He'd looked cagey. 'What do you mean?'

'Well, you're going to drive home, right?'

'Yeah, well, I'm just going to have to risk it.'

She shook her head. 'Nah, it's nothing to do with risking it, is it? You just don't have a DUI.'

'All right,' he'd admitted. 'You're right. I didn't really need you to drive.' She was still shaking her head, looking displeased. 'But just because I didn't need you to drive doesn't mean that I didn't need you. As in, *need* you. I couldn't have found Jane without you.'

'And look what happened there,' she'd said regretfully.

He'd nodded. Knowing it was true. Wishing it wasn't. 'You don't have to be a part of this, you know.'

'Hey, you don't get rid of me that easily. Just that . . .' she'd stopped. 'I don't want to be involved in any violence. Any *more* violence.'

'Well, then, this is probably the best place for you for the time being,' he'd said. 'I'll give you a call when the time is right.'

She'd nodded, thanked him, and then got out of the car and headed into her bungalow.

Not long later, he'd arrived back at his apartment at Hillview, where he'd parked, opened the trunk and frowned at the gangbanger out cold inside. Knowing from experience that moving a dead weight like that was easier said than done, he'd slammed the trunk again and let himself into the garage in search of assistance.

Moments later, he'd returned, only this time he was wheeling a metal removal trolley. With some difficulty, he'd pulled the gangbanger out of the trunk and deposited him on the trolley, closed the trunk, looked around to check he was still alone.

Not for the first time, he'd found himself feeling relieved

that the complex was mostly vacant as he'd wheeled the un-conscious gangbanger up to his apartment. The geezer was in a mess. His mouth was a mass of blood and broken teeth. As long as he could still talk. That was all Jerry cared about.

In his apartment, he'd headed through a door off the main living area into what had once been described as 'the leisure suite'. Jerry had never used the leisure suite. Leisure suites weren't really his thing. Nevertheless, he always made sure the sauna was maintained, just in case he ever had a female visitor to try to impress.

Or just in case a situation like this one should arise.

He'd wheeled the gangbanger into the sauna, tore off his sweatshirt and then nipped off to find a bike chain that he then wrapped and padlocked around the geezer's neck, chaining him to the trolley.

He'd stepped back to admire his handiwork, testing the tension of the chain and, satisfied that all was in order, shook the geezer to wake him. As the gangbanger came to his senses, Jerry stepped outside and shut the door, peering in as the guy stirred and realised that he was held fast by the chain before beginning to paw at it fruitlessly.

Bug-eyed and scared, still straining at the chain, his eyes roved around the room, taking in the wood panelling, the bench seats on either side of the small space, and then, finally, focusing through the window at Jerry on the other side.

Maybe he knew what level of serious shit he was in. Maybe not. Didn't matter. He'd get the picture soon enough.

Jerry reached to the temperature switch. 'Name?' he repeated.

'Shea,' replied the gangbanger. Although his voice was

muffled from inside the sauna, there was no mistaking the difficulty he was having talking through his broken teeth. He tried the chain again, as though it might miraculously have come loose in the last twenty seconds, and then put a hand to his mouth, gingerly dabbing at the broken teeth, and then to his head. 'It hurts,' he said, the words coming out like, *Ith hurth.*

Jerry looked thoughtful. 'Yeah, well, heads have a habit of doing that when you bump them on the trunk of a motor. Maybe that'll teach you to pipe down the next time someone locks you in a car, eh?'

He switched the sauna on, squinting at the dial. 'All right, Shea. I've put you up to 110°C. Now, that's a lot. Most people can last about a quarter of an hour at 80°C and they don't have a bike chain around their necks, heating up a treat, like you do. Let's see what you're good for.' He took a seat on a bench beneath a row of pegs and reached for his cigarettes. 'Right, let's start, shall we? Who was that guy I saw you with yesterday?'

'What guy?' replied Shea.

'White. Greasy hair. Blue suit. I think you know who I mean.'

Shea said nothing. But that was okay. And Jerry waited, watching the gangbanger as he slowly grew more and more uncomfortable. The T-shirt he wore did nothing to prevent the heat getting to his skin, the trolley heating up nicely now, bike chain doing the same.

'You're one big heat conductor in there, ain't you, Shea?' said Jerry cheerfully. 'You better hurry up and start answering.'

Shea's face reddened. And then something in him changed, as though he came to a sudden decision, and in the next moment he began talking. 'His name is Ronson Beaufoy, homeboy.' He grinned, revealing one remaining gold tooth. 'And he's going to fuck you up for this.'

'He's the big fish, is he, this Benson?'

'Ronson,' corrected Shea.

'Yeah, Benson. Looked to me like he pretty much controlled the gaff, is that right?'

'The gaff?'

'Yeah, the gaff. The place.'

'He runs CT-40, man.'

'CT-40. What's that?'

'That's our gang, homeboy.'

'Oh yeah? How come it's called CT-40, then? Because "Cedar Tree" sounds too much like a shower gel?'

'Fuck you, man. Nobody dares go up against the CT.'

Wrong. Someone dares, thought Jerry.

'Now,' he said, 'where I come from, if a geezer thinks he's protected, then that's because he's connected. Would that be the case with your mate Benson?'

Shea was beginning to sweat. Even so, the grin spread across his face. 'Oh yeah, man, and that's the reason you're going to die. That's the reason they're going to peel your skin from your body while you're still alive.'

Jerry nodded. 'Sounds messy. And time-consuming.'

'You're catching on. They're going to skin you alive.'

'Let's not jump the gun, shall we? We will get to the skinning-alive in due course. First of all, tell me what happened. Was it him who shot Jane? This Benson geezer?'

'The little girl?' sneered Shea. 'Nah, man, fuck that, it was the junkie bitch, her mom, who did that.' He was beginning to look pained, sweat coming off him in runnels. His shoulders heaved. His skin would be burning by now.

'Why – why did her mother shoot her? Were you there?' Jerry watched Shea carefully and when Shea shook his head, Jerry knew that he was lying. 'Try again. You were there. You know exactly why the mother shot her. Was he there, too, Benson? He was, wasn't he?'

'It doesn't matter what I say,' Shea was speaking with difficulty now. His mouth hot. 'Doesn't matter what I tell you. He'll kill you.'

'He'll have to find me first,' said Jerry.

'He'll find you,' said Shea.

'We'll see about that,' said Jerry. 'Your skin burning, is it?' He could see that it was. Blisters were beginning to appear above the bike chain. Shea's ears were glowing red and he wore a slight radioactive taint. 'Apparently your organs start cooking inside as well. Did you know that?'

Shea's fists were clenched. He fidgeted and writhed on the trolley, trying to make as little contact with the hot metal as possible. 'Turn it off, man,' he pleaded weakly.

'You better start singing like a canary,' replied Jerry evenly. 'Tell me what your boss had to do with shooting Jane.'

'Okay, okay, all right,' said Shea. 'Ronson was there, okay? He was talking to the mom, only she grabbed a gun and held it on the girl. I'm telling you, that's the truth. Nobody else even drew a gun but her.'

He was telling the truth, Jerry knew. It was one of his superpowers. Captain Lie Detector. He always – okay, let's not be too arrogant here – *usually* knew whether someone was telling the truth or not.

'So how did she come to shoot Jane?'

'He made her, man. He fucking goaded her. He dared her. He promised her smack. He practically made her do it.'

'I thought so,' said Jerry. 'I knew he had to be involved.' He watched as Shea gasped for air that was too hot and burned his lungs. 'Big question is why.'

'"*Why*?"' coughed Shea. 'You want to know why? Because of you – you asshole. Because you'd been round there, knocking on their door. Ronson wanted to know why.'

Jerry stood, flicked the dial of the sauna to zero, then opened the door, stepped inside and stamped Shea in the face. The gangbanger sank back, and the trolley drifted to the back of the sauna room. Engulfed by heat, Jerry took another step forward, delivered another stamp and was ready for a third.

This time, however, Shea stayed out cold. Clever lad.

Chapter Twenty-Three

'You don't mess with CT-40.'

It was a line he was to hear more than once that morning.

First, he'd called Vera, the fount of all knowledge. 'Cedar Tree Avenue,' he'd said.

'Not a nice part of town. Run by a gang called CT-40. Why do you ask?'

'Best you don't know.'

'You're not making trouble, are you, honeybunch, because this ain't Liverpool.'

'London, darlin'.'

'Whatever. The gangs in that part of town have ties with the Mexicans and, believe me, you do *not* want to mess with them. They do not fuck about with strawberries and cream and "I say, old boy, what jolly bad weather we're having."'

'Nor do I.'

'Don't give me a bad feeling about this, Jerry. If you have beef with the Mexicans, you better leave town.'

I don't have beef with Mexicans, he thought. *I have beef with this CT lot. Specifically one man.*

Next, he called on the LA guys he knew. 'I need you for a job.'

'Yeah, sure, whatever. What's the job?'

'You might call it a bit of pest control.'

'Sounds good. Who's the pest?'

Which was where things began to get a little baggy. That's when the so-called LA hard cases had a certain loss of nerve. One guy, Jimmy, said it point blank. 'I'd do anything for you – you know that.'

'But not this?'

'Uh-uh. You don't mess with CT-40. They're badass, man.'

Jerry was thinking of the guys back home. Wayne the Thug, Mad Micky Walker, Carrot Cruncher – blokes who wouldn't bat an eyelid whoever they were going up against.

'These people are in a whole different league, Jerry,' he was told. 'You're not from round here, you don't understand. You've seen *Scarface*, right? You remember the bit with the chainsaw? That's a staff training video where Beaufoy's concerned.'

Jerry visited another mate, Josh, who was similarly gungho until he knew the identity of the opposition. 'Leave it, Jerry. It's just not worth it.'

Josh paled when Jerry opened the van that he was now driving. In the back was a trolley and chained to the trolley by his neck, his flesh an angry, burned mass of peeling skin and heat blisters, lay Shea, a motorcycle helmet, back to front, covering his eyes and drowning out any noise he might be tempted to make.

Josh's mouth dropped open at the sight. Then he peered more closely and reached forward to remove the helmet, finding Shea in no position to make much noise anyway . . .

'Jerry, what have you done to his fuckin' eyes?'

'I superglued them shut,' Jerry told him, matter-of-fact.

On the trolley, Shea sniffled, his eyelids crusted with super-strength adhesive.

'Fuck me,' said Josh.

'I didn't want him identifying yous, did I?'

'Well, it doesn't matter,' said Josh. 'I can't help you, man.'

'What the fuck is going on with you lot?' said Jerry, exasperated. He slammed the van doors shut.

'You don't understand . . .'

'Because I'm not from round here? Yeah, I get it. But maybe that's what it takes. Maybe you need someone who's "not from round here" to do something about this fucking vermin.'

If he'd hoped to prick the other man's conscience, appeal to his pride a little, then he was disappointed. Josh was having none of it. 'They don't just kill you, Jerry. They kill you last. After they've killed your family. They make you watch as they—'

'Skin them alive,' Jerry sighed. 'Yeah, so I've heard. Sound like a bunch of geezers with too much time on their hands if you ask me.'

Still, the upshot was the same. He was captain of a crewless ship. What's more, he had an irate gangbanger in his trunk.

This was going to require a little thought.

★

'Are you beginning to wonder if you've bitten off more than you can chew?' asked Noah when he called, wanting, all of a sudden, to check that she was all right.

The thought hadn't even occurred to him. 'It's just a bit of a pain in the arse when everyone shits themselves when they hear the words CT-40.'

'And in the meantime?'

'In the meantime, it might be worth you steering clear. Wait until this blows over.'

'Wait – would you be saying that to Mad Micky Walker?'

He chuckled. 'No. I wouldn't say that to Micky.'

'Micky would be by your side, wouldn't he?'

'Yeah, he would.'

'Then I'll be over tomorrow morning.'

Next thing, he was back on the road, still with Shea in the van. Returning to Hillview, he parked in the garage and then used the trolley again, wheeling his prisoner back to the apartment. There, he used duct tape to bind Shea's hands and feet. Then he undid the padlock and dumped him unceremoniously to the floor, shifting the trolley out of the way.

This was not good, he reflected, looking at Shea on the floor. He'd planned to get rid of the geezer, not take him out for a morning drive only to bring him back again. What now?

Shea's eyeballs moved beneath his glued-up eyelids. Squatting, Jerry reached over and ignored the pitiful mewling as he prised open one of the eyelids, tearing the skin, but enough so that Shea could see. He thought about doing the other one but decided to leave it. Instead, he settled back in the couch and checked his phone as Shea gazed at him with one baleful eye. For a moment, the two men watched each other in silence, Jerry mulling over his next move as Shea worked his mouth, gradually dislodging the piece of tape until it was loose enough for him to tell Jerry what Ronson Beaufoy would do to him when they found him.

Jerry rolled his eyes. 'You're not going to start telling me about the fucking skinning again, are you? I'm really bored of hearing about that.'

'They have an industrial microwave, homeboy,' spat Shea. The loosened duct tape flapped at his lips. 'They'll fucking microwave your family.'

But by now Jerry was letting the abuse bounce off him. Funny, having someone rant like that reminded him of girls outside the clubs back in the day, the ones who'd start yelling at you because you'd just clomped their boyfriend, even though the reason you'd clomped their boyfriend was because the boyfriend had just slapped them. They'd be calling you all sorts of names, these birds, and it only made them even angrier, more abusive, when you stood there impassive.

It was on the doors that he'd learnt to control his temper. He was the one who never lost his cool. It had stood him in good stead.

Enough reminiscing. The big questions were what to do next? What to do with Shea?

Then the doorbell rang.

And suddenly the question was irrelevant.

Chapter Twenty-Four

For the first time in a few days, Noah was in her own car, an open-topped Jeep, climbing the approach road to Jerry's Hillview complex, when she spotted it, like a bruise in the sky.

It was only as she grew closer that she understood what she was seeing. Smoke.

At first, she didn't associate it with Jerry. Then the thought took hold and began to nag at her, a bell that tinkled to begin with, like the polite summoning of a butler in an English country house, getting louder until it was a Notre Dame clanging, saying, *The smoke – what if it's something to do with him?*

As she hit the bottom of the approach road leading to Hillview, it became clear: the smoke was coming from there. The next thing she saw was the fire truck. Then a police car. By the time she stopped and climbed out of the Jeep, her hand was over her mouth, and looking up she saw her worst fears confirmed: the source of the fire was his apartment. It stuck out like a blackened tooth in the complex, smoke-damaged, having been gutted by fire, dripping wet.

Just to her left, the fire truck was being packed up. As it drew away, she saw activity beyond, a police tent set up in the parking lot, next to it an ambulance, where paramedics were pushing a gurney, about to load it into the back of the ambulance. On the gurney was a body, sheet drawn up. As the medics stopped at the doors of the ambulance, one of the corpse's arms, dislodged, dropped from the side of the trolley.

She moved forward. 'What's happened here?' was all she could manage, feeling heat on her cheeks, fear gnawing at her gut.

A cop approached, took her by the elbow and led her gently away from the gurney. 'Ma'am, you know who lives there?' He was pointing up at Jerry's blackened apartment.

But her eyes went past him to the tent, the gurney and the arm that dangled down.

The sleeve of a camel-hair coat.

Still she nodded, *Yes, I know who lives here.*

The cop pulled a sympathetic face. 'A relation?'

'A friend.'

That was, for some reason, the right answer.

'I wonder, then, would you mind taking a look at the bodies?' he pulled a face, knowing it was a big ask.

Her eyes went to him, startled. *Bodies, plural.*

'Ma'am?' His face was a picture of concern. 'You don't have to do this. You could do it down at the morgue, or not at all, but I'm sure you understand how important it is that we identify those involved as soon as possible. Perhaps you'd like to take a moment or so to think about it?'

Sure, sure, she was nodding, stepping away, grateful for the time to readjust and make sense of the situation, thinking about that sleeve. Was she surprised? After all, she'd known what sort of guy Jerry was. If she hadn't realised before, then she knew it the moment he'd started beating a guy half to death with the trunk of his car. He was a violent guy from a violent world. And what happened to men like that? They died violent deaths.

But still. Dead. She'd only known him a couple of days. Already she wondered what she was going to do without him.

And then, as she stood there, numb with shock and disbelief, her phone bleeped. Instinctively, she reached for it. The message was from him.

'Garage,' it read. Below it, a smiley emoji.

She looked from the phone to the cop, who still watched her with concern, and then beyond him to the paramedics, who waited patiently to see if she was prepared to ID the corpse. 'Can I have five minutes?' she asked. 'Just need to get myself together, yeah?'

As the cop nodded sympathetically and the paramedics shuffled, trying not to look peeved, Noah thanked them with a raised hand, turned and made her way round the corner to the garage.

Inside, her eyes had only just adjusted to the gloom, and it was belatedly occurring to her, *What if this is a trap?* She tensed, ready to make a move, but at the same time forcing herself to trust her own instincts.

And then the shadows shifted, and the dead man made himself known.

It was him. Jerry. He was alive.

She closed her eyes. 'I thought you were . . .' she said, but stopped herself. Instead, she found herself smothered in one of his famous hugs, feeling silly, almost as though, *Dead? How could he be dead? How could she have doubted him?*

Now he put a finger to his lips, beckoning her over to the lift. They ascended to an upstairs apartment, just along from Jerry's fire-gutted place, waited until the coast was clear and then made their way to the front door and let themselves in. Once inside, they breathed a sigh of relief as Noah looked around, amazed to discover that she was in a virtual carbon copy of the last apartment: same layout, even some of the same furniture. The penny dropped. This one belonged to Jerry as well. A bolthold.

The glint in his eye told her she was correct. 'Always useful to have a spare,' he said. 'Not registered to me, either. Nobody can find us here, not that they'd ever bother looking. Hillview is the last place they'd expect us to be.'

'Us', she noticed. Not 'me'.

'Okay,' she said, relieved to be able to talk at a normal volume, 'are you going to tell me what's going on? And while we're on the subject, what the fuck is that on your face?'

Chapter Twenty-Five

There had been a knock at the door.

Jerry had moved fast. He'd crouched and clamped a hand over Shea's mouth before the gangbanger could shout and raise the alarm. Holding him down, pinning him with his knees and ignoring the excited, triumphant look in his prisoner's single open eye, he replaced the tape and was about to knock the guy cold again, just to be on the safe side, when a movement at the balcony door caught his eye.

A figure. Jerry's head jerked. That meant there were at least two of them. And whoever was knocking had been trying to set up a diversion.

Now he got a clearer look at the guy on the balcony and saw that it was the taller of the two Latinos from the All Fur Coat parking lot. The Hoodie guy. The intruder hadn't seen Jerry through the heat-reflective glass; instead, he was looking intently at the sliding mechanism of the door, trying to figure out a way in, still working on the assumption that he hadn't been spotted.

Jerry thought fast. So the guy at the front door was probably Hoodie's mate, the smaller one – Neck Tattoo. Jerry had broken his arm, made him eat a Coke bottle, probably busted his jaw. He'd be unhappy. He'd be really fucking unhappy. That's what this visit was all about: payback.

But how the fuck did they find him?

Without straightening, Jerry made for the front door. His was a double door in the Mediterranean style, the wood ornately carved and sun-bleached. But no peephole, so for now he was going to have to rely on cunning and instinct.

Why not? They'd never let him down in the past.

Right. Time to bring the pain. He grasped the door handle, giving it a rattle so that the guy on the other side was expecting him. Reason: Jerry needed him ready. He'd assumed the guy would be armed, and he wanted the gun held just right.

And now, still low, he yanked open the door to be greeted by the sight he expected: Neck Tattoo, standing there with his jaw bandaged, the other hand holding a pistol, ready to pull the trigger.

Only Jerry wasn't where he expected him to be. And by the time he realised his mistake, Jerry had grabbed his gun hand, yanked him forward and slammed the door on his arm.

Neck Tattoo yowled. And then screamed again as Jerry made sure of the job and used both hands to snap his arm across the door frame. His howl was like a wounded animal as pink-tipped bone tore through skin, protruding through the flesh of his forearm. His fingers splayed in agony. The gun dropped. His arm, when Jerry released it, hung loose, like a storm-damaged tree branch.

Not that Jerry was hanging around to admire his handiwork. Instead, he pulled the balcony door open and surged forward, launching an attack worthy of an NFL player that shoved Hoodie, still on the balcony, back so hard that he hit the guardrail.

And, with a final screech of terror, toppled right over.

There was a half-second of silence as he fell, followed by a slapping, splashing sound: the sound of Hoodie's skull splitting on the tarmac, as though Jerry had thrown a melon from the walkway to the forecourt below. And when Jerry got to the guardrail and leaned over, what he saw was the guy's body: arms and legs at strange, irregular angles, head split, pink brain matter like strawberry dessert, pulsing in the sun.

Next, he saw something else: a black Range Rover that had arrived in the parking lot below. Getting out was a guy he recognised from Sunshine Heights – Ronson Beaufoy's other minder. The new arrival was looking from the bloody, broken body of Hoodie to Jerry above, his mouth forming an O of surprise at the same time as he pulled a gun from his jeans.

For the second time in as many minutes, Jerry was thinking, *How the fuck did they find me?* but there was no time to dwell on it. As he reared back from the handrail, the last thing he saw was the guy making his way out of sight, presumably on his way up.

Shit.

Jerry turned to go back inside his apartment, aiming to grab the gun from the floor. He might have got it, too, if it hadn't been for Neck Tattoo, who was reaching to scoop up the gun just as Jerry re-entered.

It was all Jerry could do to toe-punt the gun out of Neck Tattoo's reach, slamming his fist down on the back of the guy's head at the same time. The Latino squealed but twisted, reaching to grab Jerry's legs and overbalancing him so that he came crashing to the floor.

For a moment, they wrestled, until Jerry gained the upper hand, bringing his knee up into the guy's chest, simultaneously working his thumbs into his eye sockets.

It was an old trick, popping out an eyeball. Usually, the eyeball would go back in afterwards, although you risked losing it, or blinding them. Most importantly, the guy being gouged always – but always – lost his cool as soon as the eyeball came out of its socket. Couldn't handle it. Fight ended.

Neck Tattoo's scream was high-pitched, like a terrified child, as he realised what Jerry was trying to do. At the same time, Jerry felt one of them go, the eyeball liberated from its socket and dangling on a short glistening stalk, and it had the desired effect: Neck Tattoo howled with pain and peeled off, momentarily unaware of anything, unable to process any fact other than that his eyeball was no longer where it should be. As Jerry knew, he'd still be seeing through that eyeball, even though it was currently dangling, swinging like a pendulum and hitting his cheek.

Jerry was about to go for the gun when Shea made his presence felt. Still with his arms and feet taped, he kicked out, tripping Jerry and sending him stumbling to the floor again, falling heavily and catching himself on the side of the marble coffee table as he landed.

And still Neck Tattoo wasn't quite out for the count. His hand was cupped over his gouged-out eyeball as he dived headlong for the gun, snatching it up to point it at Jerry, still on the floor, literally a sitting target.

With Shea shouting muffled encouragement, Jerry steeled

himself. *Fuck it*, he thought. Death had never scared him, never would. Matter of fact, the closer he got to death, the calmer he got. He felt it now, waiting for the bullet.

Which never came.

Because now the second gangbanger appeared in the doorway, his own gun raised. And Neck Tattoo must have seen him from the corner of his good eye, clocked the weapon, decided in that split second that he was the bigger threat, and twisted to level the gun at him.

For a moment, the two men had the drop on each other. Neck Tattoo opened his mouth to say something, but his last words went unspoken and the delay was fatal. The gangbanger opened fire.

He shot twice. And perhaps he was spooked by the sight of the dangling eyeball, or maybe he was just an inexperienced killer, but his shooting was wild and it was a miracle that he hit anything at all, but he did, and Neck Tattoo's cheek opened into a ragged, ghastly hole as he fell in a vapour of blood and shattered teeth.

Jerry saw his gun fall and was about to go for it, when, right away, the gangbanger swung his weapon and began to fire in his direction, the shots just as wild as before. *Fuck.* Jerry dived for cover beneath the coffee table, bullets spanging off the stone floor, thumping into the couch, glass smashing in the kitchen area behind them.

Trussed up on the floor, Shea saw what was happening, saw the wild firing, tried to scream a warning to his mate, attempted to wriggle out of the way.

To no avail. Blood and brain matter splattered Jerry as Shea's skull exploded. In the next instant, the gangbanger dashed across the room and, with a howl of anger and out-rage, desperate to finish the job, jumped onto the coffee table and fired downwards.

Possibly he didn't realise the coffee table was made of marble. Maybe he was too angry or too dumb to care. Either way, he paid for it with a ricochet into his own crotch, and in the next second he was screaming, dropping heavily to the table and then slithering to the stone floor, writhing in agony, his own executioner.

In the aftermath of the battle, the only sound was the gunman, mewling in torment, his hands at his crotch as blood spread on the floor around him, his movements growing steadily weaker.

Jerry cleared his throat. 'I'm not being funny,' he said, as he levered himself from underneath the coffee table, stood and dusted himself off, stepping round the pool of blood as it crept across the stone. 'But that was the worst fucking rescue attempt I've ever seen.'

'So that's what's on your face,' said Noah now.

'Yeah, it's bits of Shea's brain,' said Jerry, wiping at it ineffectually. He picked something from his temple – a tiny piece of skull fragment – and flicked it away.

'What about the guy who shot himself in the balls? What happened to him?'

'I left him there. It's not such a bad way to go, bleeding to death. Quite peaceful, so they say.'

She looked away.

'What did you expect me to do, call him a fucking ambulance? "911, come and save the life of the geezer who tried to kill me." Maybe that way he could have another crack at it when he's sufficiently recovered, eh?'

She ignored him. 'So it was you that set the fire?'

'Of course it was. Localised. I needed a couple of unrecognisable corpses, one of them wearing my coat. Should be just enough for you to identify as mine. No need to say you think it's me, mind you. Just that you recognise the coat.'

She nodded, prepared to do that, at least. 'They'll find out sooner or later, you know.'

'Yeah, but it buys me time to prepare.'

'Prepare for what?'

'War.'

Part Two

Chapter Twenty-Six

'So what's changed?' she asked him.

Noah's question intruded upon a heartbroken silence that had descended upon them both as they stood in the hospital, staring helplessly through a pane of thick glass. On the other side of the viewing window, little Jane lay hooked up to a life-support machine. Vital signs were steady, but the doctors couldn't say whether or not she'd make a recovery. Jane, who now lay half-dead in hospital, skull swathed in surgical dressing, life at the mercy of monitors and machines.

Noah cast a surreptitious sideways look at Jerry and wondered what was going through his mind just then. What was driving him? Was it rage? Guilt? Vengeance? All of the above? Either way, he remained impassive, thoughtful.

She cast her mind back to earlier that morning, when she had wandered through from her bedroom – her 'new' bedroom, although it was not too dissimilar to the last one – to the apartment living area, only to be stopped short by what she saw.

Jerry had been settled into the couch, seemingly as happy as a clam, despite everything that had occurred. He often looked pensive, she knew. His brow would knit and furrow. His eyes narrowed and his jaw would set. But she had rarely seen him like this – looking content.

It was such an arresting sight that she had spent some moments simply watching him, enjoying his enjoyment, before her eyes went from him to what he was watching. And . . .

'*The Secret Life of Puppies*,' he'd said from the sofa, as though reading her mind. 'The best show.'

'*The Secret Life of Puppies* is your favourite show? Not *The Wire* or *The Sopranos*? *The Secret Life of Puppies*?'

'Nah, don't get me wrong, I love *The Sopranos*. But *The Secret Life of Puppies* – it's just the ticket when you want to relax. Look at that,' he'd gestured, 'French bulldog. That's what you need to see when some amateurs set fire to your apartment.'

She had wandered through to the kitchen area in search of coffee, bare feet pitter-pattering on the stone floor. 'Technically, it was you who set fire to your apartment,' she'd called.

The ghastly aftermath was still fresh in her mind, having to ID the charred corpses: *Yes, I think this is him. That's his coat.* And then, *No, I've no idea who that is,* times three. *Now, if you don't mind, honey, I'm gonna have to barf.*

'Same bloody thing.'

'Anyway, what you got planned for today, then?'

There was silence. Enough to make her press pause on the hunt for caffeine. 'Fancy a visit to the hospital?' he'd said.

And seeing Jane had brought it home to them. Perhaps he, too, was thinking about the little girl in the filthy Lakers shirt. Jane's life had been shit; you didn't have to be Sherlock Holmes to work that one out. But at least she *had* a life.

Better that than what she had now, a ghostlike, half-life existence, kept alive by technology. She might never wake up, and that was bad enough. But what if she did? It would be to the knowledge that her own mother had tried to kill her.

Now Jerry looked at Noah, surprised. 'What do you mean? "What's changed?" Nothing.'

He looked back through the window. He would have liked to have moved closer, but fixed above Jane's bed was a camera, which, if his guess was correct, would feed to the police.

And that meant the cops probably suspected what Jerry already knew: that there was more to Jane's shooting than her mum going mad or an accidental discharge. Right now, it was probably best for Jane that she was in a coma and thus unable to talk. Because if the gang was as all-powerful as he was constantly being told, then they'd have hospital insiders, a nurse, a janitor, an orderly. All of them ready to inform when the situation changed. Right now, it probably wasn't worth the risk of killing her, but if she regained consciousness . . .

Not yet, darlin', he found himself urging her silently. *Stay under for a while. Just until I get things sorted.*

'So what now?' said Noah. 'If nothing's changed, then what happens now?'

'Well, all right, then. Something *has* changed. I now know I've got a leak.' He glanced meaningfully at Noah.

'Pop another one of those looks at me, and you'll be driving yourself from now on.'

He chuckled. 'Don't worry. You wouldn't be here if I thought it was you. Anyway, they think I'm dead, and I need to keep it that way for the time being, which is why I'd like you to stay in the apartment for a bit, see if the cops return and what they're up to. With any luck, they're going to decide there was a tear-up and a fire, and everybody died and that'll be the end of it, but it'd be good to know if they're still nosing about, knocking on doors and that.'

She shot him a doubtful look. 'All right, if you say so. And what will you be doing in the meantime?'

'First, I've got a bit of business to attend to. Something you're best off out of.'

'You're not even going to tell me what it's about?'

'No.'

'Why?'

'Well, you know how you disapproved when I was encouraging that geezer by nudging him with the trunk of the car?'

'Yeah.'

'That's why. I've got a bit of plumbing to do.'

Chapter Twenty-Seven

Jerry had dearly hoped he'd seen the last of the All Fur Coat club, but here he was again, installed at a stool by the bar, waiting to speak to his goatee-bearded bouncer mate.

'Good afternoon, sir.' Having been summoned by the bar staff, the guy materialised by his side. His hands were pushed into the pockets of his suit trousers, his attempt to remain stony-faced doing nothing to hide his wariness. 'How nice to see you again.'

Jerry shot him a wintry smile. 'Believe me, I'm no happier to be here than you are to see me.'

Goatee remained standing. 'This is to do with Commodore, is it? I must say, I'd considered that business to be complete.'

'Yeah, well, it is complete, you'll be pleased to hear. And this ain't anything to do with Commodore, it's to do with a couple of scrotes who came looking for me following a little disagreement in your parking lot. Now, I've been wracking my brains as to how they might have found me, and I've come to the conclusion that whatever their second step was, they must have started right . . .' he placed a fingertip to the bar top, 'here.'

Goatee shook his head slowly. 'If you're asking do I know anything about that, then the answer's no.'

And he was telling the truth. Which foxed Jerry for a moment. After all, there was no love lost between him and Goatee, and it would hardly have been a shocking turn of events if the bouncer had helped the Latinos. But he hadn't.

So if not him, then who?

His eyes travelled the room, alighting on a waitress moving between the tables. She was serving drinks, but she had half an eye on Jerry and Goatee at the bar.

It was the waitress from the other night. Ashley.

And she had a black eye.

Chapter Twenty-Eight

Lucas had been working beneath the hood of a black Corvette when Jerry appeared in the doorway of the workshop. Jerry watched his reaction carefully, and what he saw when the mechanic straightened to greet his visitor was a look of shock, or fear, or perhaps a mixture of both. It was only there for a split second before it was replaced with a broad grin (a forced, too-big grin) and a warm welcome – 'Well, well, well, Jerry O'Connell' – but it was there. And it was enough for Jerry to know that he was right.

'You're not surprised to see me, are you?' he said.

Brow furrowed (too furrowed), Lucas said, 'Nah, not surprised. Why would I be surprised? Unless there's something wrong with the bike I fixed for you. And there better not be anything wrong with that baby, I fixed it up good.' He moved in to give Jerry a fist bump, face clouding when Jerry knocked his hand away. 'Everything all right, man?'

Jerry ignored the question, crowding Lucas back into the workshop as he stepped inside. 'Yeah, the bike. You did a real good job there. You fixed it up real good. I always said that you were the best mechanic in LA. Not had a chance to give it back to Jane, yet, mind you. But when I do, I'll be sure to let her know how my good friend Lucas fixed it up. My trusted, loyal friend Lucas.'

The smile on the other man's face had turned queasy. 'What's this all about, man? Christ, you're talking even more crazy than you usually do.'

The entrance through which Jerry had entered was a small wicket door set into the main double doors of the garage. He turned and closed it with a firm clunk that echoed around the oil, grease and metal-smelling workshop. All of a sudden, the only light in the workshop was that of the inspection lamps. They cast the faces of Lucas and Jerry in shadow, accentuating menace and fear.

'Yeah, mate, thank you for that. Must take you for a spin in one of my motors to give you a proper thanks. You'll have to come round and give the collection the once-over. Another once-over, I mean. You'd like that, wouldn't you? You like my collection, don't you?'

Lucas swallowed, looking nervously from the recently closed door to Jerry. 'Now you really have lost me.'

On the workbench was a can of WD-40. Jerry had clocked it the second he walked in, just the sight of it producing in him a warm glow of nostalgia. He knew of old what a great weapon it made. The WD stood for 'water dispersal': spray it in a geezer's eyes and it dried them out, blinded him, put him out of the fight. Not quite as efficiently as gouging out his eyeball, mind you, but it did the job.

There'd be some WD-40 left in that can, he knew. Nobody ever finished a tin of WD-40.

Only one way to find out for sure.

He moved forward, grabbed Lucas at the same time as he scooped up the can and sprayed it in the other man's face. Lucas screamed and thrashed but couldn't escape Jerry's grip as the WD-40 did exactly what it said on the tin, and he was powerless to prevent Jerry dragging him across to the workbench.

'I've lost you, have I? Let's jog your memory, shall we, Lucas?' said Jerry. He smashed Lucas's head against the workbench hard enough that Lucas was half-in and half-out of consciousness as Jerry upended him, tore off a trainer and then jammed his foot in a vice, spinning the lever until the foot was wedged tight. 'How does that feel?'

Lying on the grease-stained floor, one leg elevated, foot trapped in the vice, Lucas groaned. His eyes were red, a strip of irritated skin crossed his face like warpaint, and when his hands came up as though to grasp at the vice, Jerry responded by tightening it further, producing a new shout of pain.

Next, Jerry grabbed one of the inspection lights, angling it so that he could see the mechanic's face clearly. Pulling up a work stool, he took a seat, placed a boot on Lucas's chest to pin him there – and then tightened the vice another half-turn.

Lucas screamed, his foot bulging, hands clawing as they reached helplessly for the vice. 'Please, please, Jerry, stop it.'

'It's Jeremiah to you, mate.'

'Jeremiah. Please. What the fuck are you doing, man?'

'You sent two blokes to find me, didn't you? What did they tell you?'

'I don't know what you're talking about.'

'Yeah, you do. You remember the All Fur Coat club,

right? Well, I've paid them a visit this morning. Turns out they gave your number to a pair of Latinos who were trying to find me.'

It had been Ashley, of course, threatened by the two guys. She'd got into Goatee's phone and found Lucas's number. And Lucas, having delivered cars to Jerry in the past, knew where Jerry lived.

Lucas groaned.

'Thought so. They didn't tell you that, did they? Else even a fuckwit like you would have known better than to send them my way. You thought it couldn't be traced back to you, didn't you?'

Lucas's foot had already begun to turn a strangely pale, corpse-like colour. Blood leaked from the jaws of the vice.

'They said they knew you,' he stammered through the pain, 'and that you'd mentioned me, and that I might know where you were. But I didn't know what they were planning, I swear.'

Now Jerry released the pressure of the vice a little – just a little – and waited for Lucas's pain to subside. 'What were they planning, then?' he said pleasantly. 'Cos I never told you they were *planning* anything, did I?'

'No, no,' jabbered Lucas, 'I just mean I didn't know what they were up to. They didn't tell me anything.'

'Trying to fucking kill me, that's what they were up to. That's what they were fucking doing.'

Even in his agony, Lucas looked genuinely shocked. 'I never knew that, I swear.'

'Maybe not,' and Jerry thought that, on balance, he probably believed him, 'but you knew they were up to no good, didn't you? You knew that at the very least they wanted to fuck me up.'

Lucas twisted his head. 'I didn't, man. I didn't know anything. I swear to God. I thought they were just trying to find you. For a bit of business, they said.'

'So why didn't you hit me up and let me know that these two geezers were trying to find me. Check that it was okay with me before you went giving them my fucking address? Eh?'

'I don't know, I was going to, it slipped my mind, I swear.'

'Oh, fuck off, you're lying.' He increased the pressure on the vice, producing a sickening crackling sound of compacted bone. At the same time, Lucas jerked as though an electric current was being passed through him, babbling in pain, unable to form coherent thoughts, simply wanting the hurt to stop as blood splashed liberally from the base of the vice to the shop floor. 'Why?' asked Jerry, raising his voice over Lucas's screams. 'Why d'you fucking do it?'

Something occurred to him, and he reached down, pulled up the sleeves of Lucas's overalls until he saw what he knew would be there – what he'd been expecting to see. 'You're back on the fucking scag.'

Lucas was moaning and mumbling. Tears falling freely. Snot bubbles at his nose.

'What was it they gave you? Money? Drugs? Both?'

Lucas looked up at him.

Yeah, both.

'I promise I didn't know they were going to try to kill you,' snivelled Lucas.

'Do you know what I reckon?' said Jerry. 'You thought you'd send them my way and see how it all panned out. Like if they fucked me up, maybe you could get your hands on some of my collection. That's what I think.'

Was Lucas that low? Jerry wasn't sure – he wasn't even certain he cared. All he saw was a pathetic, spineless junkie.

'Right. Next. What about the Sunshine Heights mob? The blokes from Cedar Tree?'

'What do you mean?'

'Gangsters. Oh yeah, they call themselves CT-40. You've heard of them. Have they been in touch as well, then?'

'No, man, no. I don't know what you're talking about. I promise you, man. I promise.'

Jerry believed him. He let go of the vice. 'Right. I'm going now.'

On the floor, Lucas took a deep breath, closed his eyes, and contemplated his end. 'Do what you gotta do. Make it quick, man.'

'I'm not going to kill you.'

'You're not?'

'Nah. I need you to mend my cars. Why do you think I did your foot and not your hands? And you'll be doing it for free an' all. And any other favours I decide upon.'

'Yes, yes,' wheedled Lucas. 'Whatever you want. Thank you, thank you.'

'Don't fucking grovel,' said Jerry. He spun the vice lever, loosening the jaws, and then left Lucas, letting himself out of the workshop.

For some moments, he sat in his car, thinking. So, he'd plugged one leak, only for another to appear. Not one rat, but two. One thing he knew, he wasn't just up against CT-40, he was up against the whole of Los Angeles. Or that's how it felt at least.

All of which meant that he had to switch up – and he knew how to do it. There was just one catch.

And it was a big fucking catch.

Chapter Twenty-Nine

The Mustang growled as it climbed Mulholland up into the hills. Noah drove, Jerry in the passenger seat, windows cranked down to enjoy the balmy warmth of what had been a beautiful afternoon. All in all, Jerry reflected, life would be perfect, if not for the nature of their journey.

Then again, he liked a bit of grit in the oyster. It was how you ended up with a pearl.

An uneasy silence reigned, and had done since Hillview, when Jerry had told her where they were going. 'We're off to see an old client of yours,' he'd said.

She'd known at once who he meant, of course, and although she'd thought about simply telling him to stick his Mulholland drive up his ass, she'd found herself agreeing because . . . well, just because.

So she drove, enjoying the Mustang, getting Steve McQueen-in-*Bullitt*, *Gone in 60 Seconds* feels the whole ride, just as he'd said she would. And, in the event, it felt like all too soon that they arrived at the tall, wrought-iron gates of the Sidney Frankus house.

It was a large house, even by Hollywood standards,

surrounded by well-kept grounds and beautifully manicured lawns. The front gates were tall, imposing and overlooked by CCTV cameras, and the space in front of them big enough to boast its own parking area. As for the neighbourhood – this house *was* the neighbourhood.

When they stopped and Noah killed the engine, the only noise was the distant hum of the city below, the chirruping of crickets and, from somewhere nearby, the relaxing hiss of a lawn sprinkler.

'What do you need to do here?' she asked him.

'I'm making a bank withdrawal,' he said flatly, working his mouth around the nasty taste inside.

'You – Mister Garage Full of Vintage Cars – you need money?'

He nodded. 'You might say I'm consolidating. Chances are, I'm going to need a lot of money in the near future and not a lot of opportunity to earn it. Might as well call in money owed while I've got the chance.'

'Okay. And if I ask why you need the money?'

'Then I'll tell you that all will soon be revealed.' He made to get out. 'Might be better if you wait in the motor.'

'Wait, what? Are you kidding me? I drove all the way up here just to sit in the car?'

'You want to come in, do you? Get reacquainted? Look, it's a gorgeous night. Why don't you just have yourself a little sit in the car, enjoy the evening, maybe Chris Hemsworth will wander by. He'll admire the motor, you can talk about Steve McQueen and he'll have proposed by the end of the conversation. I won't be long anyway, Scout's honour. Any more than ten minutes and I'll want to throttle him.'

She was still huffing when he let himself out and approached the pedestrian gate. At the panel, he paused a second and keyed in a code. Would Sidney have changed it? He got his answer as the gate clicked and swung inwards a little. *Typical*, thought Jerry, stepping through. *Complacent wanker.*

At the top of the drive, he pressed the doorbell, waited until at last the door opened a crack. A woman regarded him. Housekeeper by the looks of things.

'I didn't hear the intercom,' she said, suspiciously.

'Code's 1966, love,' said Jerry cheerfully. 'I kept telling him he should change it. Let him know I'm here, would you? Actually, on second thoughts, I'll surprise him.'

She looked confused, uncertain. Jerry stood respectfully with his hands clasped in front of him, smiling unthreateningly at her.

'Who are you?' she asked.

'I'm Big Jerry O'Connell. He must have mentioned me.'

She nodded. Sidney had indeed mentioned 'Big Jerry', and she recognised him from a couple of photographs in the house, but even so, she was unsure about letting him in unannounced.

'Honestly, darlin', it's something we always did back in the day,' said Jerry, feeling bad about taking advantage of her but pressing on anyway. 'He'll love it. And if he doesn't love it, I'll tell him it was my idea. You won't get in any trouble, I promise.'

She opened the door to allow him in. Jerry paused, tilting his head to check she was okay with it. Only when she nodded *okay* did he step across the threshold and into the house.

It was tidy, he thought, as he gazed around the entrance

hall, eyes following a set of stairs that led to the mezzanine above. But that would be down to the housekeeper – Sidney had never been that tidy. Not the Sidney he knew, anyway.

The housekeeper raised a hand to usher him through, but he knew where he was going, and they followed the sound of the TV to a gargantuan living area dominated by the huge television. Watching it, wearing a white towelling robe with one arm draped around a blonde with big boobs was Sidney Frankus. His eyes were fixed on the screen, and for a second or so he didn't register that Jerry had walked into the room.

And then he did.

Sidney jerked as though electricity had been passed through him, disturbing the blonde, who gave a *youch* and sat upright all of a sudden. Sidney's jaw dropped, his eyes widened, the blood draining from his face. 'What the fuck . . .?' he began, and his eyes darted from Jerry to the help as realisation dawned, about to unleash a torrent of abuse on the house-keeper until Jerry quietened him with an upraised hand.

'Don't you dare have a go at her,' he warned Sidney. 'Or we'll start off on the wrong foot, and you really don't want that, do you?'

Sidney opened his mouth, maybe to protest, maybe to demand that Jerry leave his house right away. But then he saw the look in Jerry's eyes, and he remembered what that look meant, and he bit his tongue, using the moment to compose and calm himself.

Standing to one side, the housekeeper looked alarmed, unsure of the dynamic.

'You're all right, darlin',' Jerry told her, and then, just in case she got any ideas about calling the cops, 'We're all right, ain't we?' he said to Sidney.

Sidney had composed himself, wearing his Hollywood-mogul mask once again. His large belly shifted as he gathered his white robe around himself and reached to his right for a cigar that rested in a huge ashtray, slotting it between his lips, although it wasn't lit. 'Yeah, we're all right,' he rasped.

The housekeeper departed, and in her wake the atmosphere settled. The blonde harrumphed and folded her arms across her chest. Sidney looked at Jerry warily, no doubt knowing exactly what his visitor wanted, and Jerry returned his gaze, enjoying himself.

'You're still a fan of doughnuts, I see,' he said and watched happily as Sidney glowered in response to the jibe.

The blonde regarded Jerry with disinterest. Jerry gave her a wink, was rewarded with the ghost of a smile.

Sidney, meanwhile, moved his head as though to see past Jerry, tilting it first one way and then the other, until at last he spoke. 'You're in the way of the TV, Jeremiah.'

Jerry stayed put.

Sidney rolled his eyes, raised one hand slowly and pretended to click an invisible remote control, saying at the same time, 'Alexa, please pause the TV. There seems to be a very large gangster blocking my view.'

Jerry allowed himself a half-smile. They all loved to think of him like that – as a gangster. To have a gangster for a bodyguard was one better than an ex-cop or a former soldier.

'Anyway,' drawled Sidney, 'now that you have graced my abode with your presence, how about you tell me just exactly what it is you're doing here?'

Jerry grinned. 'With pleasure, mate.'

Chapter Thirty

'So? Mission accomplished?' Noah raised her head from the headrest, still wearing her aviators, even though the sun was busily sinking below the Hollywood Hills.

'Well, I got some of the money owed to me,' said Jerry, as he slid into the Mustang. He looked across at her. Hardly in the best of moods himself, he was at least grateful that Noah's previous irritation seemed to have subsided. Maybe Chris Hemsworth really had popped by.

'That's what it was all about, was it?'

'Two hundred grand in my account tomorrow.'

'And you borrowed it from him?'

'From him? No, I fucking well did not,' said Jerry. 'He owed it to me, and a lot more. See, all the time I was body-guarding for him, along with doing other stuff, I never used to invoice him, I didn't need the money. Just let it build up. And then if I wanted something, I'd tell him to buy it for me out of what he owed me. It was a good way to shift money about, if you know what I mean. He'd borrow money off me, too. Anyway, by the time I left him, he was into me for a lot. That was me part collecting.'

'He owes you more than two hundred thousand?'

'That's just the interest.'

'And he paid it, just like that?'

Jerry winked. 'I didn't give him much choice.'

'You didn't . . .'

'I didn't threaten him, no.' He winked. 'I didn't need to.'

'Okay,' she said. She reached for the ignition, the car started with a growl, and they pulled off the gravel and onto the road, beginning their journey back down Mulholland. 'What now?'

'We're going on a trip,' said Jerry. 'Just one more thing I need to do first.'

Chapter Thirty-One

Night had fallen, but as Jerry knew, Lucas often – make that usually – worked long into the wee small hours, forever trying to scrape together the cash to pay off his debts. (Or, thought Jerry sourly, trying to raise the money to maintain his drug habit, ratting out his mates.)

Even so, the only sign of someone home was an open padlock hanging off the door. And when Jerry opened the small wicket door and, stooping, stepped inside, the workshop was dark. Too dark to see.

'Hello?' he called.

No reply. No music. No sound of machinery.

He fished for his phone, lit the torch and started to pick his way through. On the right was the Corvette, now raised on the lift, its wheels about shoulder level. On the left was the workbench. The vice. The stone below it stained with blood.

As he moved through the workshop, he saw light spilling from around a door frame at the very end. 'Mate?'

No reply. Jerry wished he was carrying one of his favoured weapons from back in the day. Boot knives, they used to have, always carried in the left shoe, so if you went down in a punch-up, you could retrieve one from the boot of a mate. They used to have CS gas, too – make sure you stand upwind when you're using that or you risk getting a face full of your own gas – as well as coshes and knuckledusters, always worn underneath a pair of gloves to keep them hidden.

Right now, though, he had nothing; instead, he looked around, found a wrench close by and then approached the door.

'Lucas,' he repeated. 'Are you there?'

Still no reply.

Slowly, carefully, he unlatched and then nudged the door inward. It opened into a tiny backroom office, the kind of place that a small business owner like Lucas might use every now and then for a bit of admin work, probably wishing he could afford an assistant to do it for him.

And Lucas was there all right. He was slumped face forward on the desk, his forehead against his crossed arms, breathing – he was alive, that much was clear – but a mere shell of a man, laid low by pain and drugs. Within reach were his works: syringe, spoon and a brown lump of cotton wool.

It was hardly a surprise. His foot was bandaged and would be painful. And what did a junkie in pain do?

Jerry laid down the wrench. 'Wake up, I need to talk to you.'

Drowsily, the other man raised his head, registered Jerry and then immediately shrank away.

'I ain't come to hurt you,' Jerry reassured him. 'I need some information, that's all. And you're going to get it for me. You're always telling me how you've got great contacts. Now's the time to use them.'

Moments later, when he'd explained what he wanted, and Lucas's eyes were drooping once more, he stood up.

'Come on, mate,' he said. 'Let's get you out of here.'

They were about to leave when another thought occurred to Jerry. 'Where do you keep the stuff?'

Lucas was groggy. 'What do you mean?'

'Come on, you can't have stuck it all into your blood-stream, and I'm guessing those two Latino wankers gave you a decent supply in exchange for grassing me up.'

The grease monkey's eyes dropped, shame upon him like a cloak. 'I'm sorry,' he mumbled.

'Yeah, I know. Now, come on, where's the secret hiding place, then?'

Half an hour later, they were sitting in the lobby of rehab, where Lucas, having heard Jerry tell the receptionist that he intended to pay for the duration of Lucas's stay, asked, 'Why are you doing this?'

'I told you, I need information. Plus, it's no good having a junkie for a mechanic, is it? Tell you what, though, don't make the mistake of thinking it's guilt, or that I'm going soft in my old age. You got exactly what you deserved.'

Plus, he thought, *you might not be so grateful when you see what I've got in store for your workshop.*

Chapter Thirty-Two

It was a Thursday night, and Lucas, with one of the two daily calls allowed by rehab, had come through with the information Jerry needed, which was how Jerry found himself sitting in the Prius across the street from Sunshine Heights, checking his watch.

There they were. Right on time. Two Range Rovers, shark-like on the approach road, gliding through the parking lot and then turning onto Cedar Tree Avenue, their occupants obscured by smoked glass.

Nice one, he thought. Lucas's information had been good. He started the engine, drawing away to follow at a distance.

What next? Lucas had given him the day, time, the fact that the deal took place at Wilmington in the Los Angeles Port, and that the port police were paid to look the other way. But what he hadn't been able to tell Jerry was which pier. Jerry would have to discover that for himself, which meant he was thanking his lucky stars that the gangsters were thoughtful enough to drive such distinctive motors. God bless them. They were the same the world over: couldn't resist flexing, even if it meant that every idiot knew exactly what they were up to.

In due course, they came to the port and Jerry drew back, pulling off the road. He killed the engine, watching as the Range Rovers stopped by the gatehouse. To the left of him, a vast container facility stretched off into infinity; to the right were cranes lining the water of the inlet, all of them bathed in blue light. From somewhere came the long, lonesome sound of a ship's horn.

Up ahead, the gate was raised for the two Range Rovers, which cruised inside.

Pier 20, then. That was the one. Some fifteen minutes later, the vehicles returned and Jerry dipped low in the seat of the Prius as they rejoined the road, passing not far from where he sat.

'Happy days,' said Jerry, watching them recede in the rear-view mirror. 'Gotcha.'

Chapter Thirty-Three

'Remember me telling you about Mad Micky Walker?'

Noah did, of course, remember Jerry mentioning 'Mad Micky Walker'. It wasn't a name you forgot in a hurry,

'Well, you're about to meet him,' said Jerry.

Jerry and Noah had crept out of Hillview early the previous morning, keeping a low profile to avoid the forensics and fire investigation teams that had taken up residence in Jerry's old apartment. The day before, having ignored a knock at the door, they'd found a card pushed through: Detective Sergeant Lowrey would like to speak to the occupants about events in the complex. Could they call? If only she knew.

After all that, LAX to Heathrow felt like an escape. Flight, in both senses of the word. For Noah, it was her first time in first class on a flight; first time she'd been to Britain. Burning with anticipation, she was enjoying the experience of walking through the terminal with Jerry by her side when she was brought up short: standing with the taxi drivers and chauffeurs was a guy wearing shorts. He held a large piece of card bearing the words 'Tom & Jerry', complete with a tragically inept drawing of a cat.

Jerry saw him at the same time and roared with laughter. The next thing Noah knew, she was stepping out of the way as the two men embraced each other.

This, then, was Micky Walker – Mad Micky Walker.

Micky greeted Noah with what seemed like exaggerated politeness. At the same time, she was trying to get a handle on his accent. In LA, nobody spoke like Jerry. She'd only been in London five minutes and so far everybody did. As for her? In LA, she felt like part of the furniture. Just another grifting girl. Here, she already felt like an exotic animal.

They reached the car – Jerry's Range Rover – and set off, Jerry quizzing Micky about various old pals: Boring Mark, Ginger Mick, Yum Yum, Popeye Phil, Booby Pete, Semtex, Chippendale Dave. *What were they doing now? Was Micky still in contact?* Micky fielding the questions as he negotiated traffic.

'And how's Mum?' asked Jerry at last.

'I saw her the other day, in Morrisons.'

'Oh yeah? What did she have to say?'

'She asked after you. I told her you was doing well in LA.'

Jerry turned back to face front, still addressing Micky. 'Was she with anyone? Apparently, she's got a new boyfriend. Some geezer called—'

'Keith,' finished Micky.

'You know him?'

'Don't know him. Know *of* him.'

'He's not a face, then?'

'Would like to be. Likes to think he is.'

'Is he handy?'

'Would like to be. Likes to think he is.'

'So . . .'

Micky's shoulders rose and fell. 'I've been seeing Keith around and about. He seems to be enjoying the benefits of the O'Connell association, you might say.'

Noah leaned forward in her seat. 'Either The O'Connell Association is a 1970s funk band I should know about, or you've got my interest.'

Micky loved to talk about the past and was about to tell the story when Jerry stopped him with a look; instead, he waited until they'd stopped at a petrol station, Jerry stepped out for a bottle of water and a packet of Marlboro Lights, and Micky's eyes found Noah in the rear-view mirror. 'Jerry's a bit of a legend in these parts, love,' he said. 'I'll tell you a story. Not long ago, he was back home and he got in a minicab, started chatting to the driver. And he says to the geezer driving, "What about trouble? Do you get any of it?" "No," says the geezer, "we don't get any trouble at all." "Why's that?" says Jerry. "Well," says the driver, "it's because the firm's owned by Jerry O'Connell." *Oh yeah*, thinks Jerry, *is that so*?

'And so, he goes along to the firm and says to them, "What's all this, you putting it about that I own the firm?" Well, the guy's all apologetic, of course, but he's a working bloke and he appeals to Jerry's better instincts, telling him that assaults on drivers, instances of non-payment, even birds vomiting in the back of the cab have dropped considerably since they put it about that he was the owner. "Must be saving you a few quid," says Jerry. "Yeah," says the bloke. "Well then, I tell you what," says Jerry, "for a couple of hundred notes a week, I'll let you carry on saying that Jerry O'Connell owns the firm. How's about that?" And that's it, they're still paying him £200 a week, just so they can say that he's involved,' finished Micky. 'That's the O'Connell association.

'And the thing is, Jerry don't even take the money, he makes the geezer email him the receipt to show him that he's donated the money to St Francis Hospice each month, which he likes to support because his uncle Bernard died there.'

'And there I was, looking forward to the next album,' grinned Noah, settling back.

Jerry returned to the car, and for some time they drove, Noah taking in the strange new view from her window, until she heard Micky ask Jerry, 'So that's why you're back, is it? You want to check up on your mum? On Katie?'

'Nah, there's more to it than that.' Jerry went on to tell Micky the tale. In the back, Noah listened, hearing the un-censored version for the first time. Once again, she found herself trying to reconcile the image of the gentlemanly guy she knew with the kind of guy who could shove a Coke bottle into somebody's mouth and then kick it shut.

Once more, Micky's eyes found hers in the rearview, as though sensing her discomfort. 'We have a saying around here, love: if Jerry did it, then the geezer must have deserved it.'

'Right,' she said, thinking, *But who gets to decide that*?

Jerry continued with his tale, updating Micky on recent events.

'And that's it, is it?' said Micky when Jerry had finished.

'Well, yeah. I mean, how much more do you want?' asked Jerry.

'All right, all right, keep your good head of hair on,' said

Micky defensively. 'You've got dead Latino guys. Dead gang members. That's a lot of bodies, is what I'm saying.'

'I didn't ask for any of it.'

'All right, then,' said Micky, 'so those guys from the strip club found you because Lucas ratted you out.'

'Correct.'

'But that doesn't explain how the geezers from Sunshine Heights got to you.'

'Nah. I got another grass.'

And in the back, it occurred to Noah: what if Jerry mistakenly believed the leak was her? She would be a victim, then, of some form of retribution, and Jerry's London mates would say that whatever Jerry had done, she must have deserved it.

'Game on, then,' Micky was saying.

'Game on,' agreed Jerry. 'Just one thing, I need a few lads, need to see who's up for it.'

Chapter Thirty-Four

'So this is Essex?' she'd said. Micky had dropped them off at a house on an estate in Romford.

'Slightly different to LA?'

'Yeah, honey,' she agreed, looking around, shivering in the cold, 'it's a bit different to LA. Wait, I'm not looking at your old family home here, am I?'

'Nah. But it was a lot like this. Practically identical. And not far from here either.'

A shadow passed across his face. She was swiftly learning that for him a visit to the past was not always an especially happy trip, particularly where his family was concerned.

Was this something else they had in common? Noah always felt that her own childhood, while not exactly unhappy – although she'd probably done herself a favour by escaping before it got that way – was, at the very least, unfulfilled. A case of unfinished business. There was something about the way Jerry spoke about his own background that told her he felt the same. He'd always stand by his family. More than once, he'd said how your father's name was all you had in life. How if that name was associated with cowardice and scumbaggery, then your kids would be associated with cow-ardice and scumbaggery, too. But if your name was respected, then that, too, would carry on.

Even so, standing by your family didn't necessarily mean you had to like them. You could still think they'd done you wrong, even when you were defending their name.

Was that it? she wondered. Was it simply the fact that they were both damaged kids at heart?

Meantime, it turned out that the house was currently un-occupied and would be their base for the duration of their visit. 'Thing is,' Jerry told her, 'I rent the property but never rent the garages.'

'Oh yeah? Why might that be? Don't tell me . . .'

He was already raising the door of the garage and, sure enough, inside sat a car so beautiful that it took her breath away.

'Now that is one fine-looking ride,' she said, impressed.

'That's a 1975 Daimler coupe XJC in British Racing Green, only about 1,200 made, only a handful in existence.'

'Yours?'

He nodded. 'This'll be our transport while we're here. So – you up for the Magical Mystery Tour? Everything you've always wanted to know about Essex but were afraid to ask?'

Chapter Thirty-Five

Detective Lowrey had asked Detective Baxter to pull into the lot in front of Sunshine Heights. Why? She couldn't say. Just that they were in the area and there was so much about the case bugging her. They parked up and she got out of the car, half-sitting on the hood, arms folded, her eyes on the Sunshine Heights apartment building as she mulled over the many unanswered questions.

Okay, for one: the whole shitshow at Hillview. Dead was Jeremiah O'Connell, two gangbangers, both of whom had connections to the CT-40 gang, plus one other random perp, yet to be identified. Now just what the fuck was going on there? The whole thing stank worse than month-old meat.

And that's if one of those corpses really was Jeremiah O'Connell. It was only a matter of time and she would know for sure, but it had not escaped her notice that the initial ID had been performed by 'a friend'.

Lowrey had called the cop who filed the report. 'Did you get the friend's name?'

'She didn't give her name, ma'am. She just ID'd the corpse

as Jeremiah O'Connell, which tallied with the name of the apartment owner.'

'But you asked her name, right?'

'Sure, I asked her name, but—'

'Don't tell me. She had a stick up her ass about providing her name. "Am I suspected of a crime?" All of that?'

'You got it. Up until then, she was co-operative, pleasant even, but no, ma'am, she didn't want to give her name.'

Figured.

Now Lowrey glanced behind, looking into the car, where Baxter sat staring at his phone. The pair of them got on well. They'd been for drinks, but by mutual and unspoken consent had decided not to take their relationship in that direction, and she was glad of that. There were things she wanted to keep very much to herself. Private things.

For instance, and she'd never told anybody on the force this, but she knew Ronson Beaufoy.

Well, okay, that wasn't, strictly speaking, accurate. She didn't exactly *know* him. But because she'd grown up in Compton, just two streets away from the Beaufoy family home, she knew *of* him. Everybody did. He was a neighbourhood legend – a legend like the bogeyman, a figure whose name alone inspired terror. The White Ghost, they called him.

She remembered one time when she was in the front yard playing stickball, and she saw a car with Beaufoy in the passenger seat, one arm dangling out of the open window. She had stopped her play, her ball bouncing at her feet and dribbling into the gutter, transfixed as his car passed. The first thing she'd noticed was the fingertips of the hand that hung from the car window. They were red with dried blood, as though he'd dipped them in paint. The second thing she noticed was that when he turned his head and caught her eye, almost as though feeling her gaze upon him – *sensing* it somehow – a wolfish, predatory smile had spread slowly across his face, a smile that was to haunt her dreams for many years to come, and in many ways still did. When the car had disappeared around the corner, she had dashed inside the house and into the comforting arms of her mother.

Most kids could reassure themselves, knowing that the monsters haunting their dreams were not real. Jason, Freddy, Chucky. They were all just characters in films. But the monster in little Minnie Lowrey's life was a real one. She lived in a neighbourhood among many bad men – men who found it easy to do terrible things in the name of business, who destroyed lives and claimed it was survival, using the streets as an excuse for cruelty. The worst of them all, though, the one who wore his sadism like a badge of honour, glorying in the hurt he caused, was Ronson Beaufoy, the White Ghost.

Then there was what happened to her friend Leon. Buddies since middle school, Leon had fallen in with the wrong guys. She knew that, but she stuck with Leon. Like many other kids, he'd begun talking about what he needed to do to get paid and win respect, the same clichés trotted out by half the neighbourhood, all of it true, yet somehow so hollow. Even so, when the cops came to investigate a break-in at his grandma's house, Leon, furious at what had occurred, and keen for justice to be done, had done his best to help their investigation.

He wasn't to know, of course, that one of the raiders was

a cousin to one of the gang leaders. And when word went round that Leon had been helping the cops, the gang leader ordered retribution.

The White Ghost was tasked with dispensing justice, and he did so by cutting out Leon's tongue and then beheading the boy by hacking through his neck, then mailing the head to Leon's grandmother and keeping the tongue as a souvenir so that everybody would know their fate if they spoke to the cops.

And after that, if there was a break-in, nobody in that part of the neighbourhood called the cops, just in case.

Lowrey was seventeen when Leon was murdered. Maybe it was the final straw for her. A year or so later, she escaped for good. Left the hood behind. But what stayed with her was her hatred of the gangs and in particular of Ronson Beaufoy.

Now, here he was in a new neighbourhood. He had a new gang. He had apparently forged connections with Tijuana and thus enjoyed a fearsome reputation – an even more fearsome reputation – because of it.

And her hatred of him had only intensified.

Now, what about this Jeremiah O'Connell? *Who are you, Jeremiah O'Connell? And what have you done to upset this lot?*

Okay, so what did she know about him? Not a lot was the answer. But an initial and, given the timeframe, slightly cursory search had turned up the fact that he was born in London and had moved to LA while working in security. He'd been a bodyguard for a bunch of celebrities, notably the producer Sidney Frankus, with whom he'd worked almost exclusively for a number of years, although latterly he made a living as a high-end debt collector and problem-solver.

None of which shed much light on how he'd run afoul of CT-40. Was he an associate? No. She hadn't spent a lifetime on the streets and then on the force without knowing when someone carried the mark of the gangs. This guy. No way. This was a lone wolf, no doubt about it.

Something struck her: maybe it wasn't them declaring war on him. Maybe it was him declaring war on them.

Her reverie was interrupted by a call from the car. 'Hey, Lowrey. We have a body in a warehouse in Downtown LA.'

She straightened, turned. 'And what do you mean by that, Baxter? "A body" covers a multitude of sins.'

'Multitude of sins is right. Torture victim by the looks of things. CSU says that whoever killed this guy did a real number on him.'

For some reason, she found her gaze going back to Sunshine Heights as he said it. She got back in the car. 'Great. Better wait until after that for lunch, then.'

She didn't know how right she was.

Chapter Thirty-Six

Within Sunshine Heights, Ronson Beaufoy sat at his desk in one of the several apartments he called his own. Opposite him sat a man who was as smart and sharply dressed as Beaufoy was unkempt, his suit well-cut and crisp, compared to Beaufoy's creased linen; his hair shaved bald, in contrast to the other man's longish, greasy locks. Even the way he sat, one leg crossed over the other, was neat and compact. A pair of thick-rimmed designer spectacles was the finishing touch. Behind them, his eyes were sharp and his gaze searching.

His name was Francis Colorado, and he worked as an attorney for the cartel, which involved having to liaise with Beaufoy. There were times that Francis Colorado wondered why the cartel bothered with Beaufoy. The man had a reputation as a sadist, and though the Mexicans were hardly above gratuitous violence themselves, they were first and foremost businessmen. Beaufoy, on the other hand, though he liked to make the appropriate noises, was nothing of the sort. Certainly, he talked about business a lot. *Talked* about it. But how did he conduct it? Arriving at Sunshine Heights that morning, it had not been lost on Colorado that there was not one but two lots of police tape, indicating different and ongoing investigations at what was supposed to be the epicentre of the Cedar Tree operation.

'It was business,' Beaufoy had insisted when Colorado mentioned it. He hissed the 's' of business dramatically through his teeth, widening his eyes at the same time. 'I needed to take care of business. You have to set an example, Francis, surely you know that?'

One of Beaufoy's associates, a character named Gridlock, had re-entered the room. 'She's gone, chief,' he told Beaufoy, referring to the female cop who'd spent the last ten minutes standing in the parking lot staring up at the building. Colorado had sat and seen it written all over Beaufoy's face: of all the times for the cops to show, it had to be when the cartel's attorney was paying them a visit.

'It would make our friends very nervous if I were to tell them what I've seen here today,' said Colorado evenly. He picked an almost invisible piece of fluff from the sharp crease of his trousers.

'Well, let's just think about that, shall we?' retorted Beaufoy. 'What can we do? How about we . . . How about we . . . I don't know . . . How about we *maybe just don't fucking tell them.*'

Colorado had every intention of telling his employers exactly what he witnessed here at Sunshine Heights. If they discovered he was lying to them, then they would kill him. No, they would kill his family, make him watch and *then* kill him. Slowly.

Nevertheless, there was little point in painting the situation to be worse than it was. After all, he'd had nothing to do with Beaufoy's appointment. To be seen as undermining him might even seem like an act of insurrection. No, his reporting would be factual and dispassionate. Ronson Beaufoy should be the architect of his own downfall. Francis Colorado needed to be able to spread his hands and say that, as the go-between, he did everything he could by reporting the facts. It was up to somebody else how to interpret those facts. In the meantime, the shipments would continue, just as they always had.

Gridlock disappeared again.

'Not one of your men I've seen before.' Colorado reached for his briefcase, preparing to leave. He was trying to remember the two who would normally accompany Beaufoy. One of them had a name like Lightning Strike, something like that.

Beaufoy shrugged, one of those big, theatrical gestures he was so fond of, as though to say, *So what? Why bother me with such trivialities?*

Something else Colorado knew, though, was that in an organisation like theirs change was never a good thing. He liked consistency, as did those to whom he reported.

He stood to take his leave. In due course, he would be making a phone call, reporting his findings.

With Colorado gone, Gridlock reappeared and sank into a sofa, wanting to reach for an Xbox controller but thinking better of it. 'You didn't tell the cartel man about the English guy then?'

Jerry O'Connell. Full name, Jeremiah O'Connell. Beaufoy felt his insides curdle at the very mention of him, thinking of the loss of Shea and Lucky Strike. 'Why would I?'

In response, Gridlock merely shrugged, although they both knew that Francis Colorado and, in turn, the Mexicans would not take lightly to being kept in the dark.

'It's just business,' said Beaufoy, as though to convince himself. 'Just a little bit of business that was taken care of. That situation is dealt with.'

Chapter Thirty-Seven

Told that they were going to 'a traditional English boozer' – another stop on their whistle-stop tour of Essex – Noah had expected something quaint and quintessentially English: a dark, dimly lit and yet, conversely, welcoming place with strangely named areas like 'snug' and 'saloon bar'; the sound of table skittles and dominoes; coughing (a lot of coughing); clouds of black-grey cigarette smoke hanging like hammocks overhead: and maybe Michael Caine at the bar, on the telephone. It would be warm and slightly alien, but most of all it would be cosy.

The reality was very different. The Marquis was a squat, modern building on the outskirts of a housing estate, once painted white but badly in need of renovation. And from the outside at least, it looked like the polar opposite of cosy.

During their travels, Jerry had been taking calls from Micky. Mostly, the calls involved setting up a meeting for the following night, and the same names kept coming up: Boring Mark, Wayne the Thug, Yum Yum – characters who had appeared in various stories told by Jerry. Some were likely to be in attendance, others seemed to have fallen off the radar. Guys like Fat Roy ('Also known as Not So Fat Roy, because he had a gastric bypass and lost all the weight. Funny thing about Fat Roy, he'd always get a black eye at Christmas whilst working the doors.'). Or Psycho Paul ('He's now in prison for murder after chopping up a drug dealer.'). Or Foreskin ('His foreskin was so big he could fit five quid's worth of 50p pieces in it.'). As well as various others.

One particular call did not involve either the meeting or somebody with a gruesome nickname; instead, it was simply Micky telling Jerry, 'He's in the Marquis.'

'Right,' said Jerry. 'Cheers, mate.' He had turned to Noah. 'I'm pretty sure I promised you a trip to a traditional English boozer? Well, now's the time.'

'And this is it, is it?' she had said as they pulled into the car park of the Marquis and she'd squinted slightly disbelievingly at the building in front of her.

'Well, it's kind of an English boozer.' He was already getting out. 'Here, we're going in the side door.'

They entered and Noah was divested of the last of her quaint olde-English pub preconceptions. Like the outside, the interior was modern yet also shabby and unloved. It was busy, too, but not a charming, convivial kind of busy. To Noah, the atmosphere seemed to have an edge, as though everyone inside had been drinking long and hard. Like the whole place could turn nasty at any second.

Right away, she felt self-conscious as all eyes turned towards them: her, because, well, she was accustomed to turning heads, her exotic-animal status suddenly a burden; Jerry, because he was Jerry. It wasn't just his size and bearing, the way he took a room and made it his own, it was the fact that he was Jerry O'Connell and, as she'd discovered during the sightseeing, even those who didn't know him seemed to know who he was.

Still, she weathered the attention, grateful that it had subsided by the time they ordered drinks and took seats at a table, becoming part of the furniture. 'If we're just here to take in the local colour, then I think I pretty much get the picture,' said Noah, casting her eyes around at the sozzled guys propping up the bar, the cackling women, the two kids feeding money into a fruit machine.

But Jerry wasn't looking at her; instead, his eyes were fixed on a point at the far end of the pub, his face dark. Following his gaze, she saw that he was watching a small group seated at a table. As she focused on them, she became aware that much of the noise in the place was emanating from that very table; indeed, from one guy in particular.

She looked back at Jerry. This time, he tore his eyes off the group to return her gaze.

'See that geezer? The guy making a show of himself?'

'Uh-huh.'

'That's Keith.'

'Your mum's new boyfriend?'

He nodded, eyes going back to the group. 'Fucking scumbag,' he murmured.

'Okay,' said Noah. 'How about I play devil's advocate here, huh? Say he's just sitting there, having a grand old time with his buddies, just sinking a brewski or two. Doesn't make him a bad guy, right? Could be that he's a great boyfriend to your mum. Who's to say he's not?'

'Let's find out, eh?'

They stood and made their way over so that Jerry was standing in front of the table where Keith held court. He was a thin, rat-faced guy, his hair greased and combed into a side-parting; he was sporting a dyed goatee with matching eyebrows, giving him the look of somebody younger than he clearly was. Noah put him at late forties, early fifties, no doubt much younger than Jerry's mum. As they arrived, he was loudly berating one of his equally drunken mates for some unknown reason, but seeing a shadow cast over the table, he looked up, saw Jerry and his whole demeanour changed.

'Jeremiah,' he said, blood draining from his face. At the same time, he looked guilty, though it wasn't apparent why. 'How are you, mate? I didn't know you were back. Your mum didn't say anything about it.'

In reply, Jerry was not unpleasant, but there was no mistaking the steeliness of his tone. The warmth he'd displayed meeting Micky, say, or the other familiar faces he'd bumped into that day was entirely absent, and there was no embrace for Keith. 'I've only been home a couple of days. I haven't seen Mum yet.' He paused. 'I haven't seen Katie yet, either.'

'Right, right,' said Keith, holding up his hands, 'well, I won't say anything either, then, not until you're ready. It'll be a nice surprise for your mum, I'm sure she'd love to see you. In the meantime, why don't you join us? I'll get you a drink.' Right away, he started fussing, gesturing to an unsteady woman at the end of the table, 'Get up, get up, this is Jeremiah O'Connell. He's standing there without a drink. Get a drink for his friend, too.' He looked at Noah and took a beat too long to do so. 'This is your girlfriend, is it, Jeremiah? She's . . .'

And thank God he left that comment unfinished, before he could do any more damage.

'Yeah, something like that,' said Jerry, 'and we ain't staying, we've got stuff to do. Tell you what, give me your number, I've got a bit of work you might be interested in. You up for that, are ya?'

As they traded numbers, Keith swelled in front of his acolytes. Of course he was available, any time you want, mate, nodding like he was a fully paid-up member of the secret society, doing all but tapping the side of his nose.

Noah almost felt sorry for him, knowing what she knew. The depth of loathing Jerry already had for him.

'Yeah, mate, yeah, a bit of work,' Jerry was saying, 'a bit of important work . . .'

Keith still preening.

'I got a toilet that needs a good scrub.'

Noah couldn't help it. She burst out laughing at the same time as Keith's drinking buddies did. Keith reddened, frowned, made an effort to take the joke in good humour but failed. His ego in a piss-stained puddle on the floor.

'Nah, I'm only pulling your leg,' said Jerry, 'it'll be a bit more involved than that. Something that requires your specific skills – once I work out what they are.'

Keith, who was still not sure how to handle the situation, not wanting to shoot back at Jerry but desperate to save face, could only manage, 'Well, whatever it is, whatever it is, just be in touch, you know where I am.'

'Yeah, I know where you are. You'll either be in here, or with my mum, right. Like a flea on a dog.'

More laughter. Keith's mouth twitching, cheeks spotted with red.

That was it. Jerry had decided that the conversation was over. Without another word, he turned and left.

Chapter Thirty-Eight

The following night, Jerry and Noah sat in the Daimler in the forecourt of a gas station in Romford. *Hold up*, Noah corrected herself. This was England, so in fact they were parked in the forecourt of a *petrol* station in Romford, having stopped off on their way to the much talked-about meeting, due to take place in a pub elsewhere in town.

Why they'd parked up, Noah wasn't sure. Yet. Only that it wasn't to get gas or fill the tyres or any of the usual reasons you might stop at a gas – beg your pardon, *petrol* – station. 'All in good time,' she was told, just as his phone pinged with a picture.

It was the crew, assembled, waiting for Jerry and raising a glass in a toast. Micky was, presumably, the photographer.

'But you know him anyway. There's a wolf in sheep's clothing, I'm telling you. Micky. Fucking hell. One of the hardest men I know. This here . . .' Jerry pointed to another guy, smartly dressed, balding. 'That's Wayne the Thug. Now, what you have to know about Wayne is that he's a family guy. He owns a demolition company. He's worth millions. The thing was, he used to work with us, and he'd turn up driving a Rolls-Royce and never collected his wages. Just liked the camaraderie of it all, standing on the door with us. Just a bit of a relief for him every now and then.

'This geezer here,' he pointed to a stern-faced larger guy, 'that's Boring Mark. There's Carrot Cruncher, Paul. Then you've got Yum Yum. Good-looking geezer, innee? Now, the reason he's called Yum Yum is all down to one night on the door, when this drunk bird was coming in, took one look at him, just goes, "Yum Yum." Cracked us up, and the name stuck.'

'So, they all have nicknames?'

'Oh yeah, they all have nicknames.'

'What was your nickname?'

'I didn't have one. They just called me Big Jerry, on account of me being the biggest. It was my pals. It was me who gave out the nicknames. Sometimes they were humorous, sometimes they related to working the door.

'It was all nicknames and rules, that job. Like the fact that we didn't hit people if we could help it. It wasn't our style. But if we did, we had a saying: only use your fists when your feet are bleeding.'

'You were kicking people instead of hitting them?'

'Kicking, stamping, yeah.'

'Jesus, I thought you Brits were all about being gentlemanly.'

'No, darlin', it ain't about being gentlemanly. There ain't no Marquess of Queensbury rules. It's about winning. And if the Old Bill come and have a look at you later, it's about not having any marks to show you've been in a fight.' She pulled a face. 'You think that makes me a thug, do you?' he asked, suddenly a little more serious, but nodding at the same time, as though giving thought to a point she hadn't actually made. 'Yeah, I get that. But what you have to remember the next time you go to a club is that if you're having a good time and you're not getting your arse pinched or your bag nicked and your boyfriend's not getting a glass pushed in his face, then more than likely it's because geezers like me are keeping the scumbags out.

'People forget that, you see, when they step outside and they see a bouncer clomping some geezer. They think, "There's the doormen, being bullies." They forget that this trouble's happening outside so that it doesn't happen inside and spoil their evening. They don't know that the guy getting the granny beaten out of him had a knife and would have stuck someone inside the club. They don't know that he was a known sex pest who was already barred and wouldn't fuck off when he was asked nicely. They think it's just us being thugs.'

Hit a nerve there, she thought, but nodded, like *point taken*.

She found herself feeling pleased that he was happy. Earlier that day, she'd been struggling with jet lag and stayed in bed while Jerry went to visit his mum. Returning, he'd seemed preoccupied and a little unsettled, as though something was bothering him, and he'd not quite been himself ever since.

She went back to the photograph. 'I guess you're not going to give him a nickname,' she said, pointing at where, looking distinctly uneasy and out of place, sat Keith. He was smiling and, like the others, raising his glass in a toast, but the smile was forced, the body language around him uncomfortable. Sitting beside him, Boring Mark was doing all but showing him his back.

'Nah, we only give the people we like and respect a nick-name,' he said, and she saw that look from earlier about to return.

'So yesterday when you were offering him work – that was all just a bit of fun, was it? Just stringing him along.'

'Not quite. You know how I went to see my mum earlier? Started asking her a bit more about Keith, didn't I? Turns out that she's a bit pissed off with our mate Keith. A number of reasons, really. Mainly I think that she's worked out he's a bit of a wanker. But there's something else . . .'

At this, he pointed to the petrol station booth, where three attendants were serving customers.

'See the one nearest us?' he said.

She nodded.

'That's her.'

'Right,' said Noah. 'So that's your kid sister, Katie?'

She peered through the windscreen of the Daimler.

'Yep, and I'm hoping she'll be able to tell me what's up.'

Noah made a small frustrated noise. 'You've lost me.'

Noah watched as his chin tucked into his chest. The next thing she knew, that look from earlier had returned with a vengeance. Dark clouds appeared to pass across his face. Fury flashed in his eyes. She'd never seen him like that before – never seen anyone like that before.

'What?' she asked, taken aback, wondering what on earth could be bothering him so much.

He took a deep breath, as though having to muster the resolve to reply. 'At my mum's, I was hoping to see my Staffordshire terrier, Angel, who I've had for thirteen years.

Only I get there and find out that she's no longer with us. My mum says that the vet put her down due to old age; that she's been waiting for the right time to tell me, knowing I'd be heartbroken.'

'I'm sorry,' said Noah, softly, resisting the impulse to reach for him.

'Yeah,' said Jerry simply, and then added, 'so am I.'

'But . . .' prompted Noah after some more moments.

'But what?'

'You think there's more to it,' said Noah carefully. 'You think Keith might have had something to do with Angel's death?'

'Don't know what to believe,' he said. 'I could sense the words coming out of her mouth weren't the full truth. That's what I'm hoping to find out.'

Looking at him, Noah wasn't so sure. From what she could see, Jerry had already decided *exactly* what to believe.

At that moment, his phone rang. Jerry put it on speaker.

'What's going on, then, Jerry?' The unmistakable, slightly tetchy tones of Mad Micky Walker.

'You still at the pub, are you?' asked Jerry.

'Yeah, we're all here. Where are you?'

Jerry rolled his eyes at Noah. 'I told you I'd be there after ten. Keith still with you, is he?'

'Yeah, what's he fuckin' doing here? Do you want us to get rid of him before you show up?'

Noah looked at Jerry sharply.

'No nothing like that,' said Jerry, 'just hold it there, will you?'

A short time later, Katie had finished her shift and stepped out in to the bright sodium lights beneath the canopy of the petrol station, crossing as though to make for the pavement, pulling on a Puffa jacket at the same time.

'Hey.' Jerry intercepted her and they embraced, before she pulled away and delivered a punch.

'You've been home a couple of days, haven't you? You've been to see Mum, even. And you haven't fucking bothered to come and see me.'

'Well, I thought you might be at home when I went to see Mum,' he said, although that was a little white lie. He'd been holding off seeing Katie until he got the lie of the land elsewhere. 'But I'm here to see you now, aren't I?'

'I can't stop, though, Jerry, I need to get off.'

'Yeah, me neither, I can't stay long, I've—'

'*Got a bit of business*,' she mimicked.

'You might say that, yes. I just wanted to see you, that's all. Look, why don't you come with me? There's somebody I'd like you to meet.'

'Aw, Jerry, I've got to go . . .'

'Look, I'll be really quick,' he insisted. 'It'll only be a minute, come on.'

He led her across to the Daimler and opened the passenger door for her to get in, Noah already having moved to the rear seat.

She glanced inside, eyes going to Noah and looking distinctly unimpressed. 'Oh yeah? I heard that you was hanging around with some Yank girl. This her, is it?' Her eyes burned with antipathy for Noah. So much so that Jerry would have felt sorry for Noah, if he didn't know that she was perfectly capable of giving as good as she got.

Sure enough, Noah was not at all intimidated. 'Hi Katie, hop in,' she said brightly.

Katie settled inside. Jerry took his place in the driver's seat. For a moment, a silence settled upon them. Noah found herself wondering how this would go, how Jerry would broach the subject, and maybe shouldn't have been surprised when he got straight down to brass tacks.

'I was hoping to see Angel this morning,' he said to Katie. His shoulders were back, chin straight.

'You know, then?'

'Yeah, I know.'

'I'm sorry about Angel,' said Katie in a small voice.

'What you got to be sorry about?'

'I'm just sorry, aren't I? That's what you say, isn't it?'

'I know it was Keith who did it,' said Jerry. His voice was cold.

'How did you know that?'

He tightened his grip on the steering wheel. 'So I'm right. It was him.'

Katie's head jerked up, knowing that she had unwittingly let the cat out of the bag – well and truly out of the bag. 'He didn't mean it.'

'It was him then?' he repeated.

'Don't do nothing. For Mum's sake.'

'Tell me what happened,' he said tightly. Noah could see that fury in his eyes again. The look had returned to his face like an unwelcome house guest.

'Only if you promise,' insisted Katie.

'Promise what?'

'Not to hurt him.'

His shoulders rose and fell as he seemed to consider. At last he spoke. 'I won't kill him.'

'Don't you lie to me,' she warned.

'I'm not lying.'

'You don't lay a finger on him.'

'I won't.'

'Or get any of your mates to do it.'

'Fucking hell, you're trying to cover all bases, aren't you?'

'Say it.'

'Okay, okay. Now tell me.'

Katie sniffed. 'Keith didn't like Angel. Since he moved in, he insisted on leaving her outside. But Angel didn't like it outside. She—'

'Whimpered and cried, didn't she?' said Jerry. Turning in his seat to face Katie, he bristled with barely contained emotion. Noah could feel it in the car. The atmosphere was thick with it. 'She cried, didn't she?'

'Yeah,' agreed Katie. 'Every night.'

'And the noise pissed Keith off, did it?'

Katie nodded. She looked down.

'And so Keith did something about it, did he?'

'He came home drunk one night, Jerry,' said Katie. 'He put Angel outside in the garden and she started crying when he tried to sleep. He went downstairs, grabbed her by the collar, dragged her up the stairs, ran the bath and drowned her.'

Jerry turned to face front. When he put his hands to the steering wheel, Noah saw that his knuckles were white. A nerve in his jaw jumped. 'Mum knew?' he said, at last.

'No, Jerry, she was in bed. Next day, he told her that he'd

had to take Angel to the vet and that the vet put her down for her own good. Mum was gutted, Jerry. She really was.'

'You didn't think to tell me?'

'I didn't want to – in case you kicked off.'

In response, he was silent, but the two of them locked eyes in an unresolved battle of wills, and as Noah looked from one O'Connell to another, she wondered what the hell she'd got herself into.

Chapter Thirty-Nine

She'd got out, watched her older brother and his American bird pull away, making sure they were out of sight before she went to the waiting BMW.

Inside, his irritation at having been kept waiting pulsing off him in waves, sat Scott. A spliff burned between the fingers of one hand, which drummed on the steering wheel impatiently, the car interior reeking of weed and his eyes – skunk eyes, she called them – rimmed red. 'Who was that in the sweet motor?' he demanded. As well as his drumming fingers, his knee jogged as though he was making a physical effort to keep his true feelings from being known.

'That was my brother,' she said.

'What did he want?'

'Just to see me, what do you think? I'm his sister.' And there was something about having talked to her brother that gave Katie greater-than-usual confidence, and so she added, 'He wanted to know about Angel.'

Scott looked at her sharply. His mouth was a thin line and a vein in his neck stood out. 'Fuck. What did you say? What did you tell him?'

'He knows Angel weren't put down.'

Scott cleared his sinuses, opened the window and gobbed outside before he spoke. 'Does he know it were me what did it?'

'Nah. I told him it was Keith.'

Scott chuckled. 'That pisshead. What's big brother planning on doing about it, then?'

Katie sniffed. 'Nuffink. I made him promise not to.'

Scott gave a contemptuous snort. 'And you think he'll stick to that, do you? Mate, he ain't gonna let it go. Not unless he's had his balls cut off in America.'

'He said he wouldn't,' she repeated.

Scott looked pensive. 'All right,' he said. 'Best if it stays that way.'

Chapter Forty

They were on the plane back to LA before Noah said it: 'I know what you did the other night, by the way.'

She was talking about the meeting. After leaving the petrol station, they had driven to the pub where it was to be held.

'Come on, Jerry, the guys are getting restless,' Micky had said. 'We'll all be pissed by the time you get here.' Hearing this, Noah had feared the worst. This, after all, was Jerry's big meeting: the very reason they'd crossed the pond in the first place. He'd been talking about getting the boys together ever since they arrived. Now it was happening and the boys were all laying into the beers.

As they'd made their way upstairs, Jerry exchanging a nod and a wink with the barman, he'd turned to her, just before they entered the room. 'You're probably wondering why I've kept them waiting, are you?'

Well, yeah, she kind of was.

'They ain't seen each other for a while. Not all together,' said Jerry, his voice was low. 'I just wanted to get them re-acquainted without me there, you know? Get a little bit of bonding going on.'

Yes, thought Noah, she knew how English dudes liked to bond. With beer and fighting.

Indeed, there came a burst of raucous laughter from behind the door and she'd readied herself.

As it turned out, she should have had more faith. It immediately became clear that Micky was only joking about the drinking. Sure, there was laughter, but as she was to discover that was only because, just like Jerry, they enjoyed a laugh. This lot, she could see, were sober as judges.

With one exception. While the other guys had a solitary bottle of beer or glass of lemonade in front of them, Keith already had three empty pint glasses and was making headway on a fourth. She saw Jerry's eyes go to him; she saw them flare and become flinty for a second before they'd glazed, as though he was once again suppressing his anger.

Which he was. Because as he'd stood there, looking at Keith and thinking *This is the man who drowned my Angel, who I had for thirteen years, and loved more than anything*, he had to restrain himself from grabbing him, biting his nose off there and then.

To make matters worse, Keith had stood from the table, face flushed and beaming, rushing over to embrace Jerry, perspiration shining on his forehead. 'Jeremiah! My future son-in-law,' he'd drawled.

Noah had winced. Looking around the table, Mad Micky Walker, Wayne the Thug, Yum Yum, Carrot Cruncher and Boring Mark all did the same, each of them anticipating fireworks.

But Jerry had remained composed. 'Sit the fuck down,' he'd growled, and there was enough of a warning in his voice to cut through Keith's drunkenness and trigger his survival instinct. He'd wiped the smile off his face and took a seat.

And Jerry began.

He'd started by outlining the situation at Cedar Tree, and how 'the CT-40 geezers think I'm dead. The cops think I'm dead. But they'll find out the body wasn't mine sooner or later. We ain't got time to hang around. It needs to happen fast.'

Wayne the Thug was nodding. 'What's the plan? We go into this Sunshine Heights gaff? Take the place apart?'

'No, they've got the place sewn up tighter than a nun's chuff. Plus, you've got residents living there and we can't afford to hurt those that don't deserve it.'

'All right. What, then?' asked Wayne.

'We have to entice them out somehow. Get them on neutral ground.'

'And how do we do that?'

'We give them a kick up the arse. Details of which I'll tell you when we get you all over to LA.'

Nods from around the table. All involved were happy to wait and more than happy to make the trip to LA.

'And what about this leak you've got?' asked Wayne.

As the only outsider, Noah had felt heat rise in her cheeks, and though they tried to be discreet, it was obvious that the room's attention had shifted her way. The nameless fear she'd had in the back of Micky's car returned, only even more intensely than before, and she found a thought, like a speck of dust, irritating her mind's eye: *How well do I really know this guy?* She was with a relative stranger, in an unfamiliar place in a foreign country. Was this it? Was she going to find herself taking the starring role in an Essex snuff movie?

And then Jerry had said it. 'I don't know who the snitch is. All I know is, it's someone in LA . . .'

Noah had swallowed.

'Could be a lot of people. Plenty of geezers know where I live. But for the time being it ain't a priority, because one thing I do know – the most important thing – the snitch ain't in this room.' Jerry reassured her by making eye contact, with a wink. 'And as long as we keep everything that happens between us, then there ain't going to be any more leaks.'

Noah knew instantly what he intended by that statement; the result was immediate: the guys around her seemed to relax. She hadn't noticed it before, the ever-so-slight resistance to a stranger in their midst – not until it suddenly wasn't there. Before, she and Keith were the outsiders of this particular group. Now it was just Keith.

'I appreciated that,' she told him as they settled on the plane. 'It brought me into the group.'

'It's just about reading people, really,' said Jerry. 'I want you along for the ride, providing you want to be there, and they need to know that you have my trust.'

'And I do, do I?'

'Like I said, you wouldn't be here otherwise.'

It felt like the flight was Jerry Airways. They were all in first class, except Keith, who was at the back of the plane, with only the toilets for company. Jerry told him there was no room left in first class. Noah almost felt sorry for him.

It was some way into the flight before she spoke her mind. 'What are you going to do with him?'

'Who?'

'You know who. Keith. I mean, why is he even with us?'

'All in good time.'

Chapter Forty-One

Lowrey was behind her desk when the phone rang. 'Detective Sergeant Minnie Lowrey? My name is Dawn Emery from the medical examiner's office. I've got two flags here, both to call you, both concerning IDs on John Does.'

'Fire away,' said Lowrey.

'First one is a burns victim out of West Hollywood. Victim thought to be a Jeremiah O'Connell. You're wanting positive confirmation.'

'Yes, that would be great.'

'Okay. Second victim is a John Doe found in a warehouse in downtown LA.'

The downtown victim was the one they were called to the day Lowrey paid her visit to Sunshine Heights. The thought of it now turned her stomach. The perp – or more likely *perps*, plural – had left the victim hanging in a disused warehouse like a side of beef, his hands and feet tied with flexicuffs, arms hoisted up and held there by a length of chain slung over a low crossbeam. The flexicuffs had dug deep into his wrists, no doubt adding to the pain as he writhed, but even so, it would have been the least of his agonies. What had they done to him? What hadn't they done? One foot had been soaked in some kind of accelerant and burned. Strips of skin taken off his face and neck. Toenails ripped out.

'Jesus, just pick a mode of torture and stick to it.' Baxter had clamped one hand over his mouth, practically gagging as they'd conducted a cursory sweep to see if they could spot anything before forensics turned up. Looked like the area was clean. No cigarette butts, those helpful carriers of DNA. Just the body left as a sign, or a warning.

'Okay, so what have you got for me?' Lowrey asked Emery now, taking a gulp of lukewarm coffee, wanting to wash that ghastly image away.

Emery continued, 'Nothing yet on whether Mr West Hollywood is really the man you think he is – we've requested dental records from England for that one – but I do have something on your downtown LA vic.'

'I'm all ears.'

'No ID yet, but I thought you might like to know two things. One, several scorpion bites. Poor guy had been stung with a scorpion several times, then whoever was torturing him administered the serum. The pain is intense and you have to know what you're doing or you risk losing your subject. I leave you to draw your own conclusions about that, but—'

'Whoever did it knew exactly what they were doing?' said Lowrey, but distantly, because her mind had already gone elsewhere, specifically to the sign of the CT-40, the tattoo that all gang members had: a scorpion. And who might well be the architect of that torture. Somebody who, like Dawn Emery said, knew exactly what they were doing?

'I would say so.'

A guy like the White Ghost, maybe?

'What else?'

'The victim already had a broken nose. I don't know if it's at all significant, but he'd clearly been in a fight a day or two before the torture began.'

Chapter Forty-Two

Jerry, Noah, Wayne and Micky had swapped Hillview for Compton, and now stood bathed in a mid-morning sun that softened the city's concrete and gave it a decaying grandeur, staring at the building in front of them.

'Who's Lucas Brady, then?' Micky, in shorts and a polo shirt, a hand shielding his eyes against the glare of the sun-blasted stone, pointed at a sign above the door that read Lucas Brady Autos.

Not for the first time, it struck Noah how incongruous they all seemed: three 'geezers' from Essex standing here in Compton, of all places. At the same time, she shared a glance with Jerry, wondering if he was going to reveal the whole sorry tale of him and Lucas.

No, was the answer. 'He's just a bloke I'm helping out right now. Putting him through rehab. I thought I'd use his workshop while he was away.'

Wayne raised a quizzical eyebrow. 'So he don't know what you're planning?' he said.

'No, of course he doesn't.'

Only Noah knew what went unspoken: *But fuck Lucas*

anyway. He ratted me out. I'm paying for his rehab. If he doesn't like it, then he can fucking dangle.

'All right, well, it's your show,' sighed Wayne. 'Let's have a look inside, shall we?'

All four of them stepped into the workshop, Jerry feeling an almost overwhelming sense of déjà vu at the smells, the same dingy feel of it. His eyes went to the black Corvette, still mid-repair. A shame, really, he thought. It wasn't right to destroy a beautiful bit of machinery like that.

Still. Needs must.

Wayne was looking around. 'So you want the whole place to blow?'

This came as news to Noah, though not a total surprise. During the meeting in Romford, Jerry had outlined the situation in bare-bones terms: 'We're going to draw them out. Meet them on our turf. Hit them where it hurts.' Well-worn phrases guaranteed to play well to the guys going into bat for him. They weren't gung-ho, exactly. In fact, what impressed her was their focus. Even so, Jerry was a wily one. He knew which buttons to press and how to press them. Evidently, his policy had been to cover the main points, get everybody onside and sweat the details later.

Then there was the journey home. At various stages of the trip, he'd been taking the men aside individually, going over elements of the plan without revealing the whole thing. Wayne, she knew, owned a demolitions firm. He was the one they called the big-bang bossman, the master blaster. And, of course, she'd wondered about that: why they might need an explosives expert on board.

Now she knew.

'So this place is going to blow?' she said.

'That's the plan,' said Jerry, who, rather than look at Noah, was directing himself to Wayne.

'Yeah, shouldn't be too difficult,' said Wayne, his gaze travelling upwards. 'How important is it that the device is hidden?'

'Well, yeah, pretty important. Can you do that?'

'Yeah, I can do that.' Wayne was studying the corrugated ceiling of the workshop. 'Plenty of places to put 'em, assuming you ain't going to be letting the bad guys do a sweep of the place.'

Jerry shook his head. 'No. Second they come in here, we detonate.'

'Wait . . .' said Noah, thinking, *There were going to be people inside?*

'I'll need visual confirmation,' Wayne was saying. 'And I don't want to be nearby when you give the word.'

'How about across the road?' asked Jerry.

'Could work.'

'Okay, follow me,' said Jerry. He led them back out into the lot, where cars stood like rusting sentinels. Shielding his eyes, he pointed across the street at an empty KFC that was gradually disappearing beneath a welter of weeds and graffiti tags, as though being slowly reclaimed by the city. 'How about if you're in there?'

'Perfect.'

Noah had had enough. She thumped Jerry to get his attention. 'Hey, mister, are you going to tell me what's going on?'

'Easy,' said Jerry. He pointed at the workshop. 'That right

there is what you might call a scumbag trap. We get Beaufoy and his mates in there, the whole lot goes up.'

For a moment, Noah considered debating the rights and wrongs of it right there before deciding it was a conversation best left until they were alone. Instead, she said, 'Oh yeah? And how do you plan to get them in there? They're going to just walk right in, are they?'

'No, they ain't.'

'So . . .?'

'We'll have bait.'

Chapter Forty-Three

At Hillview, the men had been ensconced in one of Jerry's 'other' apartments, all five and Keith, who was, naturally, a source of great frustration. Carrot Cruncher, who had been forced to room with him (he plumped for paper when he should have chosen stone), was most vociferous in his dislike for the guy. 'What the fuck is he doing here? Why have we got him on board? I wouldn't mind, like, only he keeps talking like he's fucking Ronnie Kray, thinks he's big time, don't even think he's had a fucking shower since he's been here. Hasn't lifted a finger to tidy up, or any of that shit.'

Like most of the guys, Carrot Cruncher took pride in his role. It was something Noah had noticed. Only Keith seemed to be letting the side down.

Seemingly the only reason that Keith hadn't already been given a harsh lesson in team spirit was that Jerry himself seemed to be strangely relaxed about his behaviour. At one point, Yum Yum had said to him, 'What's he doing here, then, Jerry? You wanted good drivers, you said. Wayne for the explosives. Mark for the engineering. What's his speciality?'

'Keith's speciality is being Keith,' Jerry had assured him. 'All will be revealed, don't you worry about that.'

Noah had witnessed this conversation, still wondering – worrying – about what Jerry had in mind, but knowing better than to come right out and ask. Not yet, anyway.

'This job, then?' she asked him. They were in his apartment, alone.

'The plan?'

'Yeah, the plan. The plan that everyone . . .' she gesticulated in the general direction of apartment B, where any talk not concerned with calling Keith a wanker was of *the job*. 'Like, I'm beginning to feel a bit left out, in the dark, you might even say, wondering if all your fancy words about bringing me into the team were just that – words.'

Jerry nodded sagely, acknowledging her point. 'All right, okay. CT-40 sell on behalf of the Mexicans, right?'

Noah nodded.

'So they supply and control the individual dealers in that neighbourhood, and those dealers re-up from Sunshine Heights, direct from Beaufoy. But when they themselves need to re-up, they go to the Mexicans. Got it?'

'I'm with you so far,' she said.

'Which means there's a window when the drugs are not with the Mexicans and they're not at Sunshine Heights, right? They're out in the open.'

She nodded.

'That's when I'm going to take them. I'm going to take their fucking drugs.'

'And that's the bait you were talking about?'

'That's the bait. Part of the bait.'

She looked at him sharply. 'What do you mean, *part of* the bait?'

'All in—'

'Good time. Yeah, I know.' She bit her lip, feeling, not for the first time, as though she were trying to ride a bucking bronco, clinging on, waiting to be thrown off or for the ride to finish, whichever happened first.

For a long time, nothing was said. He looked at her. 'Go on then.'

'What?'

'Say what you're going to say.'

She had a ton of things to say, a heap of questions, like repeating 'What do you mean by "part of" the bait?' And, 'Are you really – really – planning on blowing up a bunch of guys in Lucas Brady's workshop?' But right now they seemed like minor details compared to the big question, the huge fucking elephant in the room, which was . . .

'Jerry, this is not some beef on the streets of Romford. This is drug gangs in LA . . .'

He shook his head. 'Look, don't matter how many times anybody says it, I've never been scared of any gang. Do you know how geezers like that work? Fear. I know a bit about that, believe me. I know that's where all the power is. And I know that if you aren't scared of them, then they haven't got that power. You scared of them?'

'I think you'd be a fool not to be. What about the cartel?'

'You see? They have that control over you. Beaufoy knows that, too. He puts it about that the cartel have his back, and we all know that he buys his gear off them, so he's got everybody believing they have his back. But he's a salesman, that's what he is. An outlet. He flogs their products, that's all. They're not looking out for him any more than Jeff Bezos is looking out for a geezer who works in an Amazon warehouse.

'Tell you what. I bet he's shit-scared of them an' all. Is he going to tell them about me? Nah. Why would he want to admit he's got a problem with anyone – it weakens him. A lone English geezer giving him gyp. What does it say about Beaufoy that he can't sort it out, eh?'

Noah conceded the point. 'Okay, so say you're right. Say that he doesn't enjoy the kind of support that he claims. He's still a dangerous guy, cartel or no cartel.'

'Mate, I'm telling you. He doesn't know his world is about to turn upside down.'

Noah lowered her voice, even though there was no need. 'Look, the men you've brought back here, I'm sure they're the best set of English dudes in the world. But take a look at them, Jerry, they're a bunch of middle-aged guys, most of them overweight. They're ex-doormen. They have families. They're just not a match for these people. You're risking their lives by going up against them. Surely you can see how irresponsible that is. Jesus, Jerry, it's goddamn selfish is what it is.

'Look, I get where you're coming from on this. And I understand why it became your fight, I really do. But one thing I do know for sure. It's not *their* fight. It's not for them to die for a little girl they've never met and never will meet. However much you're paying them.'

He nodded, his lips pursed as though giving the matter thought, although she suspected that his mind was already so made up it might as well have been set in concrete.

'Firstly,' he said, 'I'm paying them because I'm asking them to do a job, and it doesn't matter who you are, if you do a job, you get paid for it. But, let me tell you, they'd never just do it for the money. They're doing it for me, and it doesn't matter *why* they're doing it. Doesn't matter whether it's for Jane, this needs taking care of regardless. It doesn't matter to them, because what matters is that I've asked them and we've got a bond for life. And they know full well that I'd do the same for them if things were the other way around. Like if they needed me, I'd be there for them. I can assure you, none of us are remotely concerned about any cartel. Doesn't even cross their minds.' He looked at her carefully. 'You need to have more faith in me and them. After all, have I let you down yet?'

No, she thought, but there was always a first time, and besides, she had the sneaking suspicion that right now his priorities lay elsewhere.

Chapter Forty-Four

Up until recently, when Jerry had a few spare hours and the inclination to relax, he would pay a visit to one of his favourite coffee shops, buy a skinny latte, take a seat in the sun and make friends with the dogs that customers would tether outside while they went in to buy drinks. That, to him, was a perfect way to while away a couple of hours.

As far as today went, he really should not have been out. Firstly, it wasn't as though he had time on his hands, and secondly, it was dangerous to leave Hillview at all, given that A) he wasn't exactly the most inconspicuous of men, and B) he was supposed to be dead. After all, he was the one imprinting on the guys how important it was to keep the team under the radar, and that meant a low profile.

On the other hand, he'd been given a shopping list: Boring Mark needed a piece of equipment called a 'pneumatic air punch flange'; Wayne required a certain amount of fertiliser. And this was Los Angeles. Fertiliser and pneumatic air punch flange tools were not exactly an abundant resource. So while Noah had been dispatched to buy fertiliser, he'd tasked himself with securing the tool. In truth, he'd been anticipating a long and boring citywide hunt, but, as it happened, he'd found it easily.

And it was for that reason that he found himself with time to kill.

So, yes, normally Jerry would have spent a couple of hours making friends with dogs, and almost did. But today was different – today he decided to visit the hospital. There, he took up position on the other side of the viewing glass, away from the CCTV cameras, standing watching Jane, who might as well have been suspended in time and space for all the change he saw in her. A passing nurse told him that her condition remained the same, that doctors were still hopeful she'd make a recovery, but there was little sign of it just to look at her.

Why? he wondered. Why did he feel the need to do this? Maybe because Noah had a point, and he knew that he was going up against the big boys here. Not that he was biting off more than he could chew – nothing like that. But the CT-40 were big, and they had contacts with the Cartel, and by locking horns with them, it wasn't just himself in the firing line. There were others in the crosshairs, too. And maybe by being here he was just reminding himself why he was taking that risk.

He stood there some more, the sight of her strengthening his already granite resolve, when gradually he became aware that he was not alone.

He turned. It was the cop, Lowrey, only not dressed as a cop. She wore jogging skins and a vest top soaked in sweat, which meant that unless the hospital had a gym she'd come direct from a workout of her own.

He looked over her shoulder. If he wasn't very much

mistaken, she'd come without backup, and nor was she armed.

'How did you know I was here?' he asked her, testing the water.

She shrugged, keeping her distance, wearing a smile that was nonetheless wary. Around them, the hospital corridor felt dark and quiet, as though they were the only two people in the place. 'A few days ago, I got talking to the girls on the nursing station, I asked them to keep an eye out for anything or anybody unusual. So when they told me that a big guy, good-looking, with an English accent had appeared, I came scooting right on over.'

Jerry's eyes narrowed. He even let the 'good-looking' comment wash over him. 'You came from the gym?'

'From a run.'

'And you don't look that surprised to see me.'

'I'm not.'

'Even though you thought I was dead?'

She allowed herself a smile. 'I was withholding judgement about that until it was confirmed and, as coincidence would have it, it was confirmed yesterday.'

Lowrey cast her mind back to the call. It had been Dawn Emery from the medical examiner's office again – efficient as always: 'We have an ID on your West Hollywood guy.'

Lowrey had perked up. 'Wait – weren't you waiting for dental records from England?'

'Yes, but we didn't need them because we got a match from a tattoo. Crispy and charred, but still a visible identifying mark, and one that we were able to find in our records. Guy was a small-time crook by the name of . . . um, wait.

I'll need to email that over when I lay my hands on it.'

'Point being, it wasn't Jeremiah O'Connell,' asked Lowrey.

'No. I can confirm that his name was not Jeremiah O'Connell. Okay, and on the second John Doe, your downtown warehouse guy. The man's name was Jeffrey Blaydon. Mean anything?'

It didn't.

'And I was right, what I told you the other day. He had indeed been in a fist fight in the days prior to his death.'

'Okay. Anything else?'

'Other than the fact that he was quite the fan of crack cocaine, no.'

Snapping back to the present, Lowrey watched as Jeremiah O'Connell — the definitely not-dead Jeremiah O'Connell — pushed his hands through his hair, looking cautious.

'You're probably wondering what happens now,' she said.

'No, of course not,' he lied confidently. 'I mean, it's not like I've committed a crime, is it?'

She looked up and to the left, as though thinking, searching her memory banks. 'Really? Are you sure about that?'

'Never been more certain, darlin'.'

'Really? Because I'm sure we could find one. You have, after all, left the scene of an, um, one, two, three – *quadruple* possible homicide. A quadruple possible homicide for which, I might add, we have only one major suspect.' She pointed at him.

'Well, it's funny you should mention it, because I fully intended to get in touch with yous in order to clear up what seems to have been a terrible misunderstanding.'

'Oh yeah? I'm all ears.'

'Yeah, you see, I've been away on business, returning to find that my apartment has been gutted by fire and that a friend of mine has erroneously identified me as one of those poor unfortunates who perished in the blaze.'

'That's your story and you're sticking to it?'

'That's the one.' He gestured at her running gear. 'But something tells me that you're not here to take me in anyway.'

She looked at him long and hard, like maybe she was thinking about it, and, in truth, he wouldn't have put it past her to try to take him in anyway, running gear or not. But then it was as though she reached a decision. 'No. If I took you in, we'd have to put you in the cells, and there'd be no way I could keep you safe. If I took you in, I'd be signing your death warrant.'

He pulled a face. 'I'm sure you could sort something out. I can't be the only highly desirable marked man the police have had to arrest.'

'True, true. But there's something else . . .'

'And what might that be?'

'What were you doing at Sunshine Heights?'

'Everything I've told you is true. I knocked her over.' He waved a hand towards the glass. 'I wanted to make things right by returning the bike and checking up on her.'

'And . . .'

'You were right what you said,' he told her, and she nodded.

She knew. They both did – they knew that somehow, just by getting involved, he'd fucked things up. And yet she couldn't bring herself to hate him for it. Didn't even blame him. Places like Sunshine Heights, someone needed to make a difference. Maybe it was him, and maybe that was the other reason she wasn't going to take him in.

He continued, 'You know don't you, that it was him – it was Beaufoy who made the mum do it? He made her shoot the little girl.'

Lowrey shook her head slowly, absorbing the information, thinking of the White Ghost and knowing how much it would have appealed to him to watch a mother shoot her own daughter. 'I didn't know that, no. But I'd like to know how you know.'

His mind went to Shea stuffed into a shopping trolley, a bike chain around his neck. He cleared his throat. 'Ask me no questions, I'll tell you no lies.'

She was about to press the point, then decided against it. 'I can't say I'm surprised. I'm guessing there's no way of proving it.'

'As far as I can tell, the only two people left alive are Jane and Ronson Beaufoy.'

They looked at one another meaningfully. 'You know that I grew up not far from where he lived?' she told him. 'He was a gang enforcer back then. Terror of the neighbourhood. If you're thinking of going up against him, then you're fixing to get yourself killed.'

'I keep hearing that.'

'Sure, be flippant about it. We'll all have a great laugh when we're fishing bits of you out of a twenty-gallon drum.'

'Something tells me that you're prepared to let me have a go, though.'

She sidestepped that one. 'How do you think they found you?'

'The CT-40 boys? I've got a rat. Somebody in this city's got a problem with me.' He stopped himself. 'Well, somebody *else* in this city has a problem with me.'

'You shouldn't even be here, then.'

'No,' he admitted, 'I shouldn't.' He looked through the glass at Jane. The machines.

'You need to be careful,' warned Lowrey. '*More* careful. And it's best we never had this meeting.'

'Sure.'

'Because let me tell you something,' she said. 'If I know that you're alive and kicking, then so will they.'

'Noted.'

She was about to go, then stopped. 'Good luck, Jeremiah O'Connell.'

He nodded thanks. And then they turned and went their separate ways.

Chapter Forty-Five

The lads were assembled in the main living area of one of the apartments. Jerry had sat them there partly for *The Italian Job / Reservoir Dogs* vibes – a tongue-in-cheek homage that hadn't been lost on any of those assembled – and partly because, well, he needed to get them together in order to tell them the plan, and how did you get a bunch of guys in one place for the purposes of revealing a plan without it looking and feeling like *The Italian Job* or *Reservoir Dogs*? Answer? You didn't. You couldn't. You just went with it.

He stood there waiting while they got it out of their system, with their Michael Caine impressions: 'You were only supposed to blow the bloody doors off.' 'Don't throw those bloody spears at me,' and, 'Wait till you see the whites of their eyes, lads,' as well as the inevitable arguments about who wasn't going to be Mr Pink, because what else could you do? You stood there, you joined in, you exchanged the odd look with Noah, with Micky or with Wayne, and you just waited it out.

Since they came on board, he'd briefed each man on their likely role in the proceedings, but what he hadn't done was tell them as a group. In truth, he'd wanted more time, but time was a luxury he could no longer afford. Events had moved more quickly than he had anticipated, because, as Lowrey said, if she knew he was alive, then so would CT-40, so they had to move sooner rather than later. Hence the meeting.

At last, the jollity died down. What went unspoken was the idea that any one of them could die. Of that he had warned them all individually, giving them all – apart from Keith – a get-out clause. Every single one of them had looked at him as though he were crazy. 'Are you having a laugh?' said Wayne, summing up the feelings of the group. 'I wouldn't miss this for the fucking world. It's going to be the best craic I've had in years.'

'All right, then,' said Jerry now. 'Here we are. Now, one more time for those in the restricted-view seats: does everybody know what the plan is?'

Most of them did indeed know what the plan was, and with that established they sat expectantly.

'Well, our boys, the CT-40, creatures of habit, meet at the same time every week. They vary the location, but as far as I can tell, they use one of three venues, where they've paid off the cops, the port police, coastguard, whatever.'

Jerry's information wasn't gleaned solely from his night-time excursions to Sunshine Heights and the port. At a needle exchange downtown, he'd befriended a junkie's dog and then got talking to the addict, who in turn put him in touch with a guy higher up the chain (all things being relative); they'd taken seats on a bus, sitting apart and letting the bus take them away from the neighbourhood until the guy felt safe and they disembarked, Jerry following as the guy ducked into a store. By the chillers was where the guy at last felt safe to talk.

'I know that CT-40 meet every week,' Jerry had said, 'what do you know about it?'

'Nothing.'

'Yeah,' said Jerry, rolling his eyes, 'you've come all this way for that.' Money changed hands. 'Nobody knows we are having this talk?'

'Are you kidding? I was going to say the same thing.'

'Then we understand each other.'

According to the dealer, himself an addict, CT-40 took delivery of over five million dollars' worth of crack cocaine each week, blocks that were delivered in holdalls. At Sunshine Heights was where Ronson Beaufoy's army of addicts, hookers and street people would package them up ready to sell on, the proceeds being used to buy more drugs.

Five million dollars' worth of crack cocaine, ready for the taking.

That would hurt, thought Jerry. That would hurt him good.

'How will you know which location they're using?'

The question came from Yum Yum, bringing Jerry back to the present.

'I won't. Me and Noah will be staying with CT-40 and relaying directions to you lot.'

'So we'll be waiting for your call?' Boring Mark sat deep in a sofa, hands in his lap.

'That's about the size of it. You boys are going to drive fast but drive safe. You're going to have to keep your wits about you. We can't afford to let this slip through our fingers.'

Jerry looked around the room, taking them all in, seeing their eyes gleam with excitement at the thrill of what was to come. He knew that if the roles were reversed and that if it had been one of them calling on him, then his feelings would be the same – no questions asked, everything dropped for a call to action. Even so, he couldn't help the feeling of admiration, even pride, that shot through him at that moment: their enthusiasm, their fearless outlook fortifying him.

Noah was right, he was not a man often assailed by doubt, but if he'd been feeling any, then all he needed to do was look at this lot to dispel it.

'Are we up for this?'

They looked at him.

'Fuckin' right we are.'

Part Three

Chapter Forty-Six

The guy's name was Drugstore, a big black dude who seemed as wide as he was tall, in Timberlands, black jeans and a voluminous grey sweatshirt with a cross-body bag slung over the front. Along with Gridlock, he'd found himself in one of the lieutenant's roles recently vacated by Shea and Lucky Strike (who'd turned out not to be so lucky), which for Drugstore was not a happy turn of events.

Prior to now, Drugstore had been in charge of making cash deliveries to cops in Dunkin' Donuts and Burger King, receiving information in return – what Beaufoy called 'a police liaison role' – and that had been fine with Drugstore; he'd liked that. This, however, was a promotion he didn't want, mainly because no one in their right mind would covet the role of lieutenant to Beaufoy, while, of course, he was still expected to do the police liaison stuff as well, which meant that whereas before he would have received news – good or bad – and passed it on to either Shea or the not-so-Lucky Strike to pass on to Beaufoy, now he had to deliver the news himself.

'We've got some information, boss,' he said now,

congratulating himself on saying 'we' like that; like they were all in this together, right?

'Good news or bad news?' asked Beaufoy.

'Bad news, no doubt about it. It's that guy, Jerry O'Connell. He ain't dead like we thought. Cops say it's some other guy, not him.'

Beaufoy stood. His nostrils flared. His shoulders rose and fell as he absorbed the news, not so much hearing it but *feeling* it – feeling it at a gut level. 'The guy Jerry O'Connell,' he mimicked. 'You mean the guy we sent Lucky Strike to kill, who was supposed to have burned up in the fire? That guy?'

Drugstore did his best not to shrink away, knowing that any sign of weakness would only anger Beaufoy more, and the last thing Drugstore wanted at that moment – *literally* the last thing Drugstore wanted at that moment – was Beaufoy angry.

'That would be the guy. The same one.'

'And how did this information reach us?'

Drugstore felt himself relax a little. Though Beaufoy was a man of fiery temperament, even he wasn't so hot-headed as to expect only good news from Drugstore's contacts. The point, after all, was to stay one step ahead of the game, not be subject to a constant stream of glad tidings.

'It came from the LAPD.'

'It?' Beaufoy moved around to the front of the desk, closing the gap between himself and Drugstore, who once again made sure not to flinch. 'What exactly is the *it* to which you refer?'

Drugstore spread his hands. 'Boss, the information.'

'What information?' Beaufoy held up a finger. His eyes

were wide. 'Be careful when you answer, Drugstore, be very careful. I want to know exactly *what* information.'

'That Jerry O'Connell is still alive.'

'Our contact, a man to whom we pay a regular stipend, simply told you that the Englishman is still alive, is that right?'

'Well, no, he—'

'You see? This is exactly what I mean. Think, Drugstore. *Think* about your answer. What *exactly* did he say?'

'He told me that the body had been identified, and—'

'It wasn't identified as Jerry O'Connell.'

'No. Just some guy. Some other guy.'

'But that doesn't mean to say that the Englishman is still alive, does it? Just that he wasn't dead in that particular body?'

'I guess not.' Drugstore shrugged.

Beaufoy's shoulders slumped as he pushed his chin into his hands and thought hard. 'Nevertheless, you have reached, in this particular situation, not that you can always be trusted to do so, but . . . the right conclusion, I think. He engineered it so that the body would be identified as him in order to put us, and, presumably, the cops, off the scent. Why would he do that?'

Beaufoy looked across at Gridlock, who sat on the couch, side-eyeing the Xbox controller longingly.

'Why do you think, Gridlock?' asked Beaufoy. 'Why would he want to do that?'

Gridlock and Drugstore looked at one another. 'To get us off his back.'

'Guy must be shitting himself,' chimed in Gridlock.

Beaufoy shook his head. 'No. Sometimes you meet a man and you see in his eyes that he loves a fight. Jerry O'Connell was that man. He wasn't running. But then again, he hasn't come after us either . . .'

'Only a crazy guy would come after us,' reasoned Gridlock from the couch.

Drugstore shifted, glad that he was no longer the target of Beaufoy's interrogation, until the boss rounded on them both, saying, 'He's an Englishman. They're all crazy. And I could see it in his eyes. He loves a fight. No, he wasn't running.' He paused, pulling himself up, shoving his hands in his pockets. 'He's coming after us. And he was buying himself time to do it properly.'

He looked from one to the other. His temper had abated.

'So what now?' asked Drugstore, deciding the ground was safe.

'Tonight we have the meet as usual. We don't want them knowing something's wrong. After that, we go and find our friend. We need to track down Jerry O'Connell.' Beaufoy's nostrils flared. 'He's a splinter that needs extracting.'

Drugstore and Gridlock agreed, both glad that the conversation was over, while Beaufoy regained his seat and reached for his phone.

Not that he knew it, of course, but Ronson Beaufoy would be hearing from Jerry O'Connell a great deal sooner than he anticipated.

Chapter Forty-Seven

There were only three nondescript and boring cars in Jerry's collection, and one of them was the Prius with the Uber sticker into which he and Noah squeezed themselves ready for the night ahead.

Noah wore her bomber jacket, Jerry a mid-length dark coat. Before leaving Hillview, he'd shrugged it on and stepped out onto his balcony, sipping at the evening air, absorbing the sights, sounds and scents of the evening.

There was something else, too. Something he couldn't put his finger on. An edge. Was it the fact that LA always had an edge after dark? he wondered. Or was it just his imagination, anticipating the evening ahead? He'd breathed long and hard and decided that it was a little bit of both.

Noah had appeared by his side, reaching to remove a bit of fluff from his coat, and together they'd made their way down to the garage, begrudgingly taking their places in the Prius. This was dangerous, she knew. This was dangerous, and she didn't have to be here. She could be out earning money. Matter of fact, she *should* be out earning money. And yet she didn't feel in danger. She felt safer here than she ever had with any client. She felt protected. And for some reason – or maybe it was that reason, maybe it really was as simple as that – there was nowhere else she'd rather be.

Jerry, for his part, sat beside her, radiating a sense of this being just another day at the office. His cheek worked a little however, as he chewed his lip thoughtfully, knowing that he was about to unleash hell; knowing that although he was a man who never lost, there could always be a first time.

They drove, passing the twinkling lights, blinking neon advertisements and sparkling lit-up canopies of La La Land in all its neon-lit, laid-back-yet-hyperactive glory, joking and chatting at first, becoming more serious as the glitzy sights were slowly replaced by the less salubrious delights of downtown and the Cedar Tree neighbourhood grew closer in their windshield.

Reaching the avenue, Jerry parked, keeping the Prius in the shadow of an industrial unit from where he could see across the road to Sunshine Heights. To his right, Noah settled back, yawning, letting her Converse rest on the dash.

Jerry hunkered down in his coat, enjoyed the feeling of Noah by his side, and settled in to wait. He was still chewing his lip, but now he felt something unusual in the pit of his stomach, a new and unfamiliar sensation, and recognised it for what it was – nerves. *Fucking hell*, he told himself. *They've really got under your skin, that lot, haven't they?*

As it turned out, they didn't have to wait long. Say this for CT-40, he thought, as the Range Rover appeared on the apartment-block approach road, with the black van behind, they were punctual. Jerry waited until the mini convoy had pulled into traffic, and then started the Prius engine and set off to follow.

'They're on the move,' Noah told Micky over the radio, pulling herself up, a sense of purpose coming over her.

Jerry imagined the scene back at Hillview: the boys, hyped up but collected, hanging out in the garage, awaiting the instruction to go. He changed down, checked the mirror, keeping the Prius back and once again thanking his lucky stars that drug dealers liked their vehicles on the opulent side.

Cars passed on both sides, headlights streaking the windows, the Prius virtually anonymous on the streets. He wanted to get the lads rolling, but he needed to know which pier CT-40 were using before he gave the word. Sitting there, he found that he was painfully aware that the boys were strangers in LA. Put any one of them in Essex and they knew the streets blindfold. His plan had been to get them doing the LA knowledge test in the hope of ironing out any geographical issues, but there simply hadn't been time. *Drive careful,* he thought to himself, trying to send the message telepathically. *Drive careful.* He'd been through hell with these men, fought alongside them, man and boy. Fucked if he was going to lose one of them in LA.

He waited until he was indeed ninety-nine per cent certain of the location before he asked Noah to make the call, and that was right when he was pulling in at the same spot, the container facility on his left, the cranes on his right and the entrance to the port ahead of him.

'It's location one,' relayed Noah into the radio.

'Route 1-10?' asked Micky.

'Sure, use route 1-10,' confirmed Noah.

'Copy that,' said Micky, and Jerry couldn't help but grin at Micky using the military terminology.

It was their cue to go. And, sure enough, at Hillview, the garage doors opened and the silence of the balmy night was shattered by the throaty roar of a motorcycle engine and then another bike, as well as cars revving.

First to emerge from the garage was Boring Mark astride the Ducati, smoked-glass visor, leather jacket zipped to the collar; behind came Yum Yum on a Harley, a Mustang driven by Carrot Cruncher, with the punch tool in the trunk. Behind him was Mad Micky Walker in a Thunderbird.

Each car had been checked by Boring Mark to make sure it was in the best nick, fast and roadworthy and with nothing amiss that might attract the attention of the cops. Almost as one, the headlights came on as they formed up and then took the road, heading for the lights of the city, with the docks their destination. Each was in contact, ready to respond to instructions and directions provided by Noah, and they formed a sort of convoy, careful to keep their spacing even so as not to arouse suspicion, allowing themselves to be absorbed by other traffic.

Meanwhile, in the Prius, Jerry kept one eye on CT-40, another on his rear-view mirror, awaiting the arrival of his team.

'ETA?' asked Noah into the Motorola.

'Five minutes,' returned Micky.

'Let's keep quiet until then, yeah?' asked Jerry.

Noah relayed the request, lowered the radio, looked across at Jerry and marvelled at how calm he was. Speaking for herself, she felt nothing but nerves. Her heart was hammering, her fingers drummed on the door frame, knees shaking.

'If I look calm, then it's because I trust the boys to get the job done,' he told her. 'What more can you ask?'

She nodded and then changed the subject. 'The drugs will be in the van, then?'

'That's right.'

'And will Beaufoy be in there with them?'

He scoffed. 'Not likely. He'll have a couple of drones in there who'll have to take the heat if the cops pull them over.'

'Is that likely to happen?'

'The cops pulling him over? Probably not. He'll have them in his pocket.' Jerry stopped himself, thinking of Lowrey. 'Most of them, anyway. And if he did find himself pulled over by a cop who was straight, then I'm pretty sure he could pull some strings and get his drugs back quick as a greased pig on a playground slide. End of problem for Beaufoy.'

'But if he couldn't get his drugs back?'

'Well,' grinned Jerry, 'then he'd have a big fuckin' problem, wouldn't he?'

'And that's a problem that you're planning to engineer, is it?'

Again Jerry grinned. 'Watch and learn, mate, watch and learn.'

She twisted in the passenger seat as the radio crackled and a disembodied voice said, 'Is that you I see?' The unmistakable tones of Mad Micky Walker. Looking back, she could see Mark on the Ducati. Ahead of him was Yum Yum on the Harley, and behind came Carrot Cruncher in the Mustang. Funny, she thought, swivelling back to face front. She'd only known the guys a matter of days and yet seeing them was a comfort.

In the next instant, she and Jerry were overwhelmed by a throbbing, burping engine noise as Yum Yum's Harley drew alongside the Prius. Yum Yum, glancing into the car, tipped a forefinger to his visor and then drew ahead. Watching him pull in front and then lengthen the gap, closing in on a Ford that lay between him and the CT-40 van, Jerry found that he was holding his breath. This was a manoeuvre they'd worked out in advance but never practised – again, for reasons of time – and doing it on a tabletop with boxes of matches and salt shakers was hardly a substitute for a proper dress rehearsal.

This was real now. This was happening.

'Good luck,' he said under his breath as Yum Yum, with a blip on the accelerator, pulled even further ahead, coming up on the passenger side of the black CT-40 van.

Now, this is where it gets interesting, thought Jerry, even as he eased off the gas. Past them roared the Ducati (another tip to the helmet from Mark), then Carrot Cruncher in the Mustang (nod of the head).

'Hey, hey, the gang's all here,' murmured Noah at his side, watching the other vehicles pull in front, then overtake other cars on the street, closing the distance between themselves and the black van.

Now they tensed, as up ahead Yum Yum prepared to make his move. Jerry found himself holding his breath once more, mentally calculating when he himself would do it if he were the one on the saddle. At the same time, he tried to picture the scene inside the van. Would they see the bike?

If so, would they get suspicious? The gangbangers had made this trip dozens, maybe hundreds, of times; they had the port police and cops in their pocket; they had the backing of the cartel. Whether they liked it or not, and despite everything that Beaufoy might have said in warning, they'd be less cautious than they should have been. Even so, this was CT-40. Jerry and his pals couldn't afford to get complacent. His hands were slick on the wheel, and he gripped it hard, as though trying to strangle it. He felt his heart thud against his ribcage. He knew his guys were ready. He'd flown all that way to look in their eyes and know they were ready, but even so — and for all their guts and heart — they were still going against the most feared gang in LA here.

Ahead, the gap between the Range Rover and the van widened a little. Noah leaned forward in her seat, anticipating Yum Yum's move, knowing the time was right. Jerry, saying, '*Now*. Now, mate, now.'

Sure enough, Yum Yum saw his opportunity, indicated late and pulled in sharply, slotting in between the two gangbanger's vehicles, raising a hand in acknowledgement even as the van's brake lights flared and its rear end rose slightly in response.

He was in. Now, phase two of the plan.

Yum Yum began to slow a little. Not enough to raise suspicion. Just enough.

Following, Jerry felt the speed creep down. Ahead of him was the Ducati and the Mustang in procession, both slowing.

Oblivious, the Range Rover at the head of the queue drove on, maintaining its previous speed and widening the gap. Now they approached an intersection and Jerry hoped that Yum Yum was reading the situation the same way he was.

Yes.

Yum Yum slowed. Once again, the brake lights of the van lit up as the traffic lights changed. Red. Yum Yum stopped, as did the van. Across the intersection, the Range Rover pulled away.

Now, how would they respond? Jerry knew what they *should* do: stop and wait. Safety in numbers. But he was counting on that complacency. He was counting on Beaufoy being exactly the kind of bloke he thought he was: impatient, careless, a sadist – a bloke so drunk on power that he'd rather speed ahead and then punish his team for lagging behind than be careful. A bloke who thought caution was weak.

Nothing better, reflected Jerry, than using a geezer's own flaws against him.

He steeled himself, wondering if he was going to see the Range Rover's brakes fire, the vehicle slow and wait for the van to catch up. Thinking that if it did pull up and wait, then he didn't have much of a plan B.

The Range Rover kept going, gradually getting lost in traffic, and Jerry allowed himself a sigh of relief. At the same time, he watched out for . . .

Yes. There he was.

Ahead, Yum Yum on the Harley gave way for the Mustang with Carrot Cruncher in the driving seat, so that even as the Harley peeled away, they were trading places.

Jerry strained to see up ahead. No sign of the Range Rover containing Beaufoy. *Good*, thought Jerry. *You just continue being the arrogant cunt I think you are. Because that's how I'll have you.*

228

Just as planned, Carrot Cruncher stalled the Mustang at the next set of lights, bringing the van to a halt.

Everything stopped. All traffic momentarily brought to a standstill. The leading Range Rover was long gone. Jerry felt a surge of adrenaline, knowing that his guys in the cars would be reaching for their Remington shotguns, ready to take the CT-40 van; that on the bikes Mark and Yum Yum would be checking for the Glocks they had in their jackets. They would be making their move any second . . .

Now.

Except it didn't happen, because just as the guys were about to strike, the guys in the van must have worked out that they were being set up for a score, and suddenly, with a screech of tyres that tore through the night, the CT-40 van took off.

'Shit. Get after them,' called Micky, and in the next moment he was gunning the Thunderbird as Mark and Yum Yum did the same to their bikes and Carrot Cruncher hit the Mustang throttle, its engine blatting loud on the street.

Ahead, car horns sounded angrily as the van shot through lights. Jerry put the Prius in gear and tore into traffic, throttle flat, revving the engine and cursing the low power of the Prius as up ahead the Harley, Mustang and Thunderbird shot off in pursuit of the van.

Noah was braced, one arm along the sill of the door, her other hand on the dash.

'Move your hand,' said Jerry, firmly but not unkindly.

'Huh?' she said, disbelievingly.

'If we crash and the airbag deploys, it'll break your arm, darlin'.'

She looked at him, momentarily forgetting her hatred

of 'darlin', again marvelling as he coolly negotiated traffic, trying to keep the vehicles ahead in his sights.

And up ahead, the van had crossed another intersection amid a chorus of car horns and a runner who had to dive in order to avoid being hit. It snaked left and right, cutting across lanes and jinking as it made its way deftly through traffic, its brake lights blinking on and off. Not exactly a smooth ride for its passengers, thought Jerry, but effective.

'They'll call the Range Rover,' said Noah. She had taken her hand off the dash as suggested. Instead, she gripped her safety belt.

'No doubt about it,' replied Jerry. 'Just need to make it so they can't find us.'

Ahead of them, Carrot Cruncher had shown some fine driving skills, the Mustang scything through traffic with arrogant ease as it toed up on the van.

For a moment, the road ahead was clear, and Carrot Cruncher used the opportunity to wrench on the wheel of the Mustang so that it pulled out from behind the van. Flat on the throttle, it easily overtook the van and then pulled ahead.

'What's he doing?' wondered Noah aloud.

'He's taking us off the main drag,' replied Jerry. Thinking, *Good man. Sensible.*

Sure enough, Carrot Cruncher spun the wheel of the Mustang, pulling on the handbrake at the same time. The wheels locked, smoking, as the Mustang spun and blocked the road ahead.

In the Prius, Noah and Jerry held their breath, hoping the driver of the van would turn to avoid the Mustang but knowing that he might decide to simply plough forward, even though it would mean coming to a standstill.

The driver chose the first option, and the van lurched, its rear tilting as it came to a sharp halt, before turning and pulling across oncoming traffic and into a side road. Following were the two bikes, the Thunderbird and the Mustang.

Through the open window of the Prius, Jerry heard distant police sirens as he, too, pulled into the side road behind the convoy, fighting with the wheel as the Prius's tyres shrieked on the warm tarmac.

Ahead, the van jinked. A cyclist came to grief by the side of the road. In pursuit, they were resolute. Something else reached Jerry's ears through the open window. Was that another set of sirens as well? Word would have reached the cops. Any second now, the whole of the LAPD would descend upon them – not to mention the second CT-40 vehicle.

Time to make your move, lads, he thought.

And it was as if they read his mind. Now Mark used the power of the Ducati, flying up the inside of the van and reaching into his jacket for the Glock. Noah winced and chewed her lip, as through the open window they heard the crack of the Glock. Once. Twice. Two tyres out. The van slewed. Strips of rubber were flung onto the road and it came to a stop, leaving a thick trail of rubber on the street behind it.

Mark on the Ducati roared up to the driver's side of the van. At the same time, Yum Yum drew up to the passenger door on the Harley, Micky and Carrot Cruncher slotting in behind.

Jerry pulled over. The lights turned green. Cars forced to a standstill sounded their horns, while others, sensing something wrong, began pulling around the boxed-in van and away, seeing the guns and wisely deciding they were better off elsewhere.

Now Mark and Yum Yum were levelling their weapons at the driver and passenger, while, at the back of the van, Carrot Cruncher and Micky went to work fixing the punch tool to the rear doors.

From further back, Jerry heard the shouts of Yum Yum and Mark demanding keys and any weapons be handed over. By now, most other drivers had decided to make themselves scarce, though there were some brave souls filming. Jerry and Noah, meanwhile, had climbed out of the Prius, watching proceedings but careful to maintain the impression that they were merely shocked bystanders.

Jerry watched as weapons were passed through the windows to Yum Yum and Mark.

Simultaneously, things were happening at the rear of the van. Jerry heard the *clump-thunk* sound of a neat hole punched clean through the van doors by Micky. A moment later and Micky had tossed a thunderflash inside. Down the street, Jerry heard the muffled thump and saw a lightning crack of magnesium white light through the newly made hole. Up front, Yum Yum and Mark used cable ties on the driver and passenger, cuffing their hands to the wheel, as Carrot Cruncher hefted his Remington and shouted orders through the now-smoking hole.

Jerry couldn't hear what was said but knew what it was: 'We can gas you out, or you can open the doors, chuck out your guns, phones and the drugs, and we'll be on our way. Your choice.'

They had CS gas ready but didn't need to use it because the back doors of the van opened a crack. Yum Yum and Mark joined Carrot Cruncher and Micky, all of them with guns at the ready, but the gangbangers had clearly chosen not to fight. Out came the guns, phones, a holdall of drugs, all of it snatched up. Moments later, Jerry's team were back to their vehicles.

Noah watched, amazed at their casual attitude. She and Jerry looked at each other and then back at the van, where it was as if the gangbangers were in a state of shock, the back doors hanging open, two men half-falling out, dazed looks on their faces.

And then, as the traffic restarted around them, Jerry and Noah clambered back into the Prius and pulled away. That was it. Job done.

Almost.

Chapter Forty-Eight

The kids by the grocery store at Cedar Tree Avenue listened to the wrath of the White Ghost emanating from the apartment block behind, and they looked at one another, wide-eyed with fear.

At the same time, cars were still pouring into the lot, dispensing gangbangers, who adjusted their pants, pushing guns into their waistbands, looking around themselves, grim-faced. They had been summoned by either Gridlock or Drugstore, and when Ronson Beaufoy's lieutenants got in touch to say that the White Ghost wanted them at Sunshine Heights right away, then it didn't matter what deal they were doing, who they were screwing, who needed a lesson teaching. They went.

Their attendance was required because Ronson Beaufoy had belatedly realised that war had been declared on CT-40 by Jerry O'Connell, and that war was the reason that the residents of Sunshine Heights – the innocents, the dealers, the users, the workers – had locked their doors, turned down their TVs and were keeping quiet, not knowing what had happened, aware only that it was bad; that whatever it was, it had angered Beaufoy, and each of them knew, either from painful personal experience or through the myth and legend that had grown up around him, that an angry Ronson Beaufoy was to be avoided at all costs.

And so the only people to be found milling around at the entrance to the lot were CT-40 gang members, who shook their heads no to any passing traffic – the users, the addicts and part-timers who were accustomed to pulling in and handing over their hard-earned in exchange for tiny vials of crack.

There would be no deals done today. Business was temporarily suspended, which was in itself an extraordinary turn of events, because business in this neighbourhood was never suspended, not for Thanksgiving or Halloween or Christmas Day. Never, except today, when every man who sported the Scorpion tattoo of the gang was called in.

They milled around the lot; they shuffled and posed nervously at the foot of the steps; they lined the stairs to the apartments and the walkway to the door of Beaufoy's office, and every single one of them listened as Beaufoy gave vent to his rage.

'They have taken my drugs,' he repeated for the hundredth time. Drugstore handed him a phone. 'Who is this?' he barked into it. 'Right, you tell me where my drugs are. You don't know where they are? You find them. Find them now.'

He finished the call, threw the phone, barked, 'Catch the phone,' at no one in particular when nobody did, and then was handed another by Gridlock, beginning the process again: 'Who is this? You. Tell me what you have. I want to know where he is . . .'

Sitting on the sofa, with bowed shoulders, their hands between their knees and virtually quaking with fear were the men who had been in the van. Their names were Reynard, Dario, Boo Radley and Vegas. They had yet to learn their fate, but they were all remembering what Beaufoy had done to that guy in the warehouse. How much that guy had screamed and begged for mercy; the pleasure Beaufoy had taken in torture, the craft he had applied. At the time, of course, they had laughed and joked and privately thanked the Lord that they were on his side and not the subject of his ire.

They had no such comfort today.

'What is the point of you? What is the point in having you?' Beaufoy was yelling into the phone. 'Do I need to tell you again what I will do to you if I am not satisfied? Go. Come back to me when you have answers.' He threw the phone, stared long and hard at the man who caught it, stood surveying the room, his gaze inevitably going to the four miscreants assembled on the couch. All of the men stood up, stock-still, each one hoping that whatever Beaufoy said next, it wouldn't be directed at them.

Drugstore was almost grateful when the phone in his hand bounced. He pushed up the sleeves of his sweatshirt before answering, 'Yes,' listening, eyes going to Beaufoy, then reaching out with the phone. 'Ronson. It's Francis Colorado.'

Fuck, thought Beaufoy. His jaw set. For a moment or so, it looked like he might be about to refuse the call. And then he took a deep breath, seeming to decide. 'Everybody out, apart from you and you,' he said, indicating Drugstore and Gridlock.

The men left quickly, gratefully, even – especially – the couch foursome, leaving Beaufoy alone with his two newly appointed lieutenants.

'Colorado,' he barked into the phone, trying to keep his

distaste for the lawyer out of his voice. 'To what do I owe this dubious pleasure?'

For his part, Colorado was in no mood for Beaufoy's theatrics. 'Let's get to it, shall we? Is there something you'd like to tell me, Ronson?'

'Oh, just get to the point, Colorado, what *might* I have to tell you?'

'Business in the neighbourhood currently suspended. Rumours that your shipment has been hijacked. Is that what you have to tell me?'

There was a pause. Sitting in his splendidly appointed office at home in Bel-Air, Colorado wondered whether Beaufoy would bother to lie, reflecting that the CT-40 boss pushing the panic alarm was typical of the man: a grand but self-defeating gesture that instead of solving a problem simply drew attention to it and made it worse.

Beaufoy, meanwhile, knew there was little point in trying to cover up. Okay, so Colorado had been given the bad news. But the fact was that he had needed to issue his call to arms. After all, war had been declared. Colorado was a lawyer. He had plush offices, where Beaufoy had streets; he was a tactician, whereas Beaufoy knew the true power inherent in fear, and knew how to wield it. Colorado would never understand that. He would never understand the streets like Beaufoy. And as for word reaching him, well, it was bound to, sooner or later. This conversation was always going to happen.

'Your information is correct, Colorado. Business at Cedar Tree Avenue is indeed temporarily suspended. Temporarily, mind you. A day or so is all I need to—'

'To recover the shipment.'

'Indeed.'

'So it is true, then, that you have lost the shipment?'

'I just said, didn't I, that I need to recover it? Why the fuck would I need to recover it if I hadn't lost it?' He corrected himself, 'If it hadn't been *taken* from me.'

'A hijack.'

'Right after the drop.' Beaufoy set his teeth, screwed up his face, praying that Colorado wouldn't want precise details of the hold-up.

In the event, the silence at the other end of the line was so long that he wondered if the connection had been broken, before Colorado said, 'Isn't it you, Ronson, who is always telling me that on the street the value of fear is priceless; how nobody would dare go up against the CT-40 because of your fearsome reputation. *Fearsome reputation.* Your words, I think, Ronson? First I see cops at Sunshine Heights. Now the operation has closed down and somebody has taken your shipment. Your mojo appears to be malfunctioning somewhat.'

Beaufoy knew that it was true. It had not been lost on him that he had severely underestimated Jerry O'Connell. He had known the Englishman was alive; he had correctly guessed that he would be planning some kind of offensive. But it had never – not in his wildest dreams or most torrid nightmares – occurred to him that he might try hijacking the shipment. That had been his first mistake. His second was not to order the Range Rover to stop when Gridlock told him that the van was lagging behind. Instead, he had merely looked forward to upbraiding the men for not keeping up.

It niggled him. More than he would ever have cared to admit. As an enforcer back in the day, his talent had been to read his enemy, to know when to hurt him and how. Where Jerry O'Connell was concerned, that talent appeared to have deserted him.

He was going to have to do something about that.

'It's because the shipment was taken by an outsider,' he told Colorado now.

Francis Colorado thought about this for a moment, wondering if Ronson was lying. He might be, in order to save face. But, then again, he did have a point. Who in LA would dare go up against CT-40? Even the law enforcement, if they weren't intimidated by the thought of Ronson's outfit, were likely to be concerned about his ties with the cartel.

'Then who?' he asked drily.

'There's a Limey. A guy who's tangled with me.'

'By the name of?'

'Why does his name matter?'

'You know it, then?'

'I know it.'

'Tell me.'

'Why does it matter?' Beaufoy not knowing why but wanting somehow to hide the information from Colorado.

'Why would you want to keep it secret?'

'His name is Jerry O'Connell.'

'I see. And it's this Jerry O'Connell you think has taken your shipment?'

'I know so.'

'And what are you doing about it?'

'What the hell do you think I'm doing about it, Colorado? I am going to get the shipment back, and then I'm going to get him and whoever else is responsible, and I'm going to cut bits of them off, and I'm going to cook and feed those bits to them. I'm going to make them eat themselves alive.'

Typical, thought Colorado. *All cruelty, no class.*

'You know that our friends will expect to be paid as usual next week, don't you?'

'I do,' said Beaufoy coolly, although his blood ran cold.

'How did it happen?' asked Colorado.

'They took it from the van.'

'Your men allowed it to be taken from the van?'

'Yes.'

'And those men will be suitably punished, I take it?'

'What do you think?'

'What I think is irrelevant.'

'They will be punished. Just you watch.'

'Ronson, it is my advice that you put an end to the problems you have there. This instability is making me nervous, and . . .?'

'You have no need to tell our friends in Tijuana.'

'Not *yet*,' said Colorado, who was, despite his overall policy of being absolutely truthful with the Mexicans, wondering if indeed he should keep this information to himself, 'but let this be the last time that my concerns are raised, or I might need to change my mind about that.'

'It will be sorted,' spat Beaufoy, who was thoroughly sick and tired of having his business told to him by a lawyer, even a lawyer for the cartel. He ended the call, slapped the phone down to the desktop and was about to start screaming and shouting at Gridlock and Drugstore, when it rang again.

He snatched it up, answered.

'Is that my friend, the caretaker?' said Jerry O'Connell.

Chapter Forty-Nine

'Jeremiah O'Connell,' said Beaufoy, and when he spoke, his true feelings betrayed him. They came through in his voice, like the grain in wood, like 'souvenir of Southend-on-Sea' written through a stick of rock.

And they told Jerry that he was rattled.

Good. Stay rattled, he thought. *When you're contemplating suicide, I'll give you the rope.*

Still. You had to give it to Beaufoy. He did his best to tough it out. 'Oh, the dead man.'

'You thought I was dead?' said Jerry, feeling a little surge of joy at locking horns once again. 'Just because you sent yer clowns round. They were a right fucking hoot. You should have seen one of their party pieces – he shot himself right in his own fuckin' nuts.'

Jerry could hear Beaufoy breathing hard through his nostrils, trying to control his temper. 'No, I mean that you *will* be dead.'

'Dead, eh?' he said now. 'Well, we'll have to see about that, won't we?'

'I'll get to you,' said Beaufoy.

'You don't even know where I am,' replied Jerry. *If only you fucking knew.* Because, in fact, he was sitting in a car right across the street from Sunshine Heights, where he'd been keeping a watchful, satisfied eye on proceedings, watching gangbangers arrive, enjoying the stricken looks on their faces and chuckling as they seemed to bumble about the parking lot before reluctantly making their way to the apartment blocks behind.

'I didn't say I'd find you. I said I'd get to you.'

You wouldn't call it worry, but still, Jerry paused for thought, considering the snitch situation that had been scampering around the outskirts of his brain since the situation first cropped up. Was it really the case that if Beaufoy had found him once then he could do it again? Could he *really* get to him, like he threatened? Answer: no. Surely not. Jerry had sewn things up tight. The grass had to come from outside his close circle – it had to be a geezer like Jimmy or Josh, some bloke who thought he could make a quick buck and get some brownie points off the toughest crew in town – and there was nobody outside his current team who knew where he was, or how to get to him.

Was there?

'I reckon we've got stuff to talk about,' he said, showing his own thoughts the door.

'We have nothing to discuss, save how long it will take you to die.'

'Well, in that case, you're right,' said Jerry, 'we don't need to talk, do we? See ya, mate.'

'Wait . . .' snapped Beaufoy.

Jerry grinned, left a pause. 'Yeah, what do you want?'

'I have a question.'

'Fire away.'

'What are you intending to do with them?'

'Do with what?'

'My drugs. You planning on going into business for yourself, are you?'

'Nah. I can't be arsed with that game. More than likely flush it.'

Beaufoy made a scoffing noise. 'Nobody would destroy five million dollars' worth of drugs. Nobody. Nobody. Not even you.'

'Fuck me,' said Jerry, 'you really don't get it, do you? It's not about *robbing* you. It's about *hurting* you.'

'Why?' asked Beaufoy simply.

'Why do I want to hurt you?'

'Yes.'

'I'll tell you, at the end.'

Beaufoy made a sound that was part-frustration, part-disgust. 'I see. Then how about we skip to that part now.'

'You'll be getting there sooner than you think if you can't pay the cartel, won't you?'

Beaufoy exhaled loudly. His voice rose. 'And *finally* we arrive at the reason you've decided to call me. You want to gloat.'

'Not quite. Well, partly that, yeah, to be fair. Partly to offer you a deal. An arrangement, like.'

'And what sort of arrangement might that be? No, don't tell me, it's the sort of arrangement where you want a vast amount of money in order to return my drugs to me, isn't it?'

'Now you're getting on my nerves. I've just explained to you what this is all about, and it has nothing to do with money.'

'What, then?'

'All right, how about this? You can have your crack back on condition you get out of Sunshine Heights. You give that block back to the people who live there.'

'Oh yes,' chuckled Beaufoy. 'And what happens then?'

'I don't give a monkey's.'

'What I mean is that I'll just go somewhere else. Another block.'

'No, you won't, because you'll be the bloke who had to clear out. There'll be no gang leadership for you any more. If you're lucky, you'll escape with your life, but you won't have a gang. You won't have any power. Spent force.'

'You know, don't you, that it's not a trade I would ever be prepared to make.'

'It's the only one there is.'

Jerry could almost hear Beaufoy swallow.

'You don't have yourself a deal.'

'Fair enough, mate. Be seeing you.'

Quickly, Beaufoy said, 'You can't hide five million dollars' worth of my crack cocaine in this city.'

'We'll see about that,' said Jerry.

Chapter Fifty

'I think it's about time you told me your plan,' said Noah. It was the morning after the operation and they were in his apartment, sitting at the table with cups of coffee and, as far as she was concerned at least, a ton of unanswered questions.

'Bait, remember. I'm using the drugs as bait.'

'In the workshop, yes, I remember. But how do you plan to lead them to the workshop? Breadcrumbs? A two-for-one-on-crack-cocaine deal? What?'

'I'm banking on Beaufoy having his eyes and ears, and them telling him that a bunch of Brits seem to have taken over at a workshop in Compton.' Jerry did an imitation of Beaufoy's voice. 'You won't be able to hide five million dollars' worth of my crack from me." Made me fucking laugh when he said that. I'm fucking *relying* on not being able to hide the drugs from you. I *want* you to find the fucking drugs because I want you going in that workshop.'

'Which is where Wayne comes in?'

He nodded. 'Eventually they'll find their way to the work-shop and when they do . . .' He mimed an explosion.

Noah decided to place her moral objections to one side for

a moment. 'They might suspect it's a trap,' she said.

'They might have their suspicions, but I'll be managing those. Keeping them low.'

'Oh yeah, and just how do you plan to do that?'

'I'll have a man inside.'

Noah was about to ask, when it dawned on her. And at last she realised what Jerry had meant earlier when he'd talked about the drugs haul as being 'part of the bait'.

'Not Keith?' she said.

He nodded.

'You're going to kill Keith, too?'

He looked across the table at her, and though he said nothing, his jaw was set.

She closed her mouth. Stared for a moment or so. Then quietly she said, 'That's murder, Jerry. You know that, right? I believe the term is *cold-blooded* murder.'

'Beaufoy deserves it.'

'Don't fuck around, I'm not talking about Beaufoy.'

Jerry leaned back. 'Oh, so that's your line in the sand, is it?' he said. 'It's okay that Beaufoy dies, but not Keith. One scumbag is okay, but not the other?'

'Look, honey, Beaufoy is what Beaufoy is. I wouldn't even be in the same room as you if I didn't think he deserved what's coming to him. But Keith. That's a whole different ballgame.'

Jerry's voice was steely. 'He doesn't get away with what he's done to Angel.'

'I've been thinking about that.'

'Good. I've thought about little else myself.'

'I mean that are you sure Katie was telling the truth?'

'Well, why would she fucking lie?'

'I don't know. To cover herself . . .' She held up her hand. 'I'm not saying anything. I'm just throwing it out there.'

'You think Katie's lying.'

'Come on,' pressed Noah. 'Are you really a hundred per cent certain that you've got the right guy?'

'He's a scumbag,' he insisted. 'Fucking pond life.'

'That still doesn't justify *killing* him,' she argued. 'Especially if you're not certain. Listen to me: you can't do this. That is not the man I . . .' she stumbled, looking for the word. 'Not the man I *know*. And like. And respect. Somebody being a scumbag isn't an excuse to kill them. Do you want to be the kind of unthinkingly vicious and vengeful fanatic that we're going up against here? Do you really want that?'

Nothing was said. She could see that his mind was made up.

'That's it then, is it?' she said at last, words falling like stones in the silent room. Her voice was sour. 'Decision made?'

He stayed silent.

'Then I guess there's no need to say anything more,' she said, and reached for her jacket over the back of a chair, pulled it, tugging it so violently that the chair itself dropped backwards, clattering to the floor, ignored by them both as she pushed her arms into her jacket, swept up her phone from the table, a flushed and angry flurry of sudden, frustrated activity.

He watched her, torn, as she stormed out. Moments later, he went out onto the walkway out front, looked down into the lot, where she stood, phone in hand, waiting for her car. It occurred to him to call down to her, to talk some more, but instead he just stood on the balcony, watching her. And maybe she sensed him there, because she didn't look up, not once. She just stood in the familiar pose, resting on one hip, her arms crossed, and her phone gripped in one hand, waiting until the car drew up and she got inside and was gone.

He took a deep breath and pushed himself off the railing. From behind the closed door of the neighbouring apartment came a burst of laughter, and for a second or so he considered joining them, then decided against it.

Instead, he turned, trod back into the apartment, settled into the couch and reached for the controller to watch *The Secret Life of Puppies* and think about the murder he planned to commit.

In the end, it took him about twenty minutes. Then he made the call to Wayne the Thug.

'Mate,' he sighed, when Wayne answered the phone, 'there's been a change of plan.'

'What's that then?'

'Well, you know how I was planning on using Keith as bait?'

'Yeah.'

'Well, I'm not any more. I'll plant some of the drugs in there in case they bring a sniffer dog. That should keep them busy for a bit. Otherwise we'll just have to hope they don't smell a rat.'

'All right,' said Wayne. 'It wasn't like we needed him to make it work. What you gonna do with him in the meantime?'

'Well, I was hoping you might keep up with the baby-sitting duties.'

Chapter Fifty-One

Detectives Lowrey and Baxter found themselves on floor thirty-two of the gleaming Ernst & Young building on Figueroa Street, feeling like fish out of water in the plush, vertiginous surroundings of the Vera Marlantes Agency.

Below the logo of VMA sat a receptionist who manned a forbiddingly high reception desk as though it were the console of a desolate starship and she was the last surviving crew member. Her name was Chrissy and she was beautiful (as noted by Baxter, sotto voce), but she had a bad fucking attitude (as noted subsequently by Lowrey, slightly less sotto voce, which hadn't helped matters), and right now she was regarding them dispassionately, the way a shark might assess its prey.

Thank Christ, then, for the phone, which interrupted the death stare. 'You can go through now,' said Chrissy, jerking a well-manicured finger behind her. 'That door there.' Watching them as they stood and moved to the office.

As they reached it, the door was opened and standing there was the woman herself, an almost mythical figure in Los Angeles: Vera Marlantes.

'Please come in,' said Marlantes, waving them inside the office. They took seats opposite her desk.

Though Vera Marlantes was not a tall woman, she was nevertheless famed for radiating a certain devil-may-care style, equally at home in a dive bar downtown as she was in the Chateau Marmont. Today she wore black slacks and a black shirt open at the neck. As for the bearing, however, there was precious little of that in evidence, and though she was doing her best to appear normal, there was clearly something . . . *reduced* about her. Her shoulders were sloped; there was no warmth in her eyes and they did not meet her guests as she regained her seat.

Given her business activities, she had every reason to be wary of cops, but even so, Lowrey thought there was something more. Something wrong.

'What was it you wanted to see me about?' Marlantes asked. Her eyes were dark-ringed, as though she was behind on sleep. 'It's unusual that I'm paid a visit by homicide detectives.'

'It's normally vice, is it?' said Baxter, smiling, and Lowrey shot him a warning look.

Marlantes shrugged. 'It's just not normally homicide,' she said. 'What did you want to ask me?' Her smile was thin and weak.

'You have an employee by the name of Jeffrey Blaydon,' said Lowrey, who had decided not to frame it as a question, make Marlantes believe they knew more than they actually did.

'Yes,' was what she said, simply. 'Yes, he does some work for me occasionally. Helping out, driving the girls, doing odd jobs.' A beat. 'Why?'

'When was the last time you saw Mr Blaydon, Mrs Marlantes?'

'It is *Ms* Marlantes,' she corrected, 'and now I come to think of it, it has been some time since I last saw him, yes. A few days at least. I ask again: why?'

She had finished strongly, but even so there was too much of the pantomime to her reaction. Lowrey may not have had much else in common with Jerry O'Connell, but she, too, could spot a lie when she saw one.

She was seeing one now.

'Jeffrey Blaydon is dead, Ms Marlantes,' said Lowrey. 'I'm very sorry.'

Marlantes clamped a hand to her mouth, her eyes widening, and despite the fact that she may well have had foreknowledge of Blaydon's death, the distress was very real, very raw.

Now that, thought Lowrey, was interesting.

'How?' stammered Marlantes from behind her hand. Her eyes brimmed, and then tears fell from her eyes to trickle across her knuckles. 'How did it happen?'

'I'm sorry, Ms Marlantes, this must be very difficult for you to hear, but Mr Blaydon was murdered. He was tortured to death.'

From behind her hand, she gasped. More tears, like tiny diamonds, fell from her eyes to the desktop.

Baxter leaned forward. 'Do you need to take a minute, Ms Marlantes?'

Close by was a sideboard. Bottles of water and glasses there. Lowrey indicated for Baxter to fetch one for Marlantes, who now sat stock-still, the hand that still covered her mouth trembling slightly.

The water was passed to her. She drank with a quivering hand, recovering her composure a little. It wasn't lost on Lowrey, however, that this was infamous Hollywood madam Vera Marlantes, and you didn't get to be a big player in LA without being a hard-ass. Clearly the news was coming as a shock, but why did Lowrey also get the impression that there was something else going on behind those eyes? Like maybe the news tapped into some other trauma.

She decided to restart her questioning. 'Do you know anyone – *anyone* – who would wish harm upon Mr Blaydon? Wish him that kind of treatment, for example?'

Lowrey watched Marlantes carefully, but even as she did so, something was nagging at her, something she could not quite put her finger on. It was as though the question that she wanted to ask, the one to which she really needed the answer, lay just outside her field of vision. Marlantes, meanwhile, was shaking her head no.

'Somebody did,' said Baxter. 'Somebody meant him an awful lot of harm.'

Lowrey held up a hand, quietening him. 'No need to go into the details just now.'

She was thinking about scorpions.

'You may be aware of a gang operating out of the Cedar Tree neighbourhood. CT-40,' said Lowrey. She let the question twist in the breeze, watching Marlantes, who gave a short nod. 'We have reason to believe that CT-40 may be involved in Jeffrey Blaydon's death. What happened to him bears all the hallmarks of their operation. We'll spare you the details. Did Mr Blaydon have any connections with that gang, or any drug issues that you know of?'

Marlantes shook her head. 'I never knew him have any-thing to do with drugs. Not using, not selling, nothing.'

She was lying, thought Lowrey. 'Okay, could CT-40 have been after Blaydon for another reason, perhaps?' she asked. The mists inside her mind were parting a little. Something was coming to her.

'I don't know what you mean.' Marlantes swallowed. Her tears had smeared her make-up, and all of a sudden she looked very old indeed.

'Okay, let's think about this,' said Lowrey. 'I mean, we all know what sort of business you do here. So what about this? How about CT-40 wanted *information* from Mr Blaydon?'

Marlantes' lips were pressed together, to thin white worms. By now, she seemed to have recovered complete composure. 'No. Jeffrey – Jeff, we called him Jeff – he knew nothing about the workings of the business.'

Baxter and Lowrey looked at one another. 'But that's not, strictly speaking, true, is it, Ms Marlantes?' said Baxter. 'You just told us that he drove the girls on the odd occasion. To homes. To addresses, presumably.'

Marlantes explained. 'Yes, that's true. I mean that he knew very little. Not enough . . .'

'Perhaps just enough though, Ms Marlantes,' pressed Lowrey. 'Enough for a little leverage perhaps. Do you know of any blackmail attempts, anything unusual to have occurred in the last few days?'

Marlantes shook her head no.

And then it came to Lowrey. 'The producer Sidney Frankus. You know him?'

'I know *of* him,' said Marlantes, and her ease with the reply suggested to Lowrey that it was a well-practised response. This, then, was the famed Vera Marlantes discretion at work, putting her back on comfortable terrain.

'Frankus is well known as a womaniser. Now, where in LA would a rich and famous movie producer go if he wanted to procure a woman, if not to Vera Marlantes?' said Lowrey.

'I know *of* Sidney Frankus,' repeated Marlantes coolly.

Baxter was leaning forward as Lowrey sat back, shaking her head. 'Let's, for the sake of argument, say that you know him. As in, *know* him.'

'You can say anything "for the sake of argument",' Marlantes shot back. The two cops tensed as she reached to open the top drawer of her desk; Baxter even put a hand to his waist, only for Marlantes to produce a mirror that she put on the desktop, touching her fingertips to her eyes. She reached into the same drawer, brought out items of make-up.

'Ms Marlantes, we're not finished yet,' Lowrey told her.

'Do carry on.'

Was her reaction to hearing about Jeffrey Blaydon all an act, every little bit? wondered Lowrey. Certainly, she seemed to have found her cool. Or was it that she had remembered how much was at stake here?

'Okay, so, for the sake of argument, let's say that you do know Sidney Frankus – as in, *know* him – and that you did indeed procure girls for him. That would mean you would also know Sidney's bodyguard, a gentleman by the name of Jerry O'Connell.'

'I don't know this man you're talking about,' insisted Marlantes.

Okay, thought Lowrey, not sure whether to believe her or not but pressing on anyway. 'I'm going to let you into a secret, Ms Marlantes, although knowing how well informed you are you might already know this: there is significant hostility between the CT-40 gang and this Jerry O'Connell. Now I'm seeing links between that and your man Jeffrey Blaydon and, by extension, you. Right now, these are like shark fins appearing above the water, blink and you miss them, but I'll find them, you can be sure of that. And if you're involved, then I might not be there to catch you when you fall.'

Marlantes lowered the mirror she had been looking into. When she looked back at Lowrey and Baxter, her face was hard. 'Have you quite finished?' she asked.

A short time later, Lowrey and Baxter were stepping out into the sunshine, putting the twinkling windows of the Ernst & Young tower to their backs and already feeling a great deal more comfortable with the sidewalk beneath their shoes.

'Thoughts?' asked Lowrey.

'I'm not sure,' replied Baxter. 'I'm just not sure. I want to say she's dirty. I mean, she's definitely dirty. Just how dirty is the question.'

'She sure was more upset about Blaydon than you'd expect.'

'Exactly.'

'Could be there was something more between them.'

'Could also be that those tears weren't for him.'

'They were for herself.'

'Can we draw a line between her and Jerry O'Connell?'

She thought. 'Short of either of them admitting it, I'm not certain we can. She's Madame Discretion, after all.'

'I can look into it,' said Baxter, slipping on a pair of sunglasses.

'Sure.'

As they went to step into the car, Lowrey looked up at the tower block, the windows regarded her passively in return. There was something there, she thought. No doubt about it, there was something there.

Chapter Fifty-Two

Jerry stood in the lot in front of Lucas Brady's workshop, bold as brass, a sore thumb sticking out in Compton, just the way he wanted it. He was on the blower, talking to Wayne, although Wayne was in fact just a few feet away, out of sight in the derelict KFC across the road. Just as it was important that Jerry was seen, it was crucial that Wayne stayed hidden.

Wayne and Keith had been in the KFC since dawn, at which point they'd made the unit as impregnable as possible and taken up residence, ready for the long wait, and kitted out accordingly. They now sat on foldable garden chairs that were colourful and incongruous in what had once been the dining area and was currently a dark, foul-smelling bolthole for addicts, and they had supplies of food and water as well as sleeping bags – although Jerry was insistent they wouldn't be needed – and, of course, the mobile phones Wayne was using for detonators: one for the explosives that Wayne had rigged up in the workshop, another for a second set that he'd hidden in the bottom of the holdall.

'Belt and braces,' Jerry had said. 'Belt and braces, mate. What's the point in bringing the master blaster Wayne the

Thug all the way over to LA if you're not going to get some fireworks out of it, eh?'

But even though all his ducks were in a row, there was still something on Wayne's mind. He peered through the boarded-up windows that they'd customised in order to give themselves a decent view of the workshop. Beside him sat Keith in his garden chair, cradling a bag of snacks. He wore loafers with no socks (and Carrot Cruncher had been vocal in his disgust about *that* particular crime against both hygiene and fashion) and his moustache was dusted with orange potato-chip particles. Wayne stood, excusing himself in order to move out of earshot, his nose wrinkling at the stench of urine as he retreated into the kitchen area of the KFC.

Christ, he thought. If the front was bad, it was even worse back here, because here was where addicts came to relieve themselves. Wayne had tried the main toilet, but that was a sight he could never unsee.

'What is it?' said Jerry. Across the road, he had decided that he had made his presence felt and was already clambering into his car.

'I thought the idea was that we had him in there to lure them in,' said Wayne, pinching his nose against the smell and whispering at the same time. 'He was your guarantee.'

'They'll come,' said Jerry confidently. 'Soon as they get wind that we're here, they'll come. Keith was just a bit of insurance, that's all. It'll still work, trust me.'

'You know what?' said Wayne. 'If they arrive and they're in the lot in front of the workshop, and I blow it, they're dead.'

'So even if they did smell a rat?'

'That's right. We still get fireworks night in Compton, lots of dead wannabes.'

'Well then, you do that,' said Jerry.

Wayne inclined his head, checking through the kitchen doors that Keith was nowhere nearby. 'And what about the dicksplash I'm currently babysitting?'

'I'll deal with him later.'

And with that, Jerry pulled away from the workshop, trusting that his high-visibility exercise had been enough.

Chapter Fifty-Three

Wayne finished his call with Jerry, grateful that he was able to escape the terrible stench of the kitchen area back to the slightly less terrible stench of the dining area.

There, he hunkered down at the street-facing wall, regaining his seat beside Keith, who was keeping an eye out through the holes they had improvised in the window boarding.

'Everything all right?' said Keith, looking at him inquiringly, no doubt wondering what was so important that it had taken Wayne away from his post.

'Yeah, everything is fine,' said Wayne. 'Jerry just checking in.'

'What did you tell him?'

'What do you think I told him, I told him everything was tip-top.'

'Right,' said Keith, and he lapsed into silence, Wayne happy not to have to talk to him.

And that was how they stayed for several hours, wordless, keeping an eye on the workshop across the road, occasionally reaching for a drink or a bag of potato chips, saying nothing to one another because they had little to say.

And then . . .

'Wayne?' asked Keith at last, and there was something about the way he said it, a catch in his voice that caught Wayne's attention. He looked over at him, noticing how the Keith who had been winding up Carrot Cruncher something rotten was absent now; there was no big-time gangster here, no hard-man wannabe. Keith looked like what he was − a frightened bloke, way out of his depth. Wayne didn't exactly feel sorry for him; Keith wasn't the sort of character to engender much sympathy. But still. What Wayne saw in Keith was fear.

'You all right?' he asked cautiously.

'Yeah, yeah, of course.' Keith nodded furiously. But when he raised his head, there was a stricken look in his eyes. 'I'm all right, but I'm also scared shitless.'

'Don't worry about it,' said Wayne, squinting to peer out. 'I'm shit-scared, too.'

Shit-scared was a lie − 'slightly apprehensive' pretty much covered how Wayne felt. But something told him that it would help to calm Keith's nerves. Last thing he wanted was the bloke going tonto.

'You think we'll definitely make it out of this?'

'Of course we will,' Wayne reassured him. 'Don't fucking sweat it, mate.'

Keith nodding again. 'But if we don't—'

'We will.'

'But if we don't, there's something I need to tell you.'

Wayne, who had been about to tell him to shut the fuck up even more definitively, was suddenly interested. 'Oh yeah, what's that, then?'

'It's something, like, if I die. It's something I want you to tell Jerry.'

'Tell Jerry?'

'Yeah. Something he needs to know.'

'Yeah,' said Wayne, 'you do owe him, no doubt about it. Whatever it is, you better tell him . . .' Too curious though. Too fucking curious. 'Just tell me first, though, just in case.'

But then something was happening across the road. Two black vans and a Range Rover were drawing into the work-shop lot.

'Fuck,' said Wayne. He threw a quick glance at Keith, 'This'll have to wait, but you're fucking telling me later, okay?' They both put their eyes to the window, tense now.

The passenger door of the Range Rover opened, a man in a crumpled blue linen suit stepped out.

'That's him.'

'You sure?' said Keith.

'You know how there's a famous quote about how only fools and fanatics are ever certain of themselves.'

'Yeah, kinda?'

'Well, I must be a fool, then, because I'm pretty fucking certain that's him.'

He reached for one of the two burner cells bought for the sole purpose of detonating the explosives across the road, drawing it to him. His eyes flicked, fingers worked the keys, a number appeared on the screen.

'You're going to blow it?' whispered Keith urgently, fear in his voice.

'Well, yeah, that's what we're here for. Not yet though. Need to wait until they're inside,' said Wayne thoughtfully.

'And what if they don't go inside?' asked Keith. 'Like, what if they suspect it might be a trap.'

The driver's side of the Range Rover was opening. Out stepped a big black guy dressed in the uniform of UPS.

'What the fuck?' whispered Wayne. 'Why have they got a UPS guy with them?'

Next to appear was a dog.

'There's a dog,' said Keith, somewhat uselessly.

'Yeah, we thought there'd be a dog,' replied Wayne. 'We banked on it, in fact.'

'So that they could satisfy themselves that it wasn't a trap?'

Wayne cast Keith a sideways glance, nodding. 'You're catching on.'

But now there was a new development, as the UPS guy reached back inside the van, motioning for someone still inside to get out. Wayne and Keith watched as a third figure appeared, stepping out onto the lot, looking around, and what they saw froze them.

'Fuck,' said Wayne, speaking for them both.

It was Noah.

Chapter Fifty-Four

That morning, several hours before Wayne and Keith began making frantic calls to Jerry, Francis Colorado, attorney to the cartel, had awoken in his home in Holmby Hills, Westwood.

His wife, also an attorney, but an early riser, was already long gone (fortunately, as it would turn out), while his two children, both in their mid-teens, had left for school (also fortunately).

Apart from the housekeeper, Manuela, currently busying herself in their kitchen, preparing his breakfast, Francis Colorado was alone in the home.

He dressed, listening to CNN as he went about his morning ablutions: shaving, showering – all things he did with the same careful and considered daily precision with which he carried out his legal duties – before moving through into the kitchen, where Manuela, also the picture of efficiency, had breakfast waiting for him.

'Thank you, Manuela,' he said, sitting down to eat and pulling the morning's newspaper towards him.

As he ate, the gate buzzer sounded. Manuela answered.

'UPS delivery,' she said simply.

Francis Colorado did not look up, knowing she would answer the door, which indeed she did, swiftly drying her hands on a cloth that she tossed to the side and then hurrying from the room untying her pinafore.

When she opened the door, what she saw at first was the van, retreating back down the driveway to the gate, and she was puzzled for a moment. Nothing to sign for. Nor did the van bear the usual chocolate-brown livery of UPS.

Funny, she thought, and that was before she caught sight of the cardboard box at her feet. She reached for it in order to pick it up and take it into the house, but it was too heavy; instead, she dragged it over the threshold, lips pursed, puzzled, wondering what was inside.

'Mr Colorado,' came the call.

He dabbed the corners of his mouth with a napkin. 'Yes, Manuela.'

'A delivery for you,' was the reply. 'It's too heavy for me, I'm afraid.'

His eyebrows bunched a little. 'Have you any idea what it is?' he called over his shoulder.

A pause, as Manuela investigated more thoroughly. 'Have you ordered some bowling balls?' she asked.

Colorado looked up sharply. No, he had not ordered bowling balls. Of all the sports in which Francis Colorado might care to participate, bowling was probably the last.

'I'll be there in a moment,' he told her. Standing from the kitchen table, he moved through into the hallway, where Manuela stood puzzling over the box. He looked down upon it, the beginnings of concern gnawing at his insides.

But Manuela had already scurried away to fetch scissors and, returning, busied herself with slicing through the packing tape, peeling back the flaps in order to see inside, forgetting herself a little in her eagerness.

It took her a moment or so to work out what she was seeing.

She screamed, her hand to her throat, reeling back unsteadily, and for a moment Colorado thought she might faint on the spot. He would not have blamed her, of course, for by now he had also seen the contents of the box. Staring sightlessly up at them, as though deposited in a guillotine's basket, were four severed heads. The flesh of their torn necks was ragged and almost black with dried blood.

'I will call the police,' said Manuela, collecting herself and about to hurry off, but Colorado stopped her.

'No, Manuela, this is something I need to deal with myself.' He gave her a long, meaningful look. 'I trust I can rely on your total discretion in this matter. I will, of course, reimburse you accordingly . . .'

Her eyes widened, whether in greed or in fear, he could not tell, and did not especially care either way, because now something would have to be done about Manuela. Colorado cursed the man who had done this. Finding good help in Los Angeles was next to impossible. This was inconvenient. Most inconvenient.

'What will we do?' she said, and for this Colorado had no answer, thinking that he would have to invent an excuse to tell Sarah – tell her that he had fired Manuela, perhaps caught her stealing or something, in order to explain her sudden disappearance. That in itself would take some organising.

Then it occurred to him that Manuela was referring to the heads. How to dispose of the heads.

'I will have to make some calls,' he said. 'In the meantime, perhaps you'd like to tidy the kitchen while I deal with it?'

Gratefully, she left, and Colorado reached into his pocket for his phone. As he did so, he noticed for the first time a note taped to the inside of the box, pulled it free, read it. 'This is how I deal with those who fail me.'

Strange, thought Colorado as he summoned the number and pressed to dial, did Ronson Beaufoy really think that he was inspiring fear here? The man was clearly going insane.

'Hello,' he said, when the call was answered. 'We have a problem.'

Chapter Fifty-Five

Also that morning, again several hours before Wayne and Keith, having spotted Noah, were trying and failing to talk to Jerry, Lowrey and Baxter had been at their desks, both working on terminals, each separately wondering the same thing: what happens now? There was no evidence – nothing concrete, at least – to connect CT-40 with the Jeffrey Blaydon murder. There was nothing to tie them to the death of Ruth Shepherd and the injuries done to Jane Shepherd. As far as Lowrey was concerned, in fact, she was at a standstill.

Yup. All told, it was one of those mornings where she thought to herself, *What the hell am I doing here? What is the point of me, when little girls get shot and people get tortured and everybody knows who did it but even the cops can't do a thing about it?*

Yeah, what is the point of me? What the fuck am I doing here?

And that in turn led her to thinking about a certain Jeremiah O'Connell. As a cop, she knew that guys like him were not the answer; that he was maybe just the other side of the same coin.

As a human being?

That was different. As a human being, she wanted him out there. She wanted him to – and this was the technical term – kick the White Ghost's ass.

And then it happened. Baxter had been sitting slouched in front of his computer looking how Lowrey felt: tired, morose, probably wondering if it was worth it, with his chin in his hand, the other on the mouse of his PC, doing what, Lowrey had no idea.

Until . . .

'Hey, Lowrey,' he said, suddenly sitting upright.

She looked across the desk at him, wondering if it was worth getting her hopes up, and deciding to put it on hold until she knew for sure. 'Yeah,' she replied, 'what is it?'

'You might want to come and see this.'

'This better be worth my time, Baxter,' sighed Lowrey, feeling like an old man as she pulled herself wearily to her feet. 'I mean it. No messing around, okay?'

'Scout's honour,' he said.

She found herself looking at his terminal, except that he'd placed a hand over the screen.

'I was having a look at Vera Marlantes' girls,' he explained.

'Oh yes? And exactly why were you doing that, Baxter?' said Lowrey with a raised eyebrow.

He coloured a little. 'Research. It was research.'

'And now you're telling me that your research has turned up something good, yes?'

'Oh yes. Look at this.'

He removed his hand to reveal a picture of the girl who had been with Jeremiah O'Connell at Sunshine Heights. The same girl who had identified his 'body' at West Hollywood.

'It's her, isn't it?' said Baxter.

The girl in the picture was wearing a short cocktail dress, the archetype of the kind of woman that rich businessmen, bankers, even Hollywood stars, might like to take out and then to bed. The girl that Lowrey and Baxter had met was much more casually dressed, of course, hair pulled back into a ponytail, but yes, it was her.

Definitely her.

'You know what this means?' she said.

'It means that Marlantes was full of shit,' said Baxter. 'It means that she was lying to us.'

'Yup. And you know what else it means?' Lowrey strode back to her chair, pulled her jacket from the back of it.

'What?' asked Baxter.

'O'Connell thought that he had a leak in his operation. He was sure of it.' Lowrey indicated the picture of Noah. 'And I think we've found it.'

Chapter Fifty-Six

And that very same morning, Vera Marlantes had sat at home, having decided to kill herself.

Beaufoy had told her what had happened. Poor Jeff, who, as well as being loyal to Vera and the girls at the agency, was also hopelessly addicted to crack cocaine, had been planning to score at Sunshine Heights. There, he had witnessed first-hand the problems between Jerry and Ronson Beaufoy, and seeing his chance, which meant the chance to earn money or score more drugs (he wasn't especially fussy, since the former was chiefly spent on the latter), Jeff had requested a meeting with Beaufoy during which he'd implied that if Beaufoy, needed to get to Jerry, then he, Jeffrey Blaydon, could provide Beaufoy with the leverage he needed.

That leverage being Vera.

And that was where Beaufoy had left it: that Jeff had thrown her to the wolves in exchange for more drugs.

What she had since learned – from Lowrey and Baxter, and by piecing things together in her mind – was that while Beaufoy was grateful that Jeff had come forward in order to offer his assistance, he had no intention whatsoever of paying for the information, and instead of being showered with money and drugs, Jeffrey Blaydon had been taken to a warehouse in Compton, hung on a hook and tortured. There, he had told Beaufoy about Vera.

He had told Beaufoy what was perhaps Vera's biggest secret. The one fact that she kept hidden from everybody. Armed with that knowledge, Beaufoy had come to Vera demanding information on Jerry. And Vera, with a heavy heart, but feeling she had no choice – not to mention feeling that she had been betrayed by Jeff – had given it to him.

But no more. She now knew the true cost of her . . . *betrayal*. That's what it was, wasn't it? Treachery. Jerry had never been somebody she thought of as a dear friend, but that was no excuse. What she had done was unthinkable. She always knew that she would have to live with herself for doing it; now she was beginning to realise that living with herself wasn't possible.

Vera's home mirrored her personality: big, expansive, affluent, something of a statement. And yet untidy. Borderline chaotic. A home in a state of flux, decorating style: 'just moved in'.

She sat on her couch now, watching her 67-inch HD flatscreen but at the same time not really watching it, her mind on other things. It was only mid-morning, but she had a glass of wine not far from her fingertips. She had been reaching for it more frequently of late. It helped with the feelings that came crowding in on her. *You only have yourself to blame*, she told herself. *You only have yourself to blame.*

Work, of course, was keen to get hold of her, but the calls could not raise her from her torpor, nor did she want them to. What she wanted to do was sit and graze on her own failings, wallow in them a while. And so when the buzzer for the front gate sounded, she almost ignored it, and would have done, but for the fact that she was expecting a food delivery and in that food delivery was more wine, which was why she pulled herself from the depths of the couch and schlepped slowly towards the gate panel. There on the screen was a UPS delivery guy, brown pants and jacket, brown cap, looking hopefully into the eye of the camera and smiling.

'Yes?' she said.

'Ms Marlantes?'

'That's me,' she growled. This wasn't the shopping. Not unless the store had started using UPS, which she thought unlikely. Already she was beginning to regret answering.

'I have a delivery for you. It needs a signature. If you get one of the staff . . .'

'I don't have staff,' rasped Vera. She'd decided to do without staff a long while back. Her need for absolute secrecy and discretion versus the likelihood that her trust would be betrayed. It had happened to clients of hers. Some of the girls, the higher earners, had employed staff and it had happened to them.

None of which pontificating attended to the matter at hand, which was whether or not to open the gate for the UPS guy. On the one hand, she felt like she didn't have the strength to face anyone – anyone – even a UPS guy. Like that simple piece of human interaction, opening the door, signing, thanking him, tipping him, and closing the door again, might be too much in her current state of mental anguish, not to mention slight drunkenness.

'Could you come back?' she asked.

He pulled a face. 'Well, I can come back, Ms Marlantes, just that right now I'm unable to say exactly when . . .'

Oh, for God's sake, she thought, and then, before she really knew what she was doing, she was buzzing him up. She turned away, checked her face, decided that she didn't care anyway, and waited.

She heard the van pull up the drive, paused a few moments more, then opened the door.

'Hello,' said the UPS driver, but there was something about him that wasn't quite right. Something . . . *off*.

And then she looked over his shoulder, saw the van wasn't a UPS van but a standard black thing, and that getting out of it were two men, one of whom she recognised. Ronson Beaufoy.

Too late she tried to close the door, but the UPS guy put a shoulder to it, and in the next moment all three men were barging forward, the door swinging wildly as they surged through, the third man grabbing her by the hair and pulling her to one side as Beaufoy and the UPS driver – gun in hand – steamed inside to check whether the house was empty or not.

Vera screamed and cursed, writhed and threatened, her words falling on deaf ears as the men dragged her into the main living area, where Beaufoy scooped up the remote control and switched off the TV, Vera breathing hard as she was dumped unceremoniously onto the couch.

'Vera,' said Beaufoy, smiling, shoulders rising and falling as he caught his breath. 'You and I need to have a little talk.'

'We have nothing to talk about,' snarled Vera defiantly.

Beaufoy's jaw tightened as he pretended to think. 'You probably have given us all the information you *intended* to give us. And yet there is more information that we need. Thus, we shall have to impose upon you for some extra information. Some information that, perhaps, you didn't *intend* to give us. Let's start there, shall we?'

'No,' she insisted. Her fingers went to her head, rubbing her scalp, still sore from where the bogus UPS man had grabbed her hair.

'You seem to be under the misapprehension that you have a choice in this matter,' he said to her. 'It's not "Please give me the information I need." Not "I hope you will give me the information I need." It's "Vera, you *will* give me the information I need." '

'Ah, fuck you,' she drawled. 'You have nothing over me. Go out there, do your worst. I can stand to do jail time.'

Beaufoy looked around. 'Yes, by the looks of things, you'll feel right at home. But, you see, we still have something of a crossed wire here. The time for blackmailing you is over. Now is the time for threatening you for real.'

Thoughts of Jeff crowded in on her and in the same instant Vera understood that the option of taking her own life was no longer in her own hands. She gaped, realising suddenly, terribly, what lay in store for her.

At the same time, the UPS guy standing behind the couch reached and gripped her shoulders tightly. From within his jacket, Beaufoy withdrew a knife, a wicked-looking knife, and yet even that was somehow less frightening and less disgusting than what happened next, when from his other pocket he removed a small packet, which, when he unfurled it, turned out to be a disposable rain poncho that he pulled over his head.

Vera whimpered and tried to move but was held fast by the UPS guy as Beaufoy moved his legs and sat astride her, taking a seat.

Then he went to work with his knife.

He began cutting.

And when Vera Marlantes had told him everything he wanted to know, he kept on cutting.

And even when Vera Marlantes wept and begged for death, he continued cutting.

Chapter Fifty-Seven

At around the same time as Beaufoy was using Vera Marlantes to wet his blade, Lowrey and Baxter found themselves back in the guest area of her workplace, the Vera Marlantes Agency, where below the logo of VMA and behind the tall reception desk sat Chrissy, the beautiful but forbidding receptionist.

'We'd like to see Ms Marlantes,' said Lowrey. Even asking the question felt like a triumph of hope over experience.

'I'm afraid that's not possible,' answered Chrissy.

You had to give it to her, thought Lowrey. She certainly wasn't one to be intimidated by the sight of two cops, even cops as committed as Lowrey and Baxter were right at that moment.

'Okay then,' said Lowrey, exasperated, 'how about you put us in contact with this girl instead?' She held out a print-out of the website. 'Says here her name is Skye. I'm betting her name isn't really Skye.'

The receptionist shrugged. 'Ms Marlantes never reveals—'

'Anything. Right, yeah, I know. Ms Marlantes never reveals anything.'

The receptionist's raised eyebrows said 'well, there you go'. Her ramparts remained impregnable.

'We need to find this girl,' pressed Lowrey.

The receptionist shook her head. 'To find her, you'll need the permission of Ms Marlantes, and,' she raised her hand to tick points off two fingers, 'number one, she *won't* give it to you,' that finger went down. 'And number two, she *can't* give you it.' Left upraised was the middle finger.

'Why can't she give it to us?' asked Baxter.

'Because she's not here.'

'We've established she's not here,' sighed Lowrey. 'Where is she? At home?'

'I don't know. She's not answering her phone.'

'How often does she do that?'

'Do what?'

'Not answer her phone.'

Chrissy's eyes flickered. This receptionist was accustomed to stonewalling the cops, knew Lowrey. Even so, it was clear that something was amiss.

'So that's unusual, right?' she pressed. 'Something's wrong, huh?'

'I'm sorry,' sighed Chrissy, rolling her eyes, 'but I'm going to have to call our lawyer . . .'

'You know what? I think there is something wrong,' said Lowrey. 'I think that you think there is, too. Look, you're going to have to make an independent decision. And that decision is to tell us where to find this girl.'

Chrissy shook her head at the outlandish suggestion. *As if.*

Lowrey rounded on her. 'You know, don't you, that we are trying to save lives here? Maybe even the life of this woman you call your boss. It's not about trying to protect the public image of some movie star. It is not so that some hedge funder won't get in trouble with his wife. It's about stopping people *dying*.'

The receptionist did all but roll her eyes. And then something struck Lowrey: if Marlantes knew Jerry, then there was every possibility that the receptionist did, too.

'Do you know a guy by the name of Jeremiah O'Connell?' she asked.

The receptionist gave a small start.

'You do, don't you?' pressed Baxter.

'I guess, yeah,' replied the receptionist.

'It's him,' said Lowrey, sliding the blade home. 'It's his life we're trying to save.' She paused meaningfully. 'Now are you going to help us, or not?'

Chapter Fifty-Eight

Vera was on fire with pain.

Beaufoy had started with her fingers, making small incisions on her fingertips and along the backs of each digit, peeling strips of flesh from the back of her hands, exposing the musculature, the fat and tissue of the hypodermis. After that, he had moved to other parts of her body, cutting away clothes, working at her thighs, stomach, breasts and, lastly, her face. And now she was coated in blood, awash with it. Every part of her bleeding. And she knew that if the shock didn't kill her, then the blood loss would, and very soon. Already she was losing consciousness. Waking up from her last blackout, she found herself alone. Beaufoy and his two heavies must surely have assumed that she was already dead and left.

She almost chuckled. After all, she had wanted to die. Here she was on the very precipice. One thing to do first, though. One last thing. Not that it would make things right, but she could try.

She slid from the sofa and, with her blood-soaked clothes hanging off her like tattered rags, began to crawl towards the phone handset. Each movement of her body sent pain shooting through her. She could taste the blood in her mouth and in her nostrils, feeling as though she would never escape the coppery smell of it and, of course, being absolutely right on that score.

She knew what she had to do.

Got it. The phone. Hit the button.

He answered. 'Hello? Vera? You all right?'

'Shut up,' she gasped, and then, 'Shut up and listen.'

His voice at the other end of the line was wary. 'I'm listening.'

'It was me,' she said. 'I was the one who told them where to find you. They left me no option.'

There was a long pause at the other end of the line. 'There's always an option, Vera,' he said, with steel in his voice.

She chuckled wetly, a small bubble of blood forming at one nostril. 'Well, you'll be pleased to know that I'm paying for it now. I haven't got long.'

'They hurt you?'

She looked down at herself. At her torn, blood-soaked body. Her flayed, ragged flesh. 'You could say that.'

'What did they want to know?' he asked tightly.

'They're on their way, Jerry,' was what she gasped in reply. 'They're going after Noah. Get there. Stop them.'

And that was it for Vera. She ended the call, the phone slipping from her fingers as she slumped, knowing she had no strength left, that she had done all that she could to repair the damage and knowing, too, that it would never be enough.

And as the life began to leach from her like water down a plughole, she thought about the harm she had done, and the little good she had done, and she thought about a husband

and son she had, a 'secret' family that Jeff, under duress, had told Ronson Beaufoy about, a family that Beaufoy had threatened to find, torture and kill if she didn't give up Jerry. And so she had.

When Beaufoy had cut her, he had wanted more information on Jerry and she had given up Noah. After that, he'd wanted to know where to find Vera's family as well, but that information she had refused to give him. Despite all the pain he had inflicted, she had not told him.

And she held on to that thought – that single, solitary, comforting thought – as she slipped from this world into the next.

Chapter Fifty-Nine

Jerry stared at the phone in his hand as shock percolated slowly through him. Vera. It was Vera.

Yes, of course, he'd suspected the leak might be her, but only in much the same way that he'd suspected Jimmy or Josh or any other LA contact, which was to say idly. Considering the possibility. Not wanting to rule them out. Now he found the reality of the situation hitting him harder than expected, and as he set off, he dialled for Noah, listening in frustration as it rang. And rang. And then went to voicemail.

Fuck.

As he went for the car, he found himself thinking it over. The bombshell. The reality that sat in his head like an unwelcome house guest: Vera had betrayed him. A fact that hit him harder than it had done to learn that Lucas had ratted him out. Quite why, he found it difficult to say. After all, his involvement with Vera had always been strictly business. But, then again, they liked each other. They were close enough to sink a few beers, and for her to end the night crashing on his couch. So, yes, while it was more surprising that Lucas had ratted him out, somehow it was more hurtful that Vera had done it.

Jerry reached the car and was about to try Noah again when his phone buzzed.

He'd clicked to answer and held it to his ear before he realised the caller wasn't her.

'Hello, Mr O'Connell,' said a well-spoken voice. 'You don't know me, but we may have something in common.'

'Oh yeah? Who's this, then?' asked Jerry, warily.

'My name is Francis Colorado.'

Chapter Sixty

In her bungalow, Noah watched helplessly as on the tabletop her phone buzzed. Holding her, pinning her arms back, was the man who had been referred to as Gridlock, dressed in a UPS uniform. Also in the bungalow, another guy – Drugstore, who wore a bag across his chest – and, of course, Ronson Beaufoy.

Beaufoy stood with his hands thrust into the pockets of his pants, hair greasy and awry, and in desperate need of a shave. Ronson Beaufoy, she thought absently, was not a man who could confidently rock the stubbled look; his non-beard was an incoherent mess, patchy and inconsistent, much like the man himself.

'What do you want?' she'd demanded, bitterly regretting her lack of caution when it had come to opening the door. She knew exactly why of course – why she had peeled herself from the couch and hurried to open it – and it was because she had hoped it would be Jerry, and that they could make up. Things had been different for her since Jerry O'Connell had come into her life. Better. And since walking out of his apartment the day before, she'd come to the realisation that 'better', while not being 'perfect', was still infinitely prefer-able to the way things had been before.

All of that had been racing through her mind when she came to answer the door. She hadn't even used the peephole.

Now she had let these terrible men into her home. And Gridlock stood pinning her arms behind her, and over on the table – a fact not lost on Ronson Beaufoy, who looked at it, smiled and then raised his eyes to meet hers mockingly – her phone was buzzing, rumbling on the tabletop as it rang out plaintively, uselessly, the screen displaying the name, 'Jerry'.

'You don't want to talk to him?' she asked Beaufoy. With her arms held back, she felt vulnerable, exposed, but was doing all she could to hide the fact.

'Oh yes,' said Beaufoy quickly, exposing teeth as he grinned, 'I want to talk to him very much. Very much indeed. What I don't want to do is warn him. You understand, I'm sure. You do understand, don't you? You do, don't you?'

Her eyes travelled to Drugstore, who stood not far away from the front door as though keeping guard, hands clasped in front of him. If she'd been hoping for any sign that he, too, thought something was amiss with his boss, then she was disappointed. Drugstore's face remained impassive.

'How did you find me?' she asked, and she wasn't certain that she was particularly interested in the answer.

'Your friend Vera,' replied Beaufoy pleasantly.

That information was a slap in the face. 'Vera told you? What? She just told you? Just like that?'

'No, of course not,' said Beaufoy airily. He pushed a hand through his hair. 'We had to torture her first. She couldn't tell us what we really wanted to know, of course, which is

286

how to find Jerry O'Connell. But after we cut her some more she told us where to find you, and that you might know how to find your boyfriend.'

The phone was buzzing once more. Jerry again. Looking at it, she felt the closeness of him, almost like a physical event, as though she could mentally reach out and say to him, 'I'm here – I'm here and I could really do with your help, big guy.'

'Oh, it must be so frustrating,' gloated Beaufoy. She was doing all she could to keep the frustration from showing on her features, but even so, he knew. Of course, he knew. 'Let's make things easier for you, shall we?' he said and moved over to the table. From inside his jacket came the knife and for a moment she thought he might be about to stab the phone, but instead he used it to brush the handset onto the floor, before stamping down on it hard, once, twice, a third time, his lank, oily hair flopping down over his face, until the ringing stopped.

Something on the blade of the knife caught her eye. What looked like fresh blood.

To Gridlock, Beaufoy said, 'Shall we use the couch again,' and then looked across at Noah, 'just as we did with Ms Marlantes.'

Gridlock dragged her over to the sofa, pushed her down. She didn't resist. She had decided not to give him the pleasure. This was going to hurt, she knew. Then again, cancer hurt. Childbirth hurt. With any luck, it would be over quickly.

'I'm going to the can, boss,' called Drugstore from the door.

But Beaufoy waved him away. His attention was on Noah.

'Have no misconceptions,' he was saying, 'this won't be over quickly.' He raised the knife, light ran along the blade and she saw Vera's drying blood. He moved it towards her slowly, so that it blurred in her vision. He stopped. 'Wait. My poncho . . .'

He was fishing in the pocket of his jacket when there was a sound, the front door crashing open, and Gridlock, holding Noah, tensed, hissing, *Shit*, and a voice called, 'LAPD. Freeze.'

Chapter Sixty-One

'You didn't lock the door. You didn't lock the *fucking* door.'

Beaufoy, sitting astride Noah with his knife poised, huffed like an artist disturbed in the creation of his masterpiece and glared at Gridlock, who stood behind the couch, restraining Noah with his hands on her shoulders.

And it was true, Gridlock knew, that he had indeed failed to lock the front door of the bungalow. This fact was now made terribly apparent by the two cops standing in the doorway of the living area, their standard-issue LAPD Glocks drawn and held two-handed, their feet planted wide apart, everything done by the book.

And suddenly it was as if the air was filled with electricity. As though to touch it would make it fizz and crackle. And Gridlock saw wariness, a look of animal cunning that passed across his boss's face, and knew instantly that Beaufoy was not going to allow himself to be arrested.

Gridlock knew, too, that people were going to die in this room, and he offered up a silent prayer that one of them would not be him.

From the door came the command: 'Beaufoy: drop the blade.'

Gridlock felt a whimper bubble up from inside him but suppressed it. The woman cop – he recognised her. It was the same one who'd been standing outside Sunshine Heights a few days ago. Just watching them. Gridlock hadn't said so at the time, but he was fairly sure he recognised her from back in the day, back in the old neighbourhood. Maybe, maybe not. And anyway, did it really matter now?

No.

'You heard her,' said the white cop to her right. 'Now drop the fucking knife, Beaufoy.'

The blade was held close to Noah's eye. She stared defiantly at Beaufoy, at the same time trying not to let any hint of triumph or vindication into that look. Not wanting to goad him, when, with one flick of his wrist, he could pluck out her eyeball, impale it on the end of his knife like an olive on a cocktail stick. Over his shoulder, she saw the two cops, Lowrey and Baxter, recognising them from their single tense encounter at Sunshine Heights, and vaguely wishing that she hadn't given them quite such a hard time on that occasion.

Beaufoy, still with his back to the cops and holding her gaze, brought the knife away from her face. Held it out, pointy end down.

'That's right. Now drop it,' commanded Lowrey.

His hand opened. The knife fell. With a *thunk*, the point stuck into the wood flooring.

'You,' said Lowrey to Gridlock, 'step away from the girl, put your hands on your head. You, Beaufoy, do the same.

Hands on your head, get off the girl, turn and face us. Do it all careful or we put holes in you.'

Gridlock was doing as he was told. Beaufoy began to move, too, removing himself from Noah at last. But even that feeling of release did nothing to put Noah's mind at rest. She had the uneasy feeling that there was something wrong – something she couldn't quite put her finger on right now.

Three guys have burst into your house. One of them was about to use your face for sculpture practice. Maybe that's what you think is 'wrong', Noah? Huh?

'We used to call you the White Ghost,' Lowrey was saying to Beaufoy. 'Back in the day.'

'Oh?' said Beaufoy. 'We know each other of old?'

'Well, I know you. We all did back then. Rich white kid trying to make a name for himself on our streets.'

He chuckled, standing now, his hands raised. 'Looks like I did a good job then.'

'Oh yeah. I'm looking forward to telling my mama that I bagged the famous White Ghost,' added Lowrey.

'I'm pleased for you.'

'Now, there were two vehicles outside,' she said, 'both those vehicles belong to you?'

Three men, thought Noah. *Two vehicles.*

And then it hit her. Drugstore. The guy with the bag across his chest. He was no longer in the room. *Fuck.* He'd excused himself to the can.

'Hey,' she called to the cops. But it was too late. Baxter, who had been mentally congratulating himself on getting the drop on Beaufoy, sensed a movement to his right and turned in time to see a big black guy crashing along the passageway towards him with his gun drawn and his knuckle whitening on the trigger. And it was the last thing he ever saw because Drugstore opened fire on the run and a bullet tore through Baxter's temple and destroyed his skull in a red welter of shattered bone fragments, flesh and brain fluid.

Splattered with bits of Baxter, deafened by the blast, Lowrey was caught catastrophically off-guard. She tried to turn and return fire. She registered Drugstore's second shot whistle past her right ear, thinking, *Christ, that was close*, and trying to draw a bead on him as he barrelled into the room – but failing to see that, over by the couch, Gridlock had snatched his SIG from the waistband of his jeans, aimed and squeezed off a shot that caught her in the belly and knocked her off her feet, her lone shot in reply going wide.

In the aftermath of the short battle, those left unharmed felt their ears ring from the noise. The room was heavy with the stench of gunfire. Just three shots fired, both cops down, one dead, one surely fatally injured. She lay writhing, squirming on the floor, moaning and clasping her stomach, her blood already pooling around her.

And Beaufoy was delighted.

'Well, we can certainly take some lessons away from that, can't we, gentlemen?' he said. 'Gridlock, lock the fucking door next time, but good shooting. Drugstore, make sure you spend more time in the can. Right, somebody's bound to have rung the cops, nice area like this.' He flashed an unpleasant, shark-like smile at Noah. 'Let's get out of here and go somewhere we can torture her in peace.'

Noah had remained immobile throughout, emotions flip-flopping from relief and gratitude at the arrival of the cops to the painful, sickening realisation that the parachute had turned out to be a backpack. In the pit of her stomach was a nauseous, grieving feeling – for herself and for the knowledge that she had so nearly been saved, and for the two cops who had died trying to do it.

She looked over, hardly daring to take in the horrifying abattoir of her apartment: the mortally wounded Lowrey, moaning and moving weakly, slithering in a sticky puddle of her own blood; beside her, the body of her partner, the side of his head a revolting mass of blood and hair and strangely white skull, his mouth wide open in a large O of surprise.

At that moment, Gridlock's phone rang.

'Yo,' he answered, listened, and then ended the call. To Beaufoy, he said, 'Ronson. Looks like we know where the gear is at.'

Beaufoy's eyes slid from Noah to Gridlock. 'Yes?'

'Some auto shop in Compton,' drawled Gridlock. 'Eyes on the street reckon there's been a lot of English guys hanging around. One English guy in particular.'

'Tall?'

'Our guy by the sounds of things.'

And once again Beaufoy's gaze found hers. 'Jeremiah O'Connell,' he said, as though testing out the name for himself. 'Jeremiah O'Connell.' He pushed a hand through greasy, stringy hair. 'I'm very much looking forward to meeting him again.'

Still sitting on the couch, Noah allowed herself to hope once more. This, surely, was Jerry's trap being sprung; this was things going according to plan.

'Are we going, Ronson?' asked Gridlock.

Beaufoy ignored him, stared at Noah instead, before seeming to make a decision. 'Let's go,' he told Gridlock. 'We'll take the van. You, Drugstore, finish off the cop and follow on in the Range Rover.'

'Where are we going?' asked Gridlock. He shot a queasy look at Lowrey, whose legs worked feebly on the floorboards.

'We're going to an auto shop in Compton, of course.' Beaufoy pointed at Noah. 'And we're taking her along as security.'

On the way out, he stopped by Lowrey, looking down at her with interest before delving into her pockets for ID.

'Lowrey,' he read. 'Back in the old neighbourhood. Shouldn't be too difficult to find. You can be sure that I'll be paying my respects to your mama.'

Chapter Sixty-Two

Jerry pushed the Dodge Viper fast, gambling the lights, enduring the angry horn blasts of other drivers as he cut in front of them to make turns, block-changing down, pumping the gas pedal, and always, always pushing the car onwards. Another time, he might have enjoyed the drive, got off on the thrill of it. But not today. Not now.

'Christ's sake, Vera,' he muttered under his breath, although, in truth, he didn't fully blame her, knowing that however CT-40 had got to her, they would have given her no choice; knowing also that so much of this was on him, because, with hindsight, he should have made finding his grass a greater priority than he had done.

The fact was, he'd thought that if he sewed his operation up tight, then any leak would be irrelevant and he could investigate later, in his own sweet time. But he'd been wrong about that, and now he was paying the price. Or, more accurately, Noah was paying the price.

There it was, her bungalow. Parked outside was a black Range Rover. No prizes for guessing where that came from.

Conscious of the Viper's full-throated V10, he drew to a

stop some distance away, parked in the shade of a palm tree, got out and jogged towards the bungalow. The street was empty and quiet, but as he looked around, he saw a figure flitting at a nearby window. Further along the street, a drape twitched – another neighbour peeking out. Either this area had an unusually vigilant Neighbourhood Watch committee or something had happened to put the cat among the pigeons.

His eyes went to Noah's bungalow and the lone vehicle outside, neither giving anything away. Even so, instinct told him that the shit had hit the fan. The fact that Noah's front door stood ajar did nothing to allay his fears.

He kept low as he moved to a front window of the bungalow, not caring if the neighbours saw him, every sense on high alert as he peered cautiously over the windowsill and found himself looking in upon the living area.

He saw the blood first. It was as though somebody had kicked over a can of red paint and let it ooze slowly across the floor. The second thing he saw was Lowrey. She lay in the centre of the spreading pool of blood, hands at a stomach wound, her eyelids flickering like a moth at a light bulb.

Next to her lay another body. Another cop, assumed Jerry – probably her partner Baxter, although it was difficult to tell – while above her stood a gangbanger, a guy with a bag slung across his chest. In one hand he held a pistol, in his other hand a cushion, and as Jerry watched, he reached to place the cushion over Lowrey's face, about to deliver the coup de grâce.

Jesus.

Springing forward, Jerry hit the front door, knowing it was probably too late, but determined to do something anyway.

Inside, Drugstore heard the crash, raised his gun and fired – just as Jerry burst in.

It was a quick, squeezed-off panic shot that thumped into the woodwork to the left of Jerry, who was fuelled by adrenaline and fury and a desire to help Lowrey that even he could tell was hopeless but had to be done anyway. He dived at the same time as another bullet ripped through the air above, knowing that it had passed only inches away as he took Drugstore's legs out from under him and the two men crashed to the floor just feet from the bodies of Lowrey and Baxter.

'Fuck you,' gasped Drugstore. The two of them were like mud-wrestlers, grappling in the sticky blood, as Drugstore wriggled free, drew a bead on Jerry and fired.

Jerry felt a searing pain in his thigh, felt warm blood sluice quickly down his leg, knew that the bullet had grazed him, and roared in pain and fury as he came back at Drugstore, slipping and sliding but dodging as Drugstore tried to hit him with the butt of the gun. He caught the gangbanger's hand, slammed it to the floor, and the pistol skittered away. At the same time, he lowered his head, clamped his teeth around Drugstore's head, and bit off his nose.

Drugstore let out a scream – a scream that was as much in disbelief as it was in agony.

Grimacing, Jerry's lips pulled away from blood-stained teeth as he hauled himself to his knees, gripped Drugstore's ears and smashed his head to the floor once, twice, a third time, until Drugstore's head rolled and a broken jaw hung askew, and only then did Jerry let him drop, the gangbanger's head bouncing off the boards one final time.

In the silence that followed, Jerry sat back on his haunches, breathing hard and spitting fleshy bits of Drugstore's nose from his mouth. His blood was up from the battle, but at the same time he felt a sinking feeling. *Christ, I needed the guy conscious,* he was thinking. *I need to find out where they've taken Noah,* when he heard a faint voice from behind him: 'Auto shop.'

He spun.

'Auto shop,' said Lowrey. Her voice was barely a whisper, a dying whisper. 'They've taken her to an auto shop in Compton.'

On his knees still, Jerry skidded round to face her, taking her hand, gently cupping her cheek and removing stray hair from her eyes. Her breathing was shallow. He had never seen anybody as pale as she was then. She had clearly lost huge amounts of blood.

'I don't know where . . .' she started.

'It's all right, darlin', save your breath, I'm calling you help,' he insisted. 'I know where. I know exactly where.' His hands still on her face, cradling her.

'Then go,' she said. Uttering her final words, 'Good luck, Jerry,' she drifted from consciousness, her head lolling. Would she slip into a coma? He wasn't sure. It could go either way. Whatever happened, she was out for the foreseeable future.

He sat back, shoulders heaving . . . Next, he made sure that Lowrey was as comfortable as possible, then stood and looked down at himself. Beneath a tear in his trouser, he saw flesh blackened by blood. It was just a graze. *Only a flesh wound, innit.* But it was leaking thick, viscous blood, and it hurt like it was on fire.

Still, he had no time to fix himself up, nor to wash off the blood that covered him from head to foot; his phone was ringing, but he ignored it; instead, he set off, crashing out of the bungalow and back along the sidewalk towards the Viper, thinking *Fuck knows what I look like,* but not caring. The sirens were getting louder as he reached the Viper, climbed inside, started up and then peeled away.

The paramedics, on their way to Noah's bungalow, tore past him.

Chapter Sixty-Three

'Where the fuck have you been?' demanded Wayne.

Jerry, driving with one hand, his phone clamped to his ear, caught sight of himself in the rear-view mirror. His face was caked with blood, his beard matted. 'It's a long story,' he said, the words appearing from between teeth gritted with the pain.

'Well, we haven't got time to get into it now. Beaufoy's turned up mob-handed, and you'll never fucking guess who he's got with him.'

'I reckon I can,' sighed Jerry. 'Noah. Am I right?'

'In one.'

'Have they gone in yet?'

'No, they've been fannying about in the car park outside. I reckon they suspect that it's a trap.'

'I was assuming they would.'

'That's why you put the samples of the drugs in there, was it? Right, well, you was bang on, because they weren't happy about going in there until—'

'What was it? The dog?'

'Got it in one.'

'Border collie,' said Jerry thoughtfully.

'You what?'

'Bet it was a Border collie, was it?'

'I don't know if it was a Border collie.' Sitting beside Wayne, Keith was nodding. 'Yeah, Keith reckons it was a Border collie. Anyway, the dog must have detected something because they steamed in, took Noah inside with them.'

'How many?'

'Um, let's think, you've got Beaufoy, a bloke dressed up as a UPS delivery driver, Noah, the dog bloke and a whole lot of other geezers who look a bit handy. Not good odds.'

'Ah, fuck it, we've faced a lot worse than that, eh?' As if on cue, the wound in his leg flared, sending pain shooting up his side and he bit down on a cry.

'Yeah, we have,' agreed Wayne, who was never knowingly not up for a fight against overwhelming odds.

'Right.'

'You've considered the fact that Noah might be your snitch, have you?' asked Wayne, although he felt sure he already knew the answer.

'No, she's not the one,' said Jerry. 'I found the leak.'

'Sorted it, I hope.'

'Yeah, consider it sorted.'

'All right. Where are you, anyway?' asked Wayne.

'I'm on my way over to you, aren't I?'

'Well, you better get a bloody move on. What if that dog gets wind of my bombs?'

'Nah, it doesn't work like that. It'll be a drug-sniffer dog, not an explosives dog.'

'So? It finds the drugs, then they fuck off. Either way, our window of opportunity has opened and closed.'

'It won't be as easy as that, trust me.'

Wayne sighed. 'Thing is, they're all in there now. We could blow the gaff. End of story.'

'What? With Noah in it?'

'It's a thought, Jerry.'

'No. That's not an option, Wayne. No harm is coming to Noah. You got that?'

There was a pause at the other end of the line.

'Wayne . . .?' prompted Jerry.

'Yeah, yeah,' said Wayne reluctantly. 'I got it. And if Noah leaves for some reason?'

'Then blow it.'

'Sure.'

'Wait . . .'

'What?' said Wayne.

'Not if the dog's in there.'

'Oh, come on . . .'

'I'm serious, Wayne. No explosion if Noah's in there. No explosion if the dog's in there.'

Chapter Sixty-Four

Inside the workshop, Gridlock was told to watch Noah, who was made to sit at the workbench, her hands taped. She kept an eye on Beaufoy's men as they, in turn, watched a sniffer dog move through the building, treating the animal with a respect that bordered on awe.

And sitting there, it struck her that she knew the breed – just from hanging out with Jerry. A Border collie. She found herself having to suppress a grin. How proud he'd be of her if he were here now. She could hear him in her ear, 'The thing with dogs, you see, is that they're angels without wings. That's what they are to me, mate.'

And, fuck, she wished he were here now.

'It smelt drugs, didn't it?' hissed Beaufoy. 'So why hasn't it *found* the drugs? Is the fucking dog going to find my drugs or do I need to put a bullet in its furry fucking head?'

Oh yes, she really wished Jerry were here now, just to see how long Beaufoy would have lasted after a comment like that.

The men were nervous, she saw. They were wired and wary, but Beaufoy's desire – no, his *need* – to find his hijacked wares overrode all other concerns. It wasn't just the drugs, it was pride, the need to come out on top. She could practically smell the testosterone wafting off him. Meanwhile, she thought of Wayne and Keith, who lay in wait across the road, and it occurred to her: perhaps they'd simply blow the place with her in it. They hadn't done it *yet*, of course. And presumably her presence was the reason why.

But they had to be having that conversation. They had to be considering the possibility.

Had to be.

And if that happened, if they came to the conclusion that they should set off the explosives anyway, would it be worth it? At least she would go to her death knowing that she'd been necessary collateral damage. And, after all, one dead, near-friendless hooker was a small price to pay for ridding the world of Ronson Beaufoy and his gang. It felt like a trade-off worth making. It felt like a trade-off that she would be happy with.

Question was: would they? Would they go for it?

'What have you found?' demanded Beaufoy, the sound of his voice dragging her from her grim reverie. She looked over to see that one of his men had approached him, two cracked vials of cocaine in the palm of his hand. 'Just those?' Beaufoy's blood rose. 'Just . . . *two*?'

'There's more, though, Ronson,' the gangbanger told his boss.

'What do you mean there's more?' demanded Beaufoy.

'Check it – the canine's going crazy,' insisted the gang-banger, pointing. 'There's more of it right around there. These must have been left out, I don't know, must be that junkie Lucas – I don't know.'

'Or were left out to alert whoever was looking for the whole batch,' said Beaufoy thoughtfully, his eyes going to where the collie was still going nuts. Its nose was pressed at the driver's seat of the Corvette.

He pulled his knife from inside his jacket, took two strides to the Corvette and slashed the front tyre. The vehicle lurched with a thump, sitting on its rim, indicating that there were no drugs within. The gang members looked at one another, pulling awkward, what-the-fuck faces.

'What's this, though?' said Beaufoy, squatting, running his eyes along the concrete at the same time. 'It's a fucking lift, that's what it is. How they raise up the cars to work on the underside. You fucking idiots, it's here. It's under here.' He was as excited as the dog, hair flapping as his head went from side to side, looking for something. 'There'll be a panel somewhere, to operate the lift,' he said. 'Find it, find it.'

Someone did. Moments later, there was a hydraulic clunking sound and the Corvette was rising, the noise of it drowned out by the barking of the dog.

One of the men jumped into the void. 'Ronson,' he called.

'What is it?'

'It's just a few jumbos.'

They were passed up. A handful of vials. That's all it was. Enough to drive the dog crazy.

'It's a trap,' said Beaufoy. As one, his men drew their guns, all of them scanning the workshop as though they expected ninjas to appear from the walls. Rattled, Beaufoy scooted over to Noah. 'What's going on?' he demanded to know.

She didn't answer. Behind Beaufoy, the dog was still

barking, and he wheeled round. 'Put that dog out in the van now, before I put it down.'

The man assigned to be the dog handler hurried forward, took the collie and made his way to the door. Beaufoy turned his attention back to Noah.

'Now,' he rasped, 'tell me what the fuck is going on?'

Chapter Sixty-Five

Jerry, covered in blood and driving the red Viper like a madman, pain arrowing up his leg every time he stomped on the clutch, turned onto the street, his eyes going to the workshop even as he lifted off the gas and felt the nose of the Viper rise in reply, the car almost appearing to relax as its speed decreased.

Should he call the boys? Apart from Wayne and Keith, they were all back at the apartment, still basking in the afterglow of their successful heist. There was no time to mobilise them. What he had to do, he had to do alone.

He pulled over and got out painfully. When he looked down to where his trouser leg was crusted black, he knew that he was losing too much blood. He took a deep breath, fighting a wave of light-headedness. *You've not got time for this*, he told himself. *Just fucking keep it together,* and he shaded his eyes to look along the street.

Well, the workshop was still there, at least. Wayne hadn't got an itchy trigger finger and decided to blow it anyway. His gaze travelled to the abandoned KFC, where he knew Wayne and Keith would be watching. Next, he pulled out his phone, made a call and when that was over, he called Wayne.

'I see you on the street,' answered Wayne. 'What the fuck's happened to you?'

'It ain't all my blood,' replied Jerry.

'But some of it is?'

'Yeah, some of it.'

'Mate, are you all right? You look pale. I can tell from here.'

'I'll be sure to work on my tan when this is all over. Meantime, what's going on in the workshop?'

'Noah, Beaufoy, and a bunch of gangbangers in there.'

'Situation unchanged, then. What about the dog?'

'Dog's still in there.'

'Right, well, leave it with me.'

'All right. What am I doing? Waiting for your signal?'

'Yes, mate. I'll give a thumbs-up. Oh, and one other thing. How far away from the workshop do I need to be?'

'I don't know, it ain't an exact science. As far away as possible, and with something big and heavy between you and the explosion. How's about that?'

'Right.' And with that, Jerry got back into the Viper, started up and pulled onto the road, cruising slowly down the street towards the workshop. As he watched, the door to the workshop opened and one of the gangbangers appeared with a Border collie on a lead.

'Hello, boy,' said Jerry absently. Still cruising, he watched as the handler made his way across the lot to one of the parked vans, where he deposited the collie. Meanwhile, Jerry pulled up not far away. A car passed, music blaring.

Otherwise, the street was empty as he got out of the Viper, grimacing with pain as he used the parked van as cover. He stopped, gathering himself and keeping one eye on the dog handler at the same time. Now he just had to make it over without the gangbanger seeing him, which in this shape was easier said than done. Sweat popped on his forehead as he gritted his teeth and limped as stealthily as he could.

At the last moment, the gangbanger heard Jerry coming up on him from behind and turned, mouth dropping open in surprise at the limping, blood-soaked figure towering above him. A half-second later, he was sprawled half-conscious in the dirt.

Inside the workshop, Beaufoy had taken his knife from his belt. 'Where is he?' he barked at Noah. 'Where is O'Connell?'

'I don't know,' she replied. It took all her resolve not to shrink away from him as, for the second time that day, the knife came close to her face.

'He wanted us to come here, didn't he?' snapped Beaufoy. 'He left this for us.' He held up one of the vials and then tossed it over his shoulder. 'This was bait.'

Keith was supposed to be the bait, she thought. *Keith was going to be the reason they wouldn't suspect a trap. Except that Jerry had a change of heart.*

Ruefully, she realised that, either way, she'd got in the way of his plans, and, more than ever, she wished that Wayne would just blow the place, because any second now Beaufoy was likely to reach the conclusion that the place was booby-trapped and the whole set-up was a bust.

'What are you not telling me?' he barked. The point of the

blade tickled her eyelash. With a deft flick of his wrist, he cut into the tender skin just below her left eye, making her gasp in pain. A warm droplet of blood trickled down her cheek like a single lovelorn tear. 'Where is he?' snarled Beaufoy. He wore a feral look. 'Where is Jeremiah O-fucking-Connell?'

'My God,' said Noah, at last, as Beaufoy stood before her, with his shoulders rising and falling and his hair in his eyes, 'he really has got under your skin, hasn't he?'

And then Beaufoy's phone rang.

'All right there, Mr Caretaker?' Jerry greeted him in a breezy voice that belied the pain he felt. The Viper was outside the workshop now.

'Mr O'Connell,' replied Beaufoy, 'I've been waiting to hear from you.'

'Well, I was hoping you might be interested in a trade.'

Beaufoy's mouth twisted in a grin and his eyes found Noah. 'How did I know? Don't tell me, the woman for my drugs.'

'You're a bright fella. You must have done well at school. That's exactly what I'm talking about. Oh, and I got one of your mates with me as well.' Jerry stood by his Viper, looking into the trunk, where his new captive eyed him warily. 'What's your name?' he asked, not unkindly. The guy was young and, from what Jerry had seen, he was good to the dog. For that reason, Jerry was going easy on him.

'Joey,' stammered the guy in reply.

'Joey,' repeated Jerry to Beaufoy. 'You missing a Joey?'

'I might be.'

'Well, I got him. He's up for offer in a two-for-one deal. You get Joey and the rest of your drugs. I get Noah.'

'Well, I certainly want my drugs, and I'm not at all interested in hanging on to the girl . . .'

'She there with you now, is she?' asked Jerry.

'She is, as it happens.'

'She unharmed?'

'At the moment she is, yes, although I'm not sure I can
guarantee it for much longer.'

'Put her on.'

'How about I don't?'

'Oh, what, you need to check I'm on the level, do you?
All right. Take a look out of the door . . .'

Inside, they heard the sound of an engine revving. With his
knife, Beaufoy gestured to Gridlock, who went to the door,
opened it a crack and peered cautiously outside, his gun
drawn.

Looking out, he saw the gang's vans and the Range Rover
parked on the lot. Idling on the street close by was a red
Dodge Viper, driver indistinct behind the windshield. 'Car's
out here,' said Gridlock over his shoulder. The men were
restless. Sweat shone on their faces.

'What sort of car does he have?' Beaufoy asked Noah.

She shrugged. 'He's got a load of cars.'

Beaufoy pushed his hand through his hair, his eyes wide
all of a sudden. 'What sort of car is it?' he hissed at Gridlock.

'Red Dodge Viper.'

'Yes, he has one of those,' said Noah.

Outside, Jerry saw the door open a crack and Gridlock's face
appear. He hit the throttle and pulled the Viper onto the lot.

Bringing it round, he tapped the gas, wrenched the wheel, and the back of the Viper slid round in a cloud of dust as he brought the driver's side parallel to the door and then stopped, reached across and lifted the holdall to show Gridlock.

'See in there?' he called across the seats out of the open passenger window. 'You tell Beaufoy that's his drugs, and he can have them as soon as I've got Noah safe in this here motor, all right?'

And with that he floored it, bouncing off the lot, across the sidewalk and onto the road, the rear of the car stepping out as he straightened up.

Gridlock withdrew and turned to Beaufoy. 'Yeah, that was him,' he told his boss, 'and it looks like he's got our product.'

'I see.'

'Another thing, boss.'

'What?'

'He looks in a bad way.'

Chapter Sixty-Six

Jerry called again. 'Right, Mr Caretaker, I think we understand each other now, don't we? I've got your drugs. Now put Noah on so I can check she's all right.'

Beaufoy handed the phone to Noah. 'He wants to talk to you.'

'Hello,' she said.

'You all right, darlin'?' he said. He kept his voice low.

'I told you never to call me darling.'

'Yeah,' he laughed, 'you're all right.'

He chuckled, and to her it was the sweetest sound she'd ever heard.

'Are you all right?' she asked him.

'Yeah, I'm good. What are you talking about?'

'They said you looked . . .'

He chuckled. 'It's not my blood,' he said, but she wasn't so sure when he insisted he was okay. His voice sounded strained and thin to her. The kind of voice a person might use when he was masking his pain.

'What happens next, Jerry?' she asked.

'It's like I said. We'll get you out of there. Put Beaufoy back on, would you?'

'Wait . . .'

'What?'

She spoke quickly. 'Listen, whatever you offer him, he won't abide by it, Jerry. He hates you, I mean he *really* hates you. And he's losing it, he's going nuts. Whatever happens, he's going to double-cross you, I can guarantee it . . .'

And then Beaufoy was snatching the phone out of her hand, putting it to his own ear.

Jerry spoke first. 'Is she right? You planning on double-crossing me, are you?'

Beaufoy ignored the question. 'Tell me, what's your game, O'Connell?'

'Don't know what you're talking about.'

'I mean, what do you have up your sleeve?'

'I really haven't got the foggiest what you're on about. You credit me with too much intelligence.'

'No, O'Connell, the problem is this: since I first met you, I have credited you with too *little* intelligence.'

At that, Jerry couldn't help but smile. 'You thought I was just a thug, did you? That was what they used to call me back in the day: "a thug in a suit". Well, you're not the first to make that mistake. Probably won't be the last.'

In reply, Beaufoy grunted. 'So be it. In the meantime, I want my drugs.'

'I want Noah,' replied Jerry, 'so what's the hold-up?'

'The hold-up is that you only want her because I've taken her. Before that you wanted *me*.'

'That's right.'

314

'And so you're prepared to admit defeat for the girl?' Beaufoy's eyes ranged over her.

'Let's just say that it's a case of one thing at a time.'

'I see. And so, at the conclusion of our trade, we'll have unfinished business? Is that right?'

Jerry, who was bored of talk, said, 'Are we going to do it or not?'

'Yes,' said Beaufoy. 'Let's do it.'

And when the call ended, both men knew that there would be no 'leaving it for another time'. No 'unfinished business'.

They both knew that it ended here. And it ended now.

Chapter Sixty-Seven

Noah was pushed out of the door of the workshop. Her hands were secured behind her with a cable tie, a length of duct tape across her mouth, Ronson Beaufoy close behind. The first thing they saw as they emerged blinking into the sunlight and the door closed behind them was Jerry's Viper. It had been parked several yards away, close by the workshop entrance, just off to the left.

For a moment, Beaufoy tensed, wondering where Jerry was – and then saw him. The big man had positioned himself further up the lot, almost at the halfway point between them and the vans. Held as a shield – just in case – was Joey, whose hands were bound in front of him, gripping the holdalls in which were the drugs. Jerry towered over him, but even so he seemed to stoop. Not only was he covered with blood, but he seemed to have lost some of the bearing that Beaufoy remembered from their previous encounter. Judging by his pallid look, there was more blood on the outside of him than there was on the inside.

Jerry, meanwhile, was holding it together. Just. Riding a wave of pain from his wound. Fighting the dizziness that threatened to overcome. All eyes were on him, he knew. Everyone wondering how much fuel he had in the tank.

He watched as Noah and Beaufoy appeared, noting the gag, and how both their eyes went to his Viper. He'd chosen his parking spot in consultation with Wayne, and as soon as he had him and Noah safe behind it, he was going to give Wayne the signal. Blow the gaff.

To do that, though, he needed to be close to her.

'Are you ready, O'Connell?' called Beaufoy.

'Yes, mate,' replied Jerry. He heard a pained crack in his own voice and hoped it wasn't detectable. Joey stood with his head hung low, his wrists fastened with his own belt. 'You ready, Joey?' Jerry asked, but he made no reply. 'All right,' called Jerry to Beaufoy, 'me and your mate Mikel are as ready as we're ever gonna be up here. First thing's first, though, I need to make sure you're not armed. How about you give us a twirl?'

Beaufoy held on to Noah with first one hand and then the other as he opened his jacket and turned around. Nothing at his waistband. One by one, he pulled up his trouser legs, nothing there. Hardly a thorough body-search, of course, reflected Jerry, but it would have to do.

Suddenly, Noah twisted away from Beaufoy, turning her back, almost as though she planned to run back to the workshop, before Beaufoy caught her and spun her to face front again. Her eyes were wide, as though she were desperately trying to tell Jerry something, and his mind raced, trying to figure out what. A double-cross, of course. But what shape would it take? And why had she turned her back to him like that?

'And now your turn,' called Beaufoy. 'Presumably you relieved Joey of his weapon?'

Jerry dropped the confiscated Glock to the tarmac and then did the same as Beaufoy, opening his coat, turning.

'Then let's begin,' said Beaufoy, when it was done.

He took a step forward, waiting for Jerry to do the same. He did, unable to disguise the limp, which drew a smile from Beaufoy. Like gunslingers, they moved across the lot towards one another, the four of them slowly closing the distance. Jerry kept Joey in front of him while watching the door of the workshop. At the same time, he looked at Noah, who was still trying to tell him something with her eyes, and then to Beaufoy, where he was amused to see the gang leader fixing him with a hard, meaningful stare.

The Viper was closer now. So was Noah. So was Beaufoy.

What you got in mind? thought Jerry. His leg throbbed. Blood loss threatened to overcome him. But still his senses were on high alert. Every nerve ending screaming at him. *What have you got in mind?*

Beaufoy thinking the same thing.

A discarded McDonald's wrapper, caught by a light breeze, skittered across the tarmac between them. They were close now. Jerry caught Noah's eyes and gave her a reassuring wink. He got an exasperated shake of her head in return.

'All right,' said Beaufoy when there were just a few feet between them. 'Let's trade. I'll take my drugs and my man.'

He held Noah secure with one hand, reaching for the bags with the other. Noah was trying to say something under her gag. One word she kept repeating over and over again. A word that was impossible to make out. At the same time, she was working at trying to dislodge the tape across her mouth until at last it came free and she was able to speak.

'*Knife*,' she gasped.

Just as Beaufoy made his move.

Chapter Sixty-Eight

The look in Beaufoy's eyes changed. Jerry saw it: a vicious, sly look he had seen many times in other adversaries. At the same time, Noah jerked, and Jerry could have sworn it was as though Beaufoy had put his hand up the back of her T-shirt.

And then she was propelled forward into Jerry. Simultaneously there was a ripping sound and Jerry saw pieces of duct tape flapping loose. He saw the huge knife that had appeared in Beaufoy's hand and realised that it had been taped to Noah's back the whole time.

Beaufoy attacked with the blade held in a knife-fighter's grip. Jerry shoved Joey and caught Noah at the same time, swinging her round behind him and depositing her to the ground and spinning back in time to see Beaufoy coming forward.

It all happened so fast. Getting Noah out of harm's way had cost him a precious second and he was slowed down by his wound. He felt Beaufoy's knife slice his stomach and looked down to see blood already sheeting from the wound, knowing that in a few moments' time his body would be flooded with even more pain.

He staggered back, his leg buckling, sending him to one knee. Beaufoy came forward again, his teeth bared. Madness in his eyes. The knife flashed once more. Instinctively, Jerry reached up with his left hand to parry and felt the blade slice the skin along the side of his palm, neatly parting the flesh. Jerry could feel the blood pouring from him, knowing that if Beaufoy landed one more good hit he was dead meat.

Nobody could stand this kind of attack. Not even him.

And Beaufoy saw it, too. He saw Jerry stricken, down on one knee, cut and bleeding, on the cusp of defeat. He smelled victory. He came forward, wielding the blade.

But this time Beaufoy not only telegraphed the move but overstretched, and it was all the invitation Jerry needed, the streetfighter in him seeing the opening. With a roar of pain and defiance, he rose, leading with his head.

The headbutt broke Beaufoy's nose. He staggered back, blood spurting from it as Jerry pressed home his advantage, unleashing a right and then grabbing the knife from Beaufoy's fingers as the gang leader fell away, his eyeballs swimming crazily in their sockets. Jerry reached out to grab him, stopping him from falling and at the same time bringing the knife back and then slipping the blade between Beaufoy's teeth.

Jerry breathed hard, blinked away his light-headedness. His forearm tensed, about to drive the blade home backhanded, through the roof of Beaufoy's mouth and into his brain.

Ready to do it.

Wanting to do it.

'Stop!'

The voice came from the door to the workshop, which had opened. Stepping outside, other men fanning behind him, was Gridlock, his Glock pointed towards where Jerry stood with Beaufoy.

Not far away, Noah pulled herself to her feet, her wrists still bound, Joey doing the same.

Jerry's eyes went first to Gridlock, who stood with the gun raised, his face impassive, and then to Beaufoy. Around the blade still in his mouth, Beaufoy formed a crooked victorious smile. Jerry looked at him, feeling nothing. He relaxed his grip, and Beaufoy sank to his knees, spat, and put a hand to his wounded nose.

'Kill him, Gridlock,' he ordered. 'Kill them both.'

Noah gasped. Jerry's face was neutral. Gridlock did nothing.

'Shoot him,' repeated Beaufoy, his head rising when his order was not obeyed. 'Shoot him or give me the fucking gun. Now!'

And still Gridlock ignored him. Instead, his eyes were fixed on Jerry. 'I have a call for you,' he said simply, offering Jerry the phone.

Jerry took it with hands already slick with blood. 'Would that be Mr Colorado by any chance?' he said into the phone. He watched in pleasure as Beaufoy gave a start and then paled as the realisation hit home.

'Yes, this is Francis Colorado,' said the lawyer, speaking from his home. 'I trust everything has gone according to our plan?'

'Pretty much, mate, yeah,' replied Jerry, thinking, *Yeah, give or take the knife and bullet wounds, and the trip to hospital I desperately need.*

'Good,' said Colorado. 'Gridlock knows what to do.'

'And what about me and you?' asked Jerry. He was aware

of the gangbangers who stood behind Gridlock, their guns drawn. Who knows what order they'd been given. 'Are we square?'

'That depends. Have the drugs been recovered?'

'They're here, and I've got no use for them.'

'Good. Well . . .' Colorado paused. 'On the one hand, I take a dim view of your activities. But on the other hand, they have inadvertently exposed and thus helped me deal with a weak link in our organisation, and I'm grateful for your help in bringing matters to a speedy resolution. We are, indeed, as you say, square.'

Jerry limped a couple of paces and handed the phone back to Gridlock. 'He says you know what to do.'

Gridlock nodded and came to stand behind Beaufoy, whose eyes went to Jerry.

'Before he does it,' said the condemned man, looking at Jerry. 'You never told me why.'

'What do you mean?' said Jerry, a hand at his stomach wound.

'Why did you go to war?' said Beaufoy. 'Why did you want to fuck with me so much?'

Jerry nodded, figuring that he deserved his answer. 'Two reasons really. Firstly, because no other fucker would go up against you, and some fucker needed to. And secondly, the little girl in 22B.'

And that was it. On his knees, Beaufoy's head dropped and his shoulders sagged as Jerry turned, picked up the knife and used it to free Noah. She flinched as, behind them, Gridlock put a bullet in the back of Beaufoy's head and his body crumpled to the floor.

Together they climbed into the Viper.

'Your stomach,' she said. 'Oh, Christ, your leg.'

'Yeah,' he agreed. 'Need the hospital sharpish.'

She looked across at the workshop as he started up the Viper. 'What are you going to do?' she asked, as he backed up and pointed the Viper at the street. They were being watched by the CT-40 gang members, the body of their leader at their feet. Across the street was the KFC and Jerry pictured Wayne and Keith inside, waiting for his signal.

'You mean am I going to blow the workshop?'

She nodded.

'Don't really need to now, do I? What with Beaufoy being dead an' all. But then again I think of all those poor people back at Sunshine Heights, and how if I do nothing, then that little lot will go back home tonight, and it'll be business as usual. And you know what?' He opened the window, put out his hand and gave a thumbs-up. 'I'm not having that.'

They were on the road when they heard the *crump* of the explosion from behind them. In his rear-view mirror, Jerry saw a cloud of dark smoke bloom over the building tops.

Now that, he thought, *was a good day's work.*

Chapter Sixty-Nine

There had been policeman, lots of policemen. Detectives, beat cops, all kinds of law enforcement officers. They'd stood around Jerry's hospital bed, and every single one of them had wanted to know what had happened at the workshop and at the bungalow.

Jerry gave his answers, which were true to bullshit in a ratio of about 50:50, and they had agreed with every word he'd said, nodding, thanking him for his co-operation, never once issuing a single challenge, because not one of them had been particularly interested in bringing him to justice. And besides, though the police told Jerry that Lowrey was still in intensive care and they weren't sure whether she'd pull through or not yet, they had been able to retrieve a recording she'd made on her phone when she entered the bungalow that made it quite clear Jerry had tried to save her and called an ambulance at the scene. Lowrey must have known how much danger she was in – knew there was a chance she wouldn't make it out – and found a way to record what happened either way.

The boys had come in, of course. They had left Hillview and were bound for LAX, ready for their flight back to

Heathrow, filling the room with laughter and profanity, saying their goodbyes and thanking him for a cracking holiday.

Meanwhile, his constant companion was Noah. She had waited until they knew that the transfusion had been successful before she suggested they go see Jane.

'She's woken up,' she told Jerry. 'Doctors say she's going to make a full recovery. Do you want to see her?'

She remembered how he'd come over all bashful on the walkway that time.

'Yeah, I would love to,' said Jerry, pulling himself up in the hospital bed, feeling daft in the standard-issue smock. 'Just see her for a bit.'

'That's fair enough. I thought that might be your thoughts on the matter, so I brought along a little something for you to give to her.'

'What's that, then?' he asked, intrigued.

'Wait there, I'll show you,' said Noah. She stood and left the room. Moments later, she returned, wheeling Jane's bicycle. 'Here you go,' she said. 'After all, you only ever wanted to give her bike back, didn't you?'

Jerry grinned. 'That's perfect, mate, absolutely perfect.'

Epilogue

Jerry had been back from hospital just one day when his phone chirruped and the screen told him that Wayne the Thug was getting in touch.

He took the call, dropping to the couch and watching Noah, who was in the process of pulling her overstuffed bag along the floor towards the door.

In the bag were her belongings. All of them. Why? Because she was officially moving out. The reason was that her bungalow off Sunset was still a crime scene. It wasn't as if she'd ever had any affection for the place anyway, and so the idea of living there, alone, in her crime-scene house, with the memory of that afternoon confronting her every time she walked in the door was about as appealing as dental surgery. No, she had decided firmly, she definitely wasn't going back there.

And so she'd just been resigning herself to making the rounds of the motels in the area until such time that she could find another place, when Jerry had piped up.

'You could stay here,' he'd said, 'in Hillview.'

'I can't,' she'd replied. 'I mean, I can't just stay here. Not if we're not . . .'

The moment had hung between them, neither of them wanting to say it – until Jerry had broken the ice.

'Not here. Not in this actual apartment. Nah, course not. Not if we're not . . . y'know. No, what I mean is, how about you take one of the other apartments in the complex? The one the lads were staying in. It's all yours. Just as a way of thanking you for sticking with me through all of this, putting up with me and that.'

He'd cleared his throat, feeling a little awkward all of a sudden.

'Okay,' she'd said, heart soaring even as she, too, felt herself colouring a little. I'll take it. I do really love it here.'

And now – Wayne.

'What is it?' asked Jerry, pleased to hear from Wayne but knowing also that it wasn't a social call.

'It's about Keith,' said Wayne. 'You know you wanted me to keep an eye on him?'

Jerry did indeed remember that. The Keith situation was one of those loose ends – actually the only loose end – he had yet to tie.

'What about him?'

'It weren't him who drowned Angel.'

Jerry took a deep breath. Over the way, Noah had set her bag by the door and, sensing that Jerry was having a significant conversation, stood with her arms folded.

'You know that for a fact, do you?' said Jerry.

'Yeah, I do. It was something that Keith was saying at the workshop. He didn't want to tell me at first, but I wheedled it out of him on the way home. It turns out it's Katie's boyfriend – this Scott geezer. He's the one you want.'

'That's just Keith's word for it, though,' countered Jerry.

'Fucking hell, credit me with some intelligence, would you? I did a bit of checking.'

'And?'

'What I fucking say. It ain't Keith – it's this Scott.'

'Right.'

'Do you want me to do him?' asked Wayne.

Across the way, Noah was looking over, interested – almost as though she'd heard Wayne ask the question.

'Yeah. Do him. Do the cunt,' said Jerry. 'But don't finish the job. I'll be coming over to take care of that in person.'

He ended the call. Noah stood looking at him, a dark, unreadable expression on her face.

'"Do him?"' she repeated. '"Finish the job?"'

'Yeah,' he said, without meeting her eye.

'And I'm guessing that doesn't mean "do him" as in "do him a favour"?'

'Nah, it means *do him.*'

His voice was harsh. Cold.

'This is Keith we're talking about, is it?'

He shook his head. 'No, some other cunt.'

'Oh? So Keith was wholly innocent?'

'Looks that way.'

'Jerry,' she urged. 'You almost killed Keith and he turned out to be innocent. Doesn't that tell you something?'

His jaw was set. 'That's just the way it is. That's the way it's going to be.'

She looked at him long and hard, wondering if this was what she wanted for herself. Knowing all of a sudden that she was faced with a choice: either she carried on and continued settling in next door, or she left for good and never looked back – left behind a world where problems were solved with fists and knives and guns.

Without another word, she picked up her bag, opened the door and stepped out, hearing the door thump shut behind her.

Standing on the walkway, she looked left, towards the steps that led to ground level, to the parking lot, to her Jeep. And then right, to the door of what was supposed to be her new apartment.

Okay, Noah, she told herself. *Time to make your choice.*

Meanwhile, inside his own apartment, Jerry sat on the couch, knowing exactly what was going through her head. Knowing also that it was her decision to make and hers alone, and that whatever she decided he'd respect it.

At the same time, he found himself wondering if it was time to slow down. Start saying, 'Fuck it,' a bit more often. Because the opposite of saying 'fuck it' meant that one minute you were trying to do right by a little girl, and the next minute bodies were falling. Geezers were getting shot in the back of the head. Buildings exploding.

Yeah. Maybe it was time to start taking things easy.

Then again, knowing him, maybe not.